She

He waited ~~_____~~. By this time, most men had given up on her and moved on to someone else. She searched his eyes, surprised to find genuine interest.

She took a deep breath and hoped she wasn't going to regret divulging more. "I see so many children in the ER rooms who..." She turned her head and chewed on her cuticle. When they arrived needing her care, she put aside her emotions and did the job, but afterward, she always broke down. She knew how it felt to grow up feeling different. How could a parent do that to a child?

He placed his hand over her other one on the table. "It's okay, you don't have to tell me. I can see their plight affects you." He squeezed. "I could tell when you were playing the piano; your heart is filled with sorrow."

Gina stared into his eyes. The sincerity of his words and the acceptance of her pain, even though he thought it was all for others made her want to weep. She hadn't had anyone care about her in so long, she didn't know how to act.

Jerking her hand out from under his, she stood. "I have to go."

"Wait." He snagged her hand as she grabbed her coat from the back of the chair. "Do you have a phone number?"

He held her firm but gentle. Warmth spiraled up her arm and settled in her chest. Why didn't she feel frightened or invaded by this man? She shook her head. She didn't want to see him again. If she did, it would be hard to remain faithful to her vow. He'd started to seep into the empty cracks created over the years.

Praise for *PERFECTLY GOOD NANNY*

"Ms. Jager has done an exceptional job writing this western-slanted contemporary. Her characters, the main and the secondary ones, are multifaceted and their in-depth attributes show the details Ms. Jager used to express her story so well..."
~The Romance Studio—Five Hearts!

"The strongest point of this book is the way Ms. Jager has written such wonderful characters. The reader can't help but become involved in their lives, and are drawn right into the plot."
~Fallen Angels Review—Five Angels!

Thank you for your
Support of First Book ~

Bridled Heart

by

Paty Jager

Bridled Heart

Cover Art by *Kim Mendoza*

The Wild Rose Press
PO Box 706
Adams Basin, NY 14410-0706
Visit us at www.thewildrosepress.com

Publishing History
First Yellow Rose Edition, 2011
Print ISBN 1-60154-874-5

Published in the United States of America

A Special Thank You to:

Bobby and Kate Mote
for allowing me to enter the life of
a bareback bronc rider.

Mike Carnahan
for allowing me a vicarious look
at the National Rodeo Finals.

Gloria Acuna
for her insight in an occupation
I knew nothing about.

And Opal Campbell
for allowing me to dig into the rodeo life deeper.

Chapter One

The compelling strains flowed from her fingers to the piano, soothing the demoralizing memories a simple drawing manifested. Gina Montgomery hadn't played this song in years. Not since she took control of her life.

Earlier this evening, she hadn't been able to pull her gaze from the drawing as she held it up for auction. Now, as the piano strains rent the air with sorrow, the image came back to her in painful clarity. A young woman with both arms wound tightly around her body as though holding herself together. Longing on her young face. A single tear sliding down her cheek as she watched the jubilant horse gallop away. The scene, the emotions, had catapulted Gina back in time. To a period in her life she thought she'd left behind after graduating nursing school. She opened her eyes, pushing the haunting pencil drawing from her thoughts.

Her hands moved across the piano keys with little thought as the somber concerto filled the large atrium. She'd ducked into the room for a respite from the throng of art enthusiasts and fundraising matriarchs. She looked forward to helping with the fundraiser every year and always found a chance to escape from the festivities once her job was complete. Arranging the art auction took up a large amount of time weeks before and the night of the event. Now, as the attendees were plied with champagne for their generous donations, she could take a breather.

Closing her eyes, gliding her hands across the

keys, she experienced the essence of the drawing. Her chest squeezed and all the emotions she'd tucked away flowed from her fingertips and into the chords.

Holt Reynolds followed piano music to a room at the end of the hall. He'd left the festivities in search of a quiet place to make a phone call. The moving piano strains brought back memories of his sister, the reason he'd attended the fundraiser and donated a drawing he'd made after her death.

Inside the room of marble and foliage, he spotted the source of the music. The woman who held and stared at his drawing during the auction, sat at a piano. Her dark lashes fanned over her cheeks. One tear slipped out from under a lash and slid down the side of her face. Her fingers nimbly moved across the piano keys. The agonizing, heart wrenching strains and her immersion in the music reminded him of Sherrie. His sister had spent hours playing the piano, taking herself away from a world he hadn't learned about until it was too late. Angry at his ignorance to his sister's plight, and wary the woman at the piano held secrets much like his sister, he strode toward her. The clunk of his cowboy boots echoed off the marble floor.

He walked to within five feet of the piano before she registered the sound. Her hands stopped as if frozen. She breathed deep a couple times before her eyelids fluttered up. The fear and shock in their hazel depths was quickly masked with irritation.

"I'm sorry. Didn't mean to interrupt." *Like hell.* He hadn't seen anything so breathtaking and gut-punching before in his life.

"This room is off limits to the attendees." She slid from the bench and stood. The top of her head came to his nose.

He held up his cell phone. "Just looking for a quiet place to make a call."

One eyebrow, darker than her honey blonde hair, rose as she tipped her head. "So you came into a room with someone playing a piano."

Grinning, he ducked his head, then leveled his gaze on her face. He held out his empty hand. "Holt Reynolds."

Her gaze darted from his hand to his face. With reluctance, she slid her palm against his. The friction and the brief pressure roused his senses catching his gaze. Short, clean nails weren't hidden behind nail polish. She had working hands.

"I know who you are."

For appearing down to earth, she sure acted a bit high and mighty. "You do? And how's that? You don't look like the rodeo type to me."

She pulled her hand from his. Leaving him to wonder at the extended length of time she'd left it resting in his palm.

"I'm the volunteer in charge of the art that was auctioned off tonight." She sat back down on the piano bench, playing with the keys. "It's my job to write up the bios on the artists donating their work." Still tapping out a soft, soothing song, she glanced up at him. "How does a bareback rider put that much emotion into a pencil drawing?"

So that was it. She didn't figure a cowboy could have deep feelings. "Kinda the same way you put emotion into your piano playing."

Her fingers stopped. The last note echoed in the room and died. "I see." Tears glistened in her eyes. He had an urge to pull her into his arms and comfort her, but the stiff back and icy reserve creeping into her eyes kept him at a distance.

"What's your name?" She'd be a heart stopper if her hair wasn't pulled back so tight and the flowing dress she wore hugged some of her curves. Or at least curves he was pretty sure were under there.

She hesitated. Her eyes looked everywhere but

at him. She started to raise a hand toward her face and quickly lowered it to her lap.

"I can always look it up on the program." He gave her what his grandma used to call his bullshit smile. It always seemed to warm the ladies to him.

"Gina. Gina Montgomery." She tapped out another tune on the piano.

"You live here in Portland, Gina?" The sadness of her music and her resistance to his questions intrigued Holt. He didn't see a wedding ring, which upped his curiosity. He was going to friend this woman. Just as sure as he was going to win that national title and get the money he needed to set up a ranch and retire from the circuit.

"Not really." She continued to send soft strains of music into the air.

He scratched his head. "What do you mean by that?"

Her fingers stopped. Without looking at him she said, "I don't think it's any of your business where I live."

"Brrrr." He shook himself, but smiled. "Do you always get this frosty with people getting to know you, or is it just cowboys?"

She turned. A mixture of guilt and annoyance crossed her oval-shaped face. "I'm not rude to cowboys specifically. I just don't know you well enough to tell you where I live."

"We could remedy that." The phone in his hand vibrated. He glanced at the number. "Don't go away."

As the cowboy moved away from the piano to answer the call, her fingers caressed another tune. Gina couldn't believe her rudeness to the creator of that heart-wrenching drawing. But he was a man. And she'd vowed to keep her distance from the opposite sex.

She slid a glance toward Holt Reynolds. He

leaned one shoulder against a marble pillar and crossed his muscular, denim covered legs at the ankles, revealing fancy stitching on his shiny boots. The casual stance left his unbuttoned, western-cut jacket hanging open, framing the body-hugging white shirt with pearl snaps. Skimming her gaze over the handsome cowboy, it was all she could do to keep her fingers moving slowly as her heart did staccato beats in her chest.

A genuine smile pulled at his lips and the laugh lines arrowing toward his dark brown eyes narrowed. Newly trimmed, blond, curly hair gave him a look of sophistication. He cleaned up nice for a cowboy.

Why would he donate a piece of art, which had to have been drawn with his heart, to a fundraiser for sexually abused children? She studied him as he talked on the phone. His unguarded expressions and ready smile meant he talked with a good friend. Or a girlfriend.

She shook her head at the ping of disappointment. Over the years, traveling as she did, she'd come across men who'd sparked her interest, but her vow of celibacy never allowed them close enough to see if anything would develop. Love was an overrated thing. She'd had few people in her life truly love her. Oh, they said they did, but if they loved her, then why had they hurt her?

She slipped from the contemporary piece into Beethoven's Piano Sonata No. 14 in C sharp. The somber chords flowed from her fingers when her past came back to haunt her. She held the last chord; the sad longing in the strains echoed her heart.

"That looks like a good way to work out feelings." Holt's deep voice broke into her thoughts.

Gina jerked around. She'd forgotten he was still in the room. Locking the anger of her past back in the recesses of her mind, she checked her watch and slid from the bench. "I have to help distribute the works to the new owners."

As she started past him, he touched her arm. The warmth of his palm seeped through her thin sleeve and held her feet in check. Usually a man's touch, even so innocent, sent off warning bells in her head. But this touch didn't unnerve her. She tipped her head up slightly to look into his face.

"Can we continue our conversation after you're through?" His eyes held a friendly invitation.

"Why?" What could he want to talk to her about? She mended bodies, and he tried to break his on a weekly basis.

"I want to learn more about you. Is there something wrong with that?" There it was again, that shy yet disarming smile.

"Y-yes, uh, no." She walked away.

"Well?"

"I don't know."

She had to get away from him. He intrigued her, but she couldn't pursue that and remain faithful to the path she'd chosen. The only path that could heal her lonely battered heart.

Chapter Two

Holt leaned against a marble pillar watching Gina dole out the auctioned art. Not taking his gaze from her, he hit the number one on his cell phone, dialing up Jess Karlan, his best friend and one of his rodeo traveling buddies. They rodeoed together in college until Jess married and hit the pro circuit while Holt stayed behind to finish his degrees in business and art.

After graduation, he re-joined Jess. Gradually, they added two other single, bareback riders to their group. The four traveled from rodeo to rodeo hoping to rack up enough money to be in the top fifteen money makers and attend the Pro Rodeo Circuit Association finals in Vegas. Jess won the title a couple years back. Holt had made it to the finals several times, but the title eluded him. *Not this year.*

"Talk to me," Jess's familiar voice answered curtly.

"I wouldn't happen to be interruptin' nothin' now would I?" Holt smiled. His buddy already had two small children. Any time he was home, he and his bride worked on making number three.

"You know you are. What do you want?"

"Just checking in to see if we're still headed out in two days and where you plan to meet." Holt kept his eyes on Gina as she checked receipts and handed the art work over to the new owners.

"Call me tomorrow. At a decent hour." The phone clicked.

Holt chuckled. He liked Jess's wife, Clare. She understood the travel and didn't mind either tagging along or staying home. His gaze landed on Gina. Would she...

She glanced up, and their gazes met. He smiled and she jerked her attention back to the fur-encased woman waving a receipt.

Something about Gina made him want to put a smile on her face. Sadness choked her like a lasso on a calf—not quite strangling but holding her back.

Mrs. Overmeyer, the matron behind the event, came over to chat with Gina. Her somber attitude evaporated when Mrs. Overmeyer spoke. She even acted a little bubbly. Holt smiled. There *was* some life in her.

He crossed the marble floor, walking up to the table in front of Gina and the woman.

"Mr. Reynolds," Mrs. Overmeyer exclaimed. A bangle encrusted arm and ring encased hand stretched out to him. "Thank you for your most generous donation."

He shook the hand, darted a glance at Gina, and smiled at the matron. "It was my pleasure. Any time your organization does a fund raiser let me know." He nodded toward Gina. "Any chance, Gina could skip out?"

"Oh, I didn't know you two were acquaintances!"

Gina's face reddened, and she shook her head slightly.

Mrs. Overmeyer clapped her hands, her bangles clanking. "Gina, why didn't you tell me you knew Mr. Reynolds? Now I know why you stared at his drawing so much." She winked at Holt and shooshed Gina. "Go. Go. You've put in more hours than any other volunteer. Enjoy yourself."

"It's not... We don't..." Her eyes pleaded, but he wasn't going to let this opportunity slip away.

"Come on, you heard the lady. Let's go talk about my next contribution." He grasped Gina's hand, leading her to the end of the table and around

8

to stand beside him.

She stared over her shoulder at Mrs. Overmeyer, who smiled and waved.

"I can't be so repulsive you won't join me for a drink." He smiled and drew her toward the door.

"I, uh, have to get my coat and purse." She tugged on his hand.

"Oh no, you don't. You're not ducking and running. I'm going with you." He held onto her trembling hand, following beside her down a back hallway. The storage room they stepped into had more dark recesses than an empty stable.

"I'm glad I came with you. This isn't a place for a lone woman."

She turned from the pile of coats on a table and peered at him quizzically. He let go of her hand to help her put on a gray rain jacket. After she picked up a purse, he caught her hand again. Now that she had her things, he didn't want her dashing away. Her narrowed eyes sparked with annoyance when he captured her fingers proved she'd been thinking just that.

"I don't know why you're reluctant to get to know me. I'm really a great guy, ask anyone," he said as they strolled back through the dwindling attendees. He stopped by an older couple he'd talked with briefly during the event. "Would you tell her I'm a great guy?"

Gina tugged on the hand he held, and he glanced back. The mortification on her face made him feel lower than a dog with no legs.

The older woman tsked, and the couple moved off. An apology formed on his tongue as he reached out to put his other hand on her face. She jerked back and he frowned. She was more head shy than an abused horse.

Shit! That was it.

"I'm sorry. I didn't mean to make you

9

uncomfortable. I was just trying to lighten you up."

She glared and made another attempt to pull out of his hold.

"I'll let go, if you promise to come have a drink with me." He let her fingers slip from his grasp.

Gina realized Holt Reynolds wasn't about to give up. Riding a horse took tenacity and it looked like he carried that into his personal life. She'd concede, but she wasn't going to a bar. "At a coffee shop."

"Perfect."

"There's one just down the block."

He motioned for her to lead the way.

She slid the hand he'd held into her pocket. Heat radiated through the jacket's fabric to her hip. His touch warmed her deeper than physical contact. While one level was intrigued by it, another was scared. He was exactly the type of man she should stay away from. One who only wanted a good time. She wasn't drawn into that anymore.

Yet, beyond his obvious need to make her a conquest, he seemed to understand her needs. Her insecurities. How? Why did he even care?

Gina stepped out the door he held open. She glanced down the street. Now was the perfect time to dash away. His courteous patience with the older couple exiting the building, however, tugged at her conscience. Even though her head told her to run, her curiosity to learn more about the man kept her feet rooted. He held the door for two more couples exiting the building, flashing each person with a charming smile.

"Thank you," he said, when they resumed walking.

"For what?"

He smiled that disarming smile. "For agreeing to come, and for waiting."

Guilt jiggled in her belly. He knew she wanted to bolt. How did he see things in her when they'd only just met? These idiosyncrasies along with his artistic rendering made her want to learn more. The drawing had haunted her since the first day she unwrapped it. What made a man of his occupation draw something so emotion wrenching?

"I'd be lying if I didn't say you intrigue me." She slid a glance in his direction.

His face brightened.

"Not that way." She laughed when his expression crumpled. Slapping a hand over her mouth, she stopped and stared. Did she actually laugh at a sexual innuendo? She'd not flirted or encouraged a man since she made a vow to remain celibate ten years ago. What was it about this man that made her drop years of armor?

"What? You aren't allowed to laugh?" He pulled her hand down. "You have a beautiful laugh. Just like your music, full of emotion."

She waggled a finger toward him. "You're slick. I've heard you cowboys can talk a girl into things..." *Damn!* There she went again. She had to stop flirting.

He smiled. "It's not the cowboy talking, it's me."

She changed the uncomfortable subject by pointing to a coffee shop across the street. Holt grasped her elbow as they crossed the road. He was proving to be more of a gentleman than any other man she'd been around.

At the shop, he held the door for her to enter, and then stepped beside her at the counter.

"I'll have green tea with honey and"—she eyed the pastry display—"a cinnamon roll." The sweet cinnamon scent brought memories of her mom scolding, "Gina Rose, leave some for your brother and father." She smiled, remembering her mother's love.

"Are you hungry? We could go for a late dinner?"

Holt's caring tone made her stomach quiver.

How long had it been since someone cared about her well-being other than to make sure she could do her job

"No, I had a light meal before the event." She shrugged. "I just have a weakness for pastry. Especially cinnamon rolls."

He grinned. "Something to remember." Holt ordered a large milk and cinnamon roll as well then paid for the items.

She led them to a table in the corner away from traffic. "Let me pay you for mine. This isn't a date." Holding out the cost of her half, she waited for Holt to place the tray on the table.

"Put your money away. This was my idea."

"But I don't…"

"This isn't a date. It's simply two people with a mutual interest discussing that interest."

He helped her off with her coat, and she told herself that he was only doing this now, but give him time, and he'd be like all the others. He was only being nice because he was after one thing.

"So, why did you want to talk to me so bad?" She stirred honey into her tea.

"I find you fascinating." He took a sip of milk, studying her over the rim of his glass.

Fascinating? More like a challenge. She'd had more than one man since she turned her life around think he could change her focus. Gina nodded to his choice of beverage. "For asking me to a bar, you're drinking kind of light."

He wiped the milk off his lip and smiled. "Just because I asked you for a drink didn't mean I was going to get you drunk and take advantage of you." Her gaze leaped to his face and lingered a moment before she stared into her tea.

He put the cup down. "I've got a rodeo in four days. Can't be at my best if my body's dehydrated and my reactions slow."

"But you're a cowboy. I thought you all partied hard and went for the ladies." She pulled off a piece of the roll and pushed it in her mouth, avoiding the probing eyes of Holt.

"Those are the ones that don't have their sights set on winning *National Bareback Champion*." He raised his whole pastry and took a bite.

Gina snickered and handed him a napkin. "You have frosting on your nose."

He grinned, slightly dipping his head, and wiped at the white blob. Something about his smile and the way he ducked his head as though embarrassed, tickled her.

"So this rodeo in four days, where is it?" Better to talk about him. She hated talking about herself.

"California, from there we head to Texas, then Arizona and back up to Oregon." He took another bite.

"So you'll be gone a couple months." She sipped her tea, liking the idea he wouldn't be available to pester her...yet a bit disappointed, too.

"Naw, we'll only be gone a couple weeks then back here for a week and then back out on the road again." He drank his milk then continued. "There's four of us that travel together, that way we can drive twenty-four hours straight. We take turns sleeping in the camper on the truck."

"Isn't that dangerous? What if there's an accident?" She stared at him. What must his life be like driving twenty-four hours straight and then crawling on lunatic animals and trying to stay on?

"It's as safe as riding a bucking bronc." He tipped his empty cup in a salute.

"My point exactly. Is your whole life spent being in danger?" She stared at him. How could one live day to day putting their life in jeopardy? "I spend hours on end piecing people back together as an ER nurse." She shoved her half-eaten roll to the middle of the table. The thought of such disregard for life, made her stomach churn. "How can you think so little of life to put yourself in danger every day?"

"I don't. My traveling buddies are good drivers. I trust them with my life. And I train to keep my body fit and have learned to stay on a horse." He pushed the roll back at her. "Eat."

There was more confidence than cockiness in the trust of his friends and his riding abilities. But even knowing the obstacles, you never knew when something unexpected could debilitate you—like when seeing his drawing had thrown her thoughts back twenty years.

"Do you work at a hospital here in town?"

Gina shook away the disturbing memories. "What?"

"I asked if you work at a hospital here in town." His eyes narrowed, and he peered at her with more intensity.

She sipped her tea. Her hand shook as she set the cup down. What should she tell him? He'd be on the road and wouldn't know how to contact her. Once she headed to her next assignment he'd be a memory. She smiled. A nice memory for a change, but definitely a memory.

"I work for an agency that sends me to different hospitals to work anywhere from five to nine weeks at a time." She picked at the cinnamon roll.

"Are you working, here, right now?" He tipped his cup, looked inside, and placed it back on the table.

"I'm between jobs. I always take several weeks off to help with the fundraiser."

"Why this event?" He laced his fingers together, resting his hands in front of him. His coffee-colored gaze held admiration.

Gina dropped her gaze and picked at her napkin. His interest was flattering, and he hadn't attended the event just to inflate his image. If that had been his agenda, he would have stayed to be photographed with the person who purchased his art. She peered into his smiling face. He waited so patiently for her to answer. By this time, most men had given up on her and moved on to someone else. She searched his eyes, surprised to find genuine interest.

She took a deep breath and hoped she wasn't going to regret divulging more. "I see so many children in the ER rooms who..." She turned her head and chewed on her cuticle. When they arrived needing her care, she put aside her emotions and did the job, but afterward, she always broke down. She knew how it felt to grow up feeling different. How could a parent do that to a child?

He placed his hand over her other one on the table. "It's okay, you don't have to tell me. I can see their plight affects you." He squeezed. "I could tell when you were playing the piano; your heart is filled with sorrow."

Gina stared into his eyes. The sincerity of his words and the acceptance of her pain, even though he thought it was all for others made her want to weep. She hadn't had anyone care about her in so long, she didn't know how to act.

Jerking her hand out from under his, she stood. "I have to go."

"Wait." He snagged her hand as she grabbed her coat from the back of the chair. "Do you have a phone number?"

He held her firm but gentle. Warmth spiraled up her arm and settled in her chest. Why didn't she feel frightened or invaded by this man? She shook her head. She didn't want to see him again. If she did, it would be hard to remain faithful to her vow. He'd started to seep into the empty cracks created over the years.

Hult took her coat and helped her into it. He didn't know why she'd jumped like a scared rabbit, but he'd let her go, and could only hope she'd contact him when she was ready.

"Don't move." He peered in her eyes to make sure she wouldn't bolt, then grabbed a pen and napkin from the counter to scribble on.

"Here's my cell. I have it on and with me all the time except when I ride." He tucked the paper into her pocket. "Call me. Anytime. For whatever reason."

She stared into his eyes before turning and disappearing out the door. Fear sliced through him. The hurt and confusion in her eyes tugged at his heart. He'd witnessed that same thing in another pair of brown eyes and regretted not taking the time to ask questions. His gut told him Gina was a lot like Sherrie.

He didn't do right by his sister, but, somehow, he'd do right this time.

Chapter Three

Gina stretched her aching back and wiggled her numb toes. Fourteen hours she'd been on duty in the ER. After a month on the Arizona reservation, she'd realized there was little to do outside of work and volunteered for all the extra hours. It kept her from thinking about a certain cowboy and made her so tired when she hit the mattress there was no room for dreams.

"Gina, you aren't coming in to work tomorrow," Arlene, the head nurse said, as she plucked the patient chart from Gina's hands. "You're taking the next two days off. I can see you're wearing down."

"What am I going to do for two days?" Gina plopped into the chair behind the nurse's station. She didn't like the idea of two days with nothing to occupy her thoughts. That's why she liked this job. She could work twenty-four-seven and no one cared. Until now. When she least wanted time to herself, she was being forced to take it.

"Sleep, read a good book. I don't know, but I don't want to see you inside this building." The head nurse gave her a stern look.

Gina grimaced. She hadn't even found a piano in any of the public buildings. That was the only other activity she'd ever participated in. Maybe she should see about a grant to get a piano for the common room at the hospital?

Sheila, the x-ray technician, pushed an empty wheelchair into the ER reception area.

"What are you doing tomorrow, Sheila?" Arlene asked the tall, thin redhead.

"Bud and I are going to Payson for the 'Doins'." She spun the wheelchair around and took a seat in it, glancing from Arlene to Gina and back. "Why?"

Gina shook her head at Arlene as the older woman's eyes narrowed in thought. She didn't want to tag along with anyone. Didn't care to go to any 'doins'.

"Gina needs to get out of here. How about you and Bud take her along?" The head nurse tipped her head in Gina's direction.

She sat up straight. "No, I couldn't butt into their outing." A rodeo was the last place she wanted to go. The few times she'd watched a rodeo on TV, she cringed every time a body was flung off a bucking animal. There was no relaxation in that. Not to mention the slight chance Holt could be there. She didn't want to see him again—it was hard enough as it was to get him out of her thoughts.

"That's a great idea." Sheila smiled wide. "I see your face every time I come on duty. Just because you get paid good money doesn't mean you have to work twenty-four-seven." She stood. "We'll pick you up outside the quarters at ten. It's a two hour drive, then we want to get a good parking spot and something to eat before the grand entry." Sheila stopped before leaving the area. "Did you bring any western-looking clothes? They have a great dance between performances."

"I really don't want to be a third wheel. I'll just stay here." An outing with the woman would mean forming a connection, something Gina avoided. She liked moving from hospital to hospital, making acquaintances but no friends. Friends dug into your past, and she was a locked vault on that subject.

"Nonsense!" Arlene picked up the phone. "If you don't go with Sheila, I'll call and tell Dr. Palmer you're sick and not to expect you to work for a *week*."

A week? She'd go crazy doing nothing for a week.

Gina glared. "You wouldn't."

"Try me." The phone beeped as she poked at the numbers. "Hi, Alice. Say, could I speak with Dr.Palmer?"

The hair on the back of Gina's neck prickled. She didn't like being bullied. It reminded her too much of her youth. But there was no way she could be idle for a week. What was one day at a rodeo compared to a week here with nothing to do but think?

"Okay, I'll go." She shot Arlene a glare. But she wasn't about to like any of it.

"Oh, Alice, never mind. I found what I was looking for. Thanks." Arlene hung up the phone. "One day out of this place isn't going to kill ya."

Sheila waved and headed down the hall. "Great! See you tomorrow about ten."

Gina watched the redhead until she turned a corner. Sheila wasn't too bad to be around. She'd asked few questions in the time they'd worked together. But what about her husband?

"Since you need some western duds, I'd suggest you take off now and go see what you can find at the country store." Arlene tipped her head toward the exit.

"I don't need western clothes."

She hated spending money on anything that wasn't a necessity. She lived in her brother's apartment when she was in Portland and the hospitals where she worked always provided living quarters. So she not only pulled in triple what she would working the same place three hundred sixty-five days a year, she kept her expenses low. Her bank account was climbing. Five more years and she could start up her dream. A place where sexually abused children could heal through music.

Music and a very perceptive piano teacher had pulled her though the worst times of her life. They grounded her when she wished to flee. Gave her the self worth she didn't believe she deserved. She wanted to give that anchor to others.

"Gina? Gina, you're not even listening to me. See there. You do need a break." Arlene took her by the arm. "Go clock out, and I don't want to see you here until Monday."

"But the rodeo is only tomorrow. I'll be back on Sunday and—"

"No! You might be back here, but you aren't setting foot in this hospital." Arlene pushed her down the hall. "Get."

****

The cars, noise, and boisterous atmosphere of the rodeo grounds had Gina wishing she'd caught the flu and bowed out of the trip. Sheila and Bud had kept the conversation rolling the full two hours they were on the road. She learned their favorite events and who the leading riders were.

Holt's name came up in the conversation. She'd held the questions whirling in her head. If the two even had an inkling she knew the man, they would have asked questions she couldn't answer. She barely knew him, yet, at the same time, it felt like they'd been friends forever. The whole episode with him was clearer in her mind than her shift at the hospital the day before.

Bud jockeyed his four-wheel drive truck for a parking spot on the outskirts of the rodeo grounds.

"Oh look! There's Jess Karlan!" Sheila pointed to a cowboy crossing the far end of the grass area of parked cars. "He won the National Bareback title three years ago."

Gina wondered if he knew Holt, then shoved the thought aside. Even if the cowboy was here, there was a miniscule chance they would meet in amongst the hundreds of people crowding the place.

She scanned the other rodeo spectators and

realized she was underdressed. Her belt didn't have sparkling rhinestones, no straw hat with feathers adorned her head, and her white sneakers would stand out among all the dust-dulled boots. Her teal tank top and jeans were the closest she came to dressing western.

"Come on, we'll grab a dog or two and seats by the chutes." Sheila curled her arm through Gina's, and Bud caught Sheila's free hand. "Bud likes to hear the animals snort when they charge out the gate."

Gina didn't mind being pulled around. If not for Sheila's hold on her, she would have stopped and stared, getting lost in the crowd.

They squeezed into the throng of rodeo goers purchasing massive amounts of food and beverage. The most noise came from the booths selling beer. Her gaze drifted to the tents. Young women in tight jeans, glittering chunky belts, and clingy skimpy shirts laughed and flirted with the men.

Sheila handed her a paper basket of curly fries with a hotdog on top and pushed a large iced tea into her other hand.

Fat oozed from the hot dog, dripping onto the grease saturated fries. It was a wonder the people attending this event didn't all fall over from clogged arteries. Gina sipped her iced tea and wondered if her new friend would notice if she just picked at the bun.

Sheila bumped her. "Earth to Gina." Her gaze drifted to the beer tents. "Those little ladies are called buckle bunnies. They follow the cowboys around like roadies and will do anything—and I mean *anything*—to get linked with a cowboy. No self-respecting cowboy would get within a mile of that."

Gina turned her attention to Sheila. "I thought all cowboys went for the quick easy score?"

"No way. The only cowboys those ladies will pick up are newbies or ones that care more about partying than riding. Winning rodeo cowboys are as conscious of their bodies as any other smart athlete. And focused."

Holt hadn't been filling her full of fluff when he said he wasn't drinking because of his riding. She'd thought he'd made it up to impress her. Maybe he *was* different. An emotion close to happiness floated through her at the thought.

Bud led them through the crowd to a smaller set of bleachers not far from the chutes. This close to the action, she would know if Holt were here. Her heart sped up at the thought, but she immediately squelched the feeling. A part of her hoped he was here, and another part of her prayed this wasn't one of the rodeos on his agenda. She wasn't sure how she'd act if she saw him.

They ate and settled in as Sheila gave her a running commentary of the animals and the events they'd see. Bud interjected every now and then with his own take on things.

The spectacular grand entry filled the outdoor arena with wave upon wave of colorful flags, horses, and outfits. Gina began to relax and enjoy the events. As the tension eased out of her body, however, the large iced tea she drank worked through her system. She glanced around and spotted portable outhouses.

"I gotta go." She pointed to the green buildings and crawled off the end of the bleachers.

"Not without me." Sheila jumped down beside her, and they headed to the outhouses.

She entered the hot, smelly structure with trepidation, but, nature called and she didn't have an alternative.

A few minutes later, she slipped out of the fiberglass hut and stared into the chest of a large man. Startled, she took a step back and bumped into the outhouse. A smaller man walked up beside the first man. They both smiled at her. One had a lopsided grin that tipped toward lechorous. The hair on the back of her neck prickled.

She scanned the area for help. Of all the times for the row of buildings to not have lines waiting. But she wasn't about to be a victim. Not anymore.

"You here alone, Princess?" the larger one asked.

"No." She searched the line of green outhouses for Sheila.

"You look alone and lost to me." The smaller man put out his hand as if to grab her. She jammed her hand in her purse and pulled out pepper spray.

"Step back and leave me alone." She held the can in front of her and turned, keeping the nozzle aimed at the two.

"Hey you two, bug off!" Sheila pushed her way through the two men and grabbed Gina. Arm in arm, they hurried back toward their seats.

"*That's* why you always use the buddy system at a rodeo. You never know when a drunk is gonna shrink his brain and grow a pair of balls."

Sheila's vivid portrayal of the men caused a smile to spread across Gina's face. It sure explained the mishap perfectly.

Reaching the bleachers, she put a hand on the bench to climb back up into her seat when the announcer boomed, "Next up is Holt Reynolds, an Oregon cowboy who is well on his way to making the top fifteen and vying for the National title."

Her breathing stopped, and her heart palpitated. He *was* here. Did she want to see him or keep the memory of their encounter just that—a fond memory?

The announcer kept talking, and she found herself hurrying to the fence, watching through the railing. She had to see him, if for no other reason than to dispel the hold he had over her.

A horse and rider lunged out of the chute. The crowd roared. Her gaze traveled from the large, dark muscular beast to the man, waving one arm in the air and raking his spurs on the bucking, twisting horse's shoulders. The animal leaped, twisted, and leaped again. Muscles bulged below the rolled up sleeve and mounded underneath the upper part of Holt's shirt. Fear clenched her chest. What if he fell? What if the animal came down on top of him?

His gaze was riveted on the horse's ears. The concentration on his face showed a fierce competitiveness she'd not witnessed at their first encounter.

The buzzer vibrated along her nerves like a cheese grater. Gina clung to the fence watching Holt relax his position on the horse and grab the handhold with two hands. The animal continued bucking and kicking. Her heart pounded harder with each jolt to Holt's body.

A man on another horse rushed alongside the bucking animal. Holt gripped the other cowboy around the waist, slipped from the bucking horse, and landed on his feet.

He walked toward the fence, keeping the animal in his sight...until his gaze latched onto hers peering through the fence. He stopped, stared, and a slow, surprised grin tipped his lips.

The warmth in his eyes rolled over her like an old friend. A flash behind him drew her gaze.

The horse circled back by Holt, its legs lashing out as it bucked and kicked. Her throat clogged with fear. Not a sound emitted when she opened her mouth. Her fear registered on Holt's face at the same time the horse bucked by him. A hoof caught Holt in the chest, flinging him against the fence.

"*Holt!*"

Fear and guilt surged, catapulting her over the

fence and stumbling through the loose dirt to kneel next to him. His face was pale; his breathing erratic. She unzipped his vest and gingerly felt his ribs. *I caused this.* He'd been distracted, looking at her when the horse struck.

She whisked the guilt aside and went into her professional mode.

"Lady? Lady, you can't be in here," a voice said above her.

"I know what I'm doing." She shook off the hands trying to pull her away. "Leave me alone and get the paramedics in here. He'll need x-rays." She found the pulse at his wrist, ignoring the way her own heart raced. "Holt? Holt, can you hear me? It's Gina." She looked around at the men staring at her. "Did any of you see him hit his head?" They nodded in unison.

She continued her evaluation as the ambulance drove into the arena. When the paramedic knelt beside her, she rattled off his condition and the vitals she could take without equipment.

"Sounds like you have this under control." The paramedic smiled. "Darrell, bring the stretcher."

"You're not...putting me...on a...stretcher." Holt's breathy, stubborn voice nearly brought tears to her eyes.

"Yes, they are. You could have fractured ribs and a concussion." She kept her voice firm but gentle.

He grabbed her hand. "It's good to see you, but"—he gulped air—"I 'cowboy up'." He glared at the paramedic. "You know...I don't ride out of an arena on a stretcher." He hauled down another heavy breath. "Help me up and tell your driver...to get the hell out of here...so the rodeo can continue."

"Holt, you can't be serious." Gina shuddered as he narrowed his eyes.

Determination and grit blazed in their depths.

25

Where was the compassionate man she'd visited with over a month ago? He'd been replaced by an obstinate, chest-beating male.

"I'm dead serious." He grimaced and sat up. The crowd roared, and he raised one arm in a salute. "Help me up," he said through clenched teeth as he held a hand up to the paramedic.

Gina wanted to protest but moved.

Once on his feet, Holt tugged her against him. "Let me lean on you, but look like your just hugging me." He headed to the gate held open at the side of the chutes.

She held her arms loose in case he had a fractured rib. "This is lunacy."

The heat of his body and the scent of animal, male, and his deodorant squeezed into her senses. She hid her hot face against his warm, dusty shoulder as his weight pressed down on her. Depositing him with the paramedics and disappearing into the crowd would be the best for both of them, but she couldn't shed the nagging feeling he got hurt because of her. Never one to run from her mishaps, she had to make sure he received proper treatment.

"I'm glad you're here," he whispered.

As she raised her head, three cowboys headed in their direction.

"Damn, Holt. How do you rate a good looking woman chargin' over the fence to help you?" chided the youngest looking of the trio.

"Just lucky I guess." Holt winked and her insides spun like a centrifuge.

"Or a wuss," said another cowboy two steps behind the younger man.

"Sit over here." The paramedic ushered Holt to a wooden bench in a small white tent. She unlocked her hands and let him slip away. Knowing she only held him for medical reasons didn't diminish the fact she liked the feel of his solid body and heat. A heady combination—and one she needed to shake quick.

She put on her nurse face and went to work deftly helping the paramedic place ice packs between Holt's vest and clothed torso.

"Leave the ice on these ribs until you get to the hospital and get them x-rayed." The paramedic smiled at her as she assisted. "He's lucky to have a knowledgeable person around to pick him up."

Holt stared at the beautiful woman. Gina, by his side. How did she get here—to Arizona and this rodeo? Did she know his schedule? He hadn't believed his eyes when he saw her hanging on the fence.

He studied her as she helped the paramedic. All efficiency.

Jess, Sam, and Timmy also studied her. He looked beyond the small group. Several other cowboys hung back watching. But she was oblivious to anything other than patching him up.

"Anybody hear what my score was?" He directed the question at his traveling buddies to drag their attention from Gina.

"Eighty. Should put you in good standing for tonight's flight," Jess said, tilting his head toward Gina.

Her head snapped up, and she stared at Holt. "You aren't thinking of getting on an animal again today are you?"

He liked the way the green brightened in her hazel eyes when her anger flared. "I gotta finish riding or I'll be out of the money."

"Out of the money! The announcer said you were on your way to Nationals. Why risk your health to ride?"

"Because it costs money to travel here and enter. I don't plan on leaving here in the hole."

Her lips formed a straight, disapproving line.

She stood and started to walk away.

Holt grabbed her hand and pulled her back. The movement tweaked his ribs, and he fought to keep a grimace from twisting his face. "Don't argue and don't leave."

She chewed on the edge of her finger and stared into the stands.

"Please, I could use someone to hold my hand while I get x-rayed." He squeezed her hand to get her to look at him. "You're a nurse. You can't walk away from an injured man."

"Besides"—Jess stepped forward—"Holt hasn't introduced us."

"Maybe because I don't want her knowing the likes of the hooligans I hang around with." Holt shot his friend a thank you and tipped his head toward the trio. "Gina Montgomery, this sorry lot happens to be my traveling buddies."

He pointed to their newest member of the group. "This here's Timmy Jacobs. He's a bit green, but we're breaking him in."

Timmy touched the brim of his hat and stepped forward, shaking her hand. "Pleased to meet you, ma'am."

"And this is Sam Foster, he's the reason I have to ride tonight, he's on my tail in the standings."

"Miss." Sam tipped his hat, but kept his distance. "And this is my long-time friend and rodeo buddy, Jess Karlan."

"You're the one Sheila pointed out when we parked." Gina glanced at Holt. "She's going to be upset when she finds out I met him."

It eased his mind knowing she came to the rodeo with another woman, rather than a guy.

"I'm pleased to meet you, Gina. Where did you and Holt meet?" Jess never beat around the bush about anything.

"Sheesh, Jess, you could have at least waited

until I was back resting in the camper."

Holt pushed to his feet, and Gina immediately moved to his aid. He smiled and waggled his brows at his three friends.

"Gina! Gina!" A man's voice bellowed. Holt turned to the sound and watched the biggest guy he'd ever seen walk toward them. *Shit!* She did come with a man. And a mountain of one at that.

Chapter Four

Holt caught the humor in Jess's eyes and felt Gina pull away from him as the man reached them.

"Sheila sent me to make sure you were okay." The giant eyed them all and his face broke into a smile as wide as a truck bumper. "Holy shit! Do you know who that is?"

Gina smiled and nodded. "Yes, Bud, that's Jess Karlan."

"You didn't say you knew him." Bud gave her a disappointed head shake.

"I didn't know him then. I'm acquaintances with Holt Reynolds." She gestured to him.

Bud, thrust his hand out. "Pleased to meet you." He stared down at Gina. "That's why you launched over the fence to help him."

Holt liked the way her face turned pink and gradually deepened to a sunset red. "I didn't know she was attending this rodeo." He raised his arm to shake hands. Pain burned up his ribs, but he held his face straight. No way would he show any weakness. Obviously, the man didn't have a claim on her or he wouldn't have been so ready to shake hands.

"My wife is going to go to the moon when I tell her who I've been talking to." That bumper-size smile was back.

"Bud, I'll come find you and Sheila after we get Holt x-rayed." Gina slid under his shoulder, wrapping her arm around his back.

Her hold was supportive but not intrusive. He grinned. Gina's nursing instincts gave him a chance to get near her.

"Don't hurry on our account," Bud said, pointedly glancing at Holt. "We'll be here for the evening performance. We'll round you up when it's over."

Holt liked the way the man thought. He could use a little distraction from his aches and pains. "We'll keep an eye out for you," he said, winking at the man over the top of Gina's head.

Bud saluted and headed back through the cowboys milling around behind the chutes.

Jess stepped to Holt's other side. "So, how *did* the two of you meet?"

Holt glanced at Gina, but she kept her attention on moving him toward the parking lot. He shrugged as best he could with sore ribs. "At the charity auction in Portland."

"That's the night you called me and interrupted—"

"Yeah, that night." Holt slid a peek toward Gina.

She peered around him at Jess. "Why did he call you?" Her hands tightened on his ribs and he grimaced.

"Hell if I know." Jess fell into step beside them. "But he put Clare right out of the mood."

"I called to find out about the schedule while I waited for you to finish doling out auction items." His answer seemed to appease both of them.

Rounding the trailers, two of his adversaries stood their ground in front of the camper. He didn't feel like verbally sparring with the two, but he couldn't allow them to see how banged up he was. Half a ride was mental preparation, and he wasn't about to let the two in front of him think he wasn't in top form.

"How come you got such a pretty medic?" Phil asked.

"I'm just lucky." Holt winked at Gina. Luckily

she didn't see it. He didn't doubt for a second if she had, she'd have been headed back to her friends. "You better draw a rip snorter on the second go-round 'cuz it'll take one hell of a ride for you to get past me."

"You ain't ridin' with them injuries." Willie peered at Gina for confirmation.

"She fixes me up. She doesn't say whether I ride or not. And I'm riding."

He heard her intake of breath and felt her arms slip from around him.

"I'd say the little lady has a different idea," Phil said, smiling like he'd found a new can of chew in his shirt pocket.

Holt grasped Gina's hand before she could say anything and towed her around the men. Jess conversed with the two, keeping them from following and harassing him anymore.

"Can you drive a truck with a camper?" Holt asked Gina, moving to the driver's door and handing her a set of keys.

"Yes. Why?" Her narrowed eyes studied him.

"'Cuz, you're going to drive me to the hospital for an x-ray." He opened the door and waved her in. It wasn't wise to do too much if his ribs were fractured. But he also needed to know if he had to pull out of the competition. He could ride with bruised ribs, but he wouldn't chance being out the rest of the season by puncturing a lung.

She slid in behind the wheel. "I'm glad you're coming to your senses."

He shook his head and grinned. She thought she'd won. That was fine by him. Hot pain seared his ribs as he climbed into the passenger side. He slumped back in the seat, breathing shallow and willing the pain to ease.

Gina started the truck and pulled up to the main street. "Which way do I go?"

"Take the highway north into town and there should be signs to follow." He leaned his head back against the seat. Why hadn't he noticed the jack hammer behind his eyes earlier?

"It's comforting to know you haven't been there before."

Her sarcastic remark made him smile. "I rarely get bucked off, and I usually make a clean get-a-way." He rolled his head to watch her profile as she drove. "If I hadn't seen you, would you have let me know you were at the rodeo?"

She dashed a sideways glance at him and stared at the road. "I don't know."

"If nothing else, you're the first honest woman I've ever met." He closed his eyes, trying to block out the aches. It didn't help. Watching Gina was more soothing.

"I wondered if you would be here. Kind of wanted to see you ride..." She slipped a peek at him again. "Are you okay? You're getting pale."

"My head feels like there's a bull dancing around in it."

"Are you feeling nauseous?" She scanned his face matter-of-factly before returning her attention to the road.

"A little I guess." He'd had a concussion before. This didn't feel quite the same, but who knew if they all had the same side effects. "This ice is getting damn cold."

"Let me know if I need to pull over. Oh, there's a sign for the hospital."

Gina followed the signs, praying Holt didn't have injured ribs, yet knowing if he didn't, he'd ride again, possibly exacerbating the concussion.

This was her fault. If she hadn't been standing at the fence, he wouldn't have seen her. Her pulse picked up. Watching him ride had been as thrilling as it was nerve wracking. The power, skill, and ferocity it took to stay on the horse contradicted the mellow man she'd first met.

She glanced over noting his color paled more each time she looked at him. By the way his face pinched, he fought the pain. Why did men always have to be so tough? She wasn't sure she could stick around and watch him climb up on another horse tonight. As far as she was concerned, that was destructive behavior. She knew all about destructive behavior. Thank God for her piano teacher.

Gina pulled to the emergency room doors and parked the truck. "I'll get a wheelchair and come get you." She opened the door.

"No."

The one firm word drew her attention. She twisted and glanced over her shoulder. She'd heard that tone before—by her father. It froze her in a moment from her past.

Holt's spurs jingled when he shifted in the seat, drawing her back to the present. This was why she stayed far away from males other than doctors and patients. Too many unwelcome memories could immobilize her from the smallest incident.

"Just come help me walk in." His voice softened, and his eyes beseeched her to help.

"Damn it, Holt. You aren't at the arena any more. You don't have to, what did you call it? 'Cowboy up.'" She slid out of the truck. Before she made it to the front of the vehicle, the passenger door opened, and he slid his feet to the ground. The impact whitened his face and closed his eyes. She rushed to his side, fearful he would faint.

"Why are you so stubborn?" She let his armpit rest on her shoulder as she slid her arm around his back to help him into the building. His protective vest made actually touching his torso unattainable. For that reprieve she was grateful. She wasn't sure how her overwrought emotions would deal with intimate contact right now. He'd started out as more than a patient, and she found it hard to keep a professional demeanor around him.

"I'm not stubborn. Just don't want anyone to see me vulnerable." He stared into her eyes. "I think you can understand that."

She stared back. How could he know her that well after their one brief meeting?

"Your cowboy get bucked off?" A young, well-groomed man in a white doctor's coat pushed a wheelchair up to them.

"He's not my cowboy. And no, he didn't get bucked off, he was kicked." Gina narrowed her eyes and read the name tag on the young intern. "Dr. Morris, he needs his ribs x-rayed and two hundred milligrams of ibuprofen for the pain."

"Ma'am, I'm the doctor, I'll do the diagnosing." He motioned for them to enter a room with several draped areas.

"I've been a practicing ER nurse while you've been in med school and know how to decide what's needed when a doctor is busy." She eased Holt onto the gurney and pulled the ice packs out of his clothing.

The man snorted and headed back out to the desk. She'd had her battles with interns before. It took a couple years for some new doctors to get over themselves and realize nurses, especially ER nurses, did know a thing or two and could free up their time.

"You shouldn't make him mad. He could take it out on me."

She glanced at Holt. A smile wavered on his lips.

"I don't care for incompetent people in the medical profession."

"How do you know he's incompetent? He hasn't done a thing yet to prove otherwise." Holt stopped her hand when she reached up to remove his vest.

"I've seen a few interns with his attitude. They

think wearing a white coat makes them God. They don't put one hundred percent effort into their work."

His hand dropped, and she removed his vest, trying to make him move as little as possible. Holt grimaced and her stomach clenched, knowing she caused the pain. Her hands stalled at the pearl snaps of his shirt. If he were a patient she didn't know, she would have had him stripped and headed to the x-ray department by now. This man made her emotions churn—she didn't dare touch his warm flesh under that shirt.

A pretty blonde woman holding a clipboard stepped through an opening in the drapes. "We need papers filled out before we can even look at you." Her gaze landed on Holt. Her smile broadened, and her eyes lit with interest. "You're lucky things are slow today. Everyone's over at the Doin's and no one's drunk enough yet to do anything stupid."

Gina stepped away from the gurney. A small knot formed in her stomach. She had no rights to Holt, but watching the other woman flirt with him swirled up jealousy. An emotion she'd never had before toward a person. The acid in her stomach burned ten times stronger.

She started to turn away, flicking a glance at Holt. His pain-filled eyes caught her attention. He responded to the woman's questions, but his eyes never left hers.

He needed her. No one ever needed her except in a professional capacity. It unnerved her to think this man she barely knew seeped through her barriers and had her voluntarily doing uncharacteristic behavior. He held out a hand, and she stepped back to his side, placing her hand in his.

The woman's tone changed from flirtatious to professional. Was that why he took her hand? To stop the woman's flirting, or did he really care and want her close? She had to remember... men, from her experience, used more than they gave.

The doctor pushed through the curtains. "Got all you need Jeannie?" He smiled what Gina was sure made the old ladies swoon, but it came across as cocky to her.

"Yes, doctor. Just sign here, please." She held the clipboard in front of Holt. Gina glanced at the form while Holt signed his name. He'd put a woman with his last name as contact. Who was that? Ex-wife, sister, mother? There was so much about the man she didn't know and shouldn't be interested in.

"Get him out of that shirt and into this wheelchair if you want him to get an x-ray." The doctor motioned to the wheels and seat peeking through the curtain. His attitude told her she'd overstepped on their first meeting.

Holt just grinned at her and winked. The rascal knew she didn't want to undress him. She cleared her throat and pulled the snap at the top of his shirt. Looking over his shoulder, she moved her hands down the shirt band, pulling the material away from his body, feeling his heat. She'd undressed male patients before, but touching this man triggered sensations she'd locked away.

"You'll have to tug it out of my pants if you want to finish taking it off." His voice whispered, only for her ears. She dashed a glance at his face. He didn't mock her. In fact, he looked as unsure as she felt.

She tugged on his shirt and grasped the warm tail as she unsnapped the last snap. Her gaze fell on the white tank T-shirt clinging to his muscular torso. It would have to be peeled from his body as well. Taking a breath, she rolled the bottom up, exposing a tan belly with a thin line of blonde hair that widened as it climbed to his chest and spread across well-formed pecs. She inhaled sharply at the sight of two perfectly-formed hoof marks on the right side of his chest just below his puckered nipple.

"You'll have to lift your arms." She licked her lips and stepped closer, into the V of his legs, to help navigate his arms through the holes and slip the whole garment over his head.

"Thank you." His voice was rough as his dark eyes stared unblinking into hers.

Gina stepped back, dropping her gaze. The heat swirling in her body was a bad sign. She didn't want to desire this man. Any man.

"Get in the chair." She tried to keep her voice even as she pointed to the wheelchair. Control was something she'd worked hard to attain. Control over her circumstance and control over her body. She didn't like the way she lost power over her emotions around Holt.

When he was settled in the contraption, she wheeled him down the hall, following the signs to the radiology department.

Sitting in the waiting area, she came to a conclusion. As soon as she handed him over to his friends, she'd find Sheila and Bud and never attend another rodeo. She couldn't chance running into him again somewhere. He was the first man she couldn't shut out. The emotions he triggered warmed her. That not only scared her, it threatened her vow of celibacy.

Something that defined her and defied her past.

Chapter Five

Eyes closed, Holt leaned back in the seat, wishing Gina would say something. He ached all over, but the doctor had good news. There weren't any fractures in his ribs. He still needed to be monitored for twenty-four hours for any complications from hitting his head though. He'd hoped Gina would volunteer for the job, but after helping him with his shirt, she'd been more standoffish than their first meeting.

His lips tipped in a smile. There'd been no mistaking the interest in the depths of her golden-brown eyes when she peeled his undershirt off.

Gravel crunched under the tires, signaling their return to the rodeo grounds. Time to cowboy up. He opened his eyes, raised his head, willed the pills the doctor gave him to kick in, and sat straighter in the seat.

"Are you really going to ride again tonight?" she asked, putting the truck in park and narrowing her eyes.

"I told you before. There's nothing broke, I have money invested in this event. I intend to do my best to win back my money and then some."

He put his hand on the door handle just as Timmy yanked it open.

"What'd the doc say?" His young face creased with worry.

"I'll be buying you a steak dinner on Sunday night." Holt held his face poker still as he eased his body out of the truck.

"You only got a couple hours till they start the

next performance," Jess said, showing up behind Timmy.

"Good, gives the painkillers more time to kick in." He smiled and turned to find Gina stomping away from the group.

"Hey! Where're you going?" Ignoring his aches, he jogged after the woman, grabbed her arm, and spun her toward him.

"I'll not stand around and watch you do more damage." The fury in her voice belied the fear in her eyes.

She'd probably bolt, but he had to hold her. Raising his arms hurt, but he wrapped them around her and drew her against his chest.

"Shhh. I'm sorry, you feel that way, but it's how I make my living. I can't just quit because I have a couple bruises."

"And a possible concussion." Her arms folded between their bodies kept him from experiencing the closeness he desired.

The derision in her voice made him chuckle. Her attitude only proved she *did* care about his well-being.

"Please, keep me company until I ride. You don't have to watch. In fact, I'd prefer you not be around the arena when I ride. I'd be wondering if you'll jump the fence if I break a nail."

A small feminine chuckle escaped.

"Besides," he added, playing his ace. "The doctor said I need to be monitored for twenty-four hours. I think the best person for that is a bona fide nurse." Placing a finger under her chin, he made her look at him. "Please? I promise not to do whatever it is that makes you bolt."

Her eyes widened, and she sucked in her breath. Her body tensed, and he opened his hold to let her go. He wasn't sure what happened in her past. A boyfriend, husband, father who abused her, he didn't know, but he knew a head shy filly when he saw one.

Holt grasped her hand. "Come on, let's go sit with the boys."

Timmy already had the folding chairs out of the camper and set up on the shady side of the truck. Jess placed bottled water and chips on the small aluminum table.

She glanced at the open area, the other people, and slowly nodded.

Air released from his lungs. He smiled, tugging her along behind him and wishing the darn throb in his head would go away.

He placed Gina in the outside chair and took the one between her and Jess. Timmy sat next to the table and the food.

"Where's Sam?" he asked, handing Gina a bottle of water he'd opened.

"He's calling in to see what round we drew at next week's rodeo." Jess took a swallow of his drink and scanned Holt's body. "What did the doc really say?"

"Ribs are just bruised. Hurt like hell. And there's a possibility of a concussion." He smiled at the woman sitting next to him. "Said I needed twenty-four hour monitoring. Pretty handy having a nurse by my side."

She glared at him. "I think you're an idiot to ride when you could do more damage not only to your ribs but your brain as well."

"Ma'am, no offense, but he couldn't addle his brain much more than it is," Timmy offered, giving everyone a good laugh and making a smile touch her lips.

The laughter caused his head to throb worse. Holt bit his bottom lip, hiding it behind the raised water bottle. Damn, how was he going to get on a horse and concentrate with this pounding pain? He'd had a good ride and had a good chance of winning, or at least coming in the money. He had to ride again.

"Holt? Hey man, are you with us?" Jess's voice yanked him from his thoughts. His friend looked ready to jump up and help him.

Gina placed a hand on his forearm, drawing his attention and peering at him intently.

"Yeah, I'm here, what did you say?" Holt shoved the pain away and focused.

"I gathered your rigging from the last ride. You want me to check it over?" Jess eyed him as closely as Gina.

"Yeah, if you don't mind." He rubbed a hand across the back of his neck. He felt Gina rise. "Don't…"

"I'm going to massage your neck and head."

She stood behind his chair. Her cold fingers made him jump.

"Sorry." Her fingers trembled against his skin a moment before she began kneading the sore muscles.

He glanced across at the envy on Timmy's face, then smiled, closed his eyes, and let his body relax under her experienced hands. The throb in his head eased as her long, slender fingers moved up the back of his head, pushing his hat down over his face and into his lap. He couldn't have stopped its decent to the ground if his life depended on it. Her magic fingers had turned his whole body to mush.

"I'd pay you to do that to me."

He heard the jest in Jess's voice, and if anyone but his happily married buddy had made the suggestion he'd been on his feet, ready to fight.

"He won't pay you as good as I can." The minute his words hit the air, he knew they were a mistake. Her fingers stopped abruptly. The heat of her body withdrew, and the air grew thick and cold with her retreat.

"Damn, I didn't mean it that way." He implored

Jess to help him out.

"Holt's got more ready cash than I do. With my wife and kids, I'm not the rich bachelor he is." Jess shrugged his shoulders staring past Holt, looking as sincere as a dog that chewed a hole in a chair.

Holt and Timmy snorted at the same time.

"Sheesh, Jess. You won the National title and have four major sponsors. How can you say you got less money than Holt?" Timmy shook his head. "Damn modest."

Holt burst out laughing, and his head pounded but less than before. "Timmy, don't make me laugh." He reached behind the chair to take Gina's hand, holding his breath and willing her to place her hand in his.

She didn't.

He twisted and pointed to the chair beside him.

"Jess, Timmy, would you mind taking a walk so I can have a little time with Gina. Alone."

Timmy grinned like a fool, but Jess nodded and stood.

"Come on, Timmy. Let's go see what Sam's up to. He should have finished that call by now." The two wandered off through the trucks in the lot.

Gina watched the two disappear. She didn't know what Holt planned to say or do, but she had to stay unattached. *Sure, like you did when you massaged his neck and head.* Her fingers still tingled from running them through his short, curly hair and kneading the toned muscles on his neck.

A quiver started low in her abdomen. The sensation just about shot her out of the chair. This was all wrong. She didn't want to feel anything for this man. She couldn't.

"Whoa... I haven't said anything and you're spooked." He reached out, taking her hand into his rough, solid one.

"I-I really should leave." Even as she said the

words, her legs worked against her, turning rubbery when she needed them to carry her away.

"No, there is no reason for you to leave. Your ride will come get you after the evening performance, unless you decide to stay and monitor me the full twenty-four hours. Didn't you take some oath to help the injured or something?" His smile warmed her heart and sent panic clogging her throat. She couldn't go backwards, couldn't let this smooth talker make her go against the course she'd set.

"Yes...no...ohhh." She pulled her hand from his and covered her face. What should she do? She enjoyed his company, and her body craved his touch. She needed to run, to stay strong. But guilt ate at her because his possible concussion *was* her fault. If he hadn't noticed her at the fence, he wouldn't have been distracted.

"Hey."

His presence in front of her chair, his voice level with hers, proved he knelt before her.

His gentle fingers peeled her hands from her face. "You don't have to stay if it's going to upset you." He placed her trembling hands on her legs, settling his warm hands on top. His thumbs gently caressed her skin.

What was wrong with her? She hadn't fallen apart like this in over a decade. And this man hadn't done anything to cause panic. She swallowed, shoving her uncertainties back down her throat and raising her face to look into his eyes. The gentle uncensored gaze gave her the strength to utter the words he wanted to hear and her conscience wouldn't allow her to ignore.

"No, I'll stay until the rodeo is over, tonight—no longer." His concerned eyes warmed her chest and brought embarrassment. "I want you to know, I'm not always this...well, this strange."

"I know something in your past makes you skittish." He gently gathered her hands into his, resting them in her lap. "I just want you to know I've never raised a hand to a woman, and I'd never push my attentions on you." That heart-pitching smile he used more often than she liked, slid across his face. "But I am persistent, and plan to wear you down to where panic doesn't flit across your face when I flirt."

"Oh my—it doesn't, does it? I mean my panic shows?" How embarrassing. Obviously, she wasn't as good at hiding her emotions as she'd always thought.

"Don't worry. I seem to be the only one who notices." He smiled and ducked his head, disarming her once again.

That was the problem. He did notice more than anyone she'd ever been around. And that scared her. How could she keep her past hidden when he saw through her?

"Could you hop up in the camper and find something a little more filling than these chips?" He stood slowly and lowered his body into the chair next to her, rearranging the ice packs the doctor replaced between his shirt and vest.

"Shouldn't we wait for the others to return? They might not like me climbing into their home." She glanced at the camper and wondered how four men could live in the small confines. She stood. "I'll just wander down to the food venues and get something."

"No, I don't want you wandering around by yourself." The firm response made her look down at him. His right arm cradled his left ribs. Worry creased his brow over dark eyes regarding her.

"I can take care of myself." She thought of the two men earlier and Sheila's comment.

"I'm sure you could, but right now I don't need to be worrying about you. I've got enough to think about. I have to pull off two more good rides to be in the money tomorrow—"

"You're riding tonight *and* tomorrow?" She shook her head. Fear for him evolved into anger. How could he even consider climbing on a horse the shape he was in? "You're even crazier than I thought."

"If I don't make all three rides, I won't be able to compete against the scores of those who make three rides. I told you, I plan to place in the money. The only way I'll live with placing out of the money is if I draw a bad horse. Because that's out of my control."

"What if you do more damage?" She placed her hands on her hips and stared down at the man. Why would he punish his body so?

"The most I could do is be out for a week with a concussion. And there's only small purses the next couple of weeks so that wouldn't be that big of a deal." He shrugged and took a sip of water.

"Is money all you care about?" She stood in front of his chair. Pain dulled his eyes, and his breathing was shallow. "Your health will give you a happier life than money. And you could end up in a coma if you bang that hard head of yours again." Her chest constricted at the thought of him lying in a coma.

The firm set to his mouth told her it was useless to argue.

She pointed her thumb over her shoulder to the camper. "What kind of food were you thinking of?"

"Whatever you can find that is filling and won't jar my head when I eat it." He ran a hand over his face. "It's just starting to calm down."

Gina nodded and grasped the door to the camper. She still didn't like climbing into what she considered four men's home, but Holt needed nourishment. Especially if he planned to ride a horse again today.

As she pushed the door open, she was accosted

by an aroma worse than a locker room. Sweat, sour feet, manure, and something she didn't care to know.

She peered around the edge of the camper. "You sure I couldn't just hit a hotdog stand or something?"

A grin curved one side of his lips. "That bad?"

"Yeah, that bad." She slammed the door shut and walked to where her purse sat on the ground by her chair.

"Okay, but wait until Jess can go with you." He grabbed her wrist. She glared and he released her. "Please."

"What are you worried about? I'm a big girl, I can handle myself." She looked into his eyes and realized it wasn't just about her. He didn't want to be left alone. "How about you use that cell phone you said is always on you and call Jess. Ask him to bring something back with him?"

He ducked his head. "You'll have to dig in the glove box. That's where I put it when I get ready to ride."

Grasping the handle on the truck, she pulled the door open as two men, one in a security guard uniform and another older man dressed like all the other cowboys, approached Holt.

"Reynolds, what can you tell us about the crazy woman that hopped the fence after your ride?"

Chapter Six

Gina snapped the glove box shut and walked over to Holt. She held the cell phone out to him and studied the men. What did they want with her?

"Chet, Wally, I don't know who she was." Holt sent her a look that said don't say a thing.

She wanted to ask why, but this was his territory and, for now, she'd abide by his rules.

"If we've got an overzealous fan on our hands we need to know." The security guard stared at her.

She slowly sat in the chair next to Holt. So that was it. She didn't want escorted out of the area. She'd lose her ride back to the reservation. Gina avoided eye contact with the men and tried to act like what they talked about didn't matter.

"You don't have to worry about that." Holt motioned to her. "This here is a friend of mine, Miss Montgomery." Holt tipped his head toward the cowboy and then the security guard. "Gina, this is Chet and Wally."

"She looks kind of like the woman..." Chet began.

"I guarantee this woman is no threat to me or anyone else," Holt said in a tone that brooked no discussion.

The security guard cleared his throat and shuffled his feet back a step.

"What about your injuries? We haven't got word you're pulling out." Chet scratched his gray chin whiskers.

"I'm not pulling out. A few bruises, a knock on my head. Nothing to keep me from taking your

48

money." Holt waved his arm toward the arena. She noticed the twinge in his jaw and the dullness in his eyes at his actions, but she doubted the men did.

"Well, if you see that woman, let security know," Chet said.

"Will do." Holt saluted the two, and they shook their heads as they walked away.

"What was that about?" she asked when they were out of earshot.

"First things, first." He flipped his phone open, punched a button, and waited. "Jess, could you bring some decent food back with you? Yeah, that's fine, just nothing greasy. Okay. Thanks."

He shot her that disarming smile. "Food's on the way."

"The men?" She nodded her head in the direction the two men had departed.

"Most rodeos don't take kindly to spectators hurdling fences and landing in the arena during a performance." He shrugged. "That's why you're staying here, at the camper, when I ride again."

"I'm not going to bolt over the fence again. I've learned my lesson." She shot him a nonchalant look when she felt like giving him a lecture. "You don't want help. You want to destroy your body and become a crippled old man."

He smiled. "I don't plan on destroying my body. If you saw the ride, I didn't get thrown. The ornery cuss kicked me. I was minding my own business."

Yeah, staring at me. Guilt punched her stomach as solid as a fist.

He put her purse on the ground and motioned for her to sit. "This is the first time I've been this beat up in the last four years." His eyes gleamed with pride. "There's a reason I've been to the National Rodeo Finals the last three years. That's because I stay on the horse and make the ride."

"How long do you plan to beat up your body?"

She raised a hand to halt his words when his eyes snapped with indignation. "You may not fall off a horse, but you have to admit just staying on one is hard on the body. Your shoulder is jerked, the whipping of your spine, not to mention I saw some rider's heads practically bounce off the rump of the horse he was riding, he'd leaned back so far."

"My plan is to win the championship this year and retire to my ranch." His eyes took on a different gleam, one of contentment. "I plan to raise rough-stock and work on my art."

"Rough-stock? What's that?" She settled into the chair, curious to hear more about the man and his passion.

"Rough-stock is the bucking stock—bulls, horses. I plan to keep my hand in rodeoing by providing bucking horses." Holt grinned. "Less wear on the body and still some profit."

He glanced at Gina. Her head was tipped back, her eyes closed. The waning evening light reflected traces of red in her hair. She had the thick, straight strands pulled up into a ponytail today. The style made her look more youthful, more approachable.

"What are your plans for the future? Are you always going to be an ER nurse, traveling, never settling down?" A flicker of irritation crossed her features before she opened her eyes and stared into the blue sky.

"I don't plan to travel indefinitely, and I don't plan to be an ER nurse indefinitely." Her voice held conviction and a passel of resentment.

"You don't like being a nurse?"

Her head snapped around, eyes wide as they searched his.

"I heard it in your voice."

She slumped into the chair like a sack of feed with a mouse-sized hole.

"How is it you see and hear things I don't say?"

She didn't look at him.

It tickled that she realized he saw through her. "I've spent a good deal of my time around all sorts of people and enjoyed not only studying them for composition—would they make an interesting person in a drawing—but also the emotions on their faces."

"Like the picture at the auction." She turned to him, her gaze intent. "Who was the girl in the drawing? Is she someone you know?"

Very few knew the truth behind Sherrie's death. The realization he could have saved her plagued him. He stared at the woman next to him. Her insecurities and demons almost masked in her eyes. Holt took a deep breath. If he wanted her to open up to him, he had to do the same. "That was a drawing of my sister."

"Oh."

She looked away, then back, her gaze assessing him. What was she thinking behind those hazel eyes?

"How do ribs and baked potatoes sound?" Timmy said loudly as the trio of riding buddies appeared between parked cars.

Holt had forgotten about his growling stomach as he concentrated on getting closer to Gina. Their timing was crappy.

"Good. Sounds good." He glanced at Gina. She still cogitated on what he'd said. What about the picture had captured her? And why did finding out it was his sister, push her deeper into herself?

Jess set the bags down on the table and handed foam boxes filled with a whole meal to everyone. Gina hesitated, then took it at Jess's urging.

"The place has started to fill up already," Sam said, glancing between him and Gina. Holt knew his traveling buddies had been speculating on the woman who sat in the chair trying to appear invisible.

"You know what I've been thinking?" He looked at the others but kept an eye on her.

"It's hard to answer that these days," Jess said, glancing toward Gina and back at him. "You've been full of surprises lately."

"Jess should drive Gina to the motel before the bronc riding starts." In his peripheral vision, he saw her head snap up and felt her gaze bore into him. "That way when I need more nursing, Gina would be at the motel to check me out and make sure I'm fit to ride tomorrow."

Timmy and Sam snorted. That was sure to set Gina in panic mode. He sent the two a scathing glower.

"I meant, get her a room. We can drop her off—" He turned to her and almost grinned at the steely glare directed at him. "Where is it you're working right now?"

"You don't need to know, since I'll be leaving here tonight with Sheila and Bud." Her voice dripped with ice.

"It's not a bad idea, if you don't have to be back till after the final ride tomorrow," Jess said, setting his container down and picking up a bottle of soda. "He could aggravate that concussion by riding. If you checked him out, you could tell him if he shouldn't ride the last ride."

"Like he'd even listen to me." Her gaze locked onto Holt's. He felt more than her anger, he felt fear. She was worried he'd do more damage. Was it the nature of her nursing or because she cared for him?

"He may not listen to you, but we've been friends long enough, I won't let him risk his health. We'd"—Jess pointed a thumb at Timmy and Sam— "tie him up so he couldn't compete."

Holt didn't doubt it for a minute. They'd been through a lot together. Jess wouldn't let him ruin his life by being stupid. But would Gina believe his friend?

"They would, too, if for no other reason than to keep me from beating them." He wanted her to stay. Wanted to get to know her better, help her heal the scars.

She studied Jess's face then trained her gaze at him. Her hand froze mid-air before she dropped it into her lap. He grinned at how she caught herself before chewing on her nail, a nervous trait he found endearing.

"I'm not riding in that truck or camper for two hours with all of you."

Holt's heart banged around in his chest like a runaway colt. Was she conceding to stay?

"I'm going to drop out for the next two weeks and heal. I'll rent a car, take you to your hospital, and fly home."

"I didn't—" She looked from him to Jess and back again. "I didn't mean that—" Her eyes narrowed, and she stood. "We need to talk." She stomped to the hood of the truck, standing with her back to them.

"I'm not sure why you're pushing her, but I do believe you need someone looking out for you this weekend," Jess said as Holt stood stiffly to go see what burr was under her saddle.

"I'm not pushing, just trying to get her to hang around long enough I can learn more about her." Holt shot a glare at the other two. "Contrary to popular belief, not every woman is meant to be slept with. Some just need friends."

"That's new." Sam scowled. They'd had a set-to when Sam first joined the group. Right after Sherrie's death, Holt hit the bottle and wound up in bed with a buckle bunny who happened to be Sam's fiancée. Ever since, they kept a polite distance from one another's women.

53

Holt waved him off even though he was still embarrassed over the whole incident. He headed to Gina; he wanted to be her friend first. When she accepted that, he'd work on the physical aspect of the relationship.

He stepped in front of her. The crossed arms and grim set to her lips wasn't a good sign. It was obvious she didn't want the others to see or hear what she was going to say. Holt wanted to rub a hand up and down her arm, but had enough sense to keep his distance.

"What did you want to say?" He leaned against the truck hood, making sure all the weight settled on his back and not the bruised ribs.

"I—" She glanced at him then away. She took a deep breath, and her gaze finally stalled on his. "I won't be some conquest. I'm not a groupie. I only came to this rodeo because the head nurse told me not to show my face at the hospital for two days because I've been working so much overtime. And Sheila happened along saying she was coming here, and the next thing I know, I'm sitting in a truck hearing all about this fantastic rodeo event I'll never forget." She swung her hands in the air. "I didn't know you'd be here. Didn't know I'd climb a fence to see if you were dead or alive."

She huffed out a low growl and wrapped her arms around her body. "I'm the reason you were hurt."

He started to speak, but she raised a hand.

"You were staring at *me* when you were kicked. If I hadn't stood at the fence you'd be fine, and I wouldn't be about to make what I'm sure is a big mistake." She sighed, a deep weary sound. "But I can't in all good conscience walk away from something that was my fault in the first place." Her eyes stared into his. "I like you. You're nice and funny. But"—she nibbled on a fingernail—"I won't

54

take this any farther than a friendship. No matter what you or your buddies think."

Holt nodded. He heard her words, saw she believed in them. Her body on the other hand, showed him her deeper attraction. Her nipples pushed at the tight top, her cheeks flushed. Yet, something in her past made her think she shouldn't feel this way.

"I told you earlier, my goal is to win Champion Bareback Rider at Nationals in December. That's my focus right now. But I have time for a friend." He peered into her eyes. "I promise, if you stay, you get your own room, and I'll take you back to your hospital tomorrow." Holt winced as he pushed away from the truck. "Besides, this body of mine is in no shape to do the horizontal mambo."

She chuckled. "I just don't want you thinking...you know. Because I won't change my mind."

"You're too young to say something like that. Lives change." And he hoped to be the one to change her mind.

She shook her head and clutched her arms tighter to her body. "That's the one thing that irritates me the most. You thinking you know me. You don't and stop trying to think you do!" She turned, walking up to Jess.

"I'm ready to go to that motel. I could stand to get out of this heat. But I need to find Sheila and Bud and tell them the change of plans." She scanned the arena area. "There, I see them already in the stands where we'd sat earlier."

Holt stopped behind her. "Go tell them what's happening. Then Jess will take you." He watched her all the way through the parked vehicles to the mountain of a man, Gina called Bud, and his redheaded wife in the bleachers. Gina pointed in their direction and he nodded. The woman's red head bobbed, and her face pointed their direction several times while Gina's motions became more and more stilted. He could almost feel her agitation through her robotic gait back to the parking lot.

Holt met her at the back of the truck. Her bristling behavior made her all the more endearing. He ached to reach out, wrap his arms around her, and soothe away her worries He may tell Gina and his buddies, he just wanted to be her friend, but his heated body and lonely heart wanted more. Her professionalism while doctoring him, the beautiful music that flowed from her fingers, and her quick wit were all qualities he admired.

As Jess headed for the driver's side, Holt opened the passenger door, placing a hand on Gina's arm to help her in. She glanced at the contact and a deeper shade of pink spread across her cheeks.

She may not be in his arms any time soon, but, if he went slow, he had a strong feeling she would be well worth the wait.

Chapter Seven

Holt ignored the searing pain in his ribs as he climbed into the truck. The dun mustang tried his damnedest to buck him off, twisting and stomping, but he'd hung on for a score in the seventies. Holt clutched his side and grinned. A seventy kept him in the running for the money tomorrow.

Timmy and Sam headed off with a group of bull riders to check out a local bar while Holt rested his head on the back of the seat waiting for Jess to finish loading their gear in the camper. The pounding in his head made him nauseous. By the way his ribs burned and ached, he was sure all the meat and muscle had been ripped from them. All he wanted was a hot shower and a bed.

Jess rocked the vehicle climbing in and started the engine. The rumble of the diesel motor excited him when he was awake and raring to go, and soothed him into sleep when he was tired. Tonight, the deep rumble comforted and gave him a buffer of solitude.

"She isn't Sherrie," Jess's low voice said above the hum of the truck motor.

"I know." Damn, this was a heck of a time for Jess to become a psychologist.

"Then stop treating her like she's fragile. I've a feeling Gina has more grit than you give her credit for. Saving people's lives every day, I'd say she knows the value of life and won't throw hers away."

"I know she isn't going to commit suicide like my kid sister." He rolled his head, staring at his friend. "But something has hurt her. She's as skittish as a head shy horse."

"You don't have to save her. It wasn't your fault Sherrie did what she did. It was that bastard your mother married."

Jess had never liked Holt's stepfather.

Hell, he didn't even like the man.

He'd tolerated his stepfather. His mother didn't get interested in anyone until eight years after his father died. That led Holt to believe it was a love match. Funny thing was, Holt had felt in his gut something wasn't right with his new stepfather. But he'd headed off to college so it didn't matter. He only had to be around the man on holidays.

He squeezed his eyes shut, begging the pounding in his head to cover the memory of Sherrie's pleading when she called and asked to spend the summer with him. But he'd just joined the PRCA and didn't want to run herd over his teenage sister, and the rodeo circuit wasn't any place for a teenage girl who wasn't a participant.

A month into summer, he got the call that haunted him every day and most nights. She'd killed herself. His guts still turned inside out every time he thought of that call.

"You couldn't have known what he was doing to Sherrie, you were at college. Hell, your mom was the one who should have done something."

Jess grew up motherless and was proud of the fact he and his siblings made it just fine. A fact he didn't mind bringing up every time the matter of Holt's mom not stopping her husband came into the conversation.

"Do we have to discuss this right now? My head has enough trouble dealing with it when it isn't rattled." Holt wanted to have Gina's hands massage his neck and scalp, like earlier in the day. He wanted to feel those soothing hands and know someone cared.

"I just don't want you messing this *friendship* up by treating her like a jumper. Because I don't believe she is." Jess parked the truck in front of the motel.

His friend's comment penetrated the dull throb of his head. "Why do you care if I mess this up?"

Jess smiled. "I like the guy she brings out in you. You've been smiling more today than a bunch of bachelors at Hooters. And that's with being in pain. Can't imagine what you'd be like if you were healthy."

"Well, don't go getting any ideas. We're friends, and that's as far as the lady wants to take it." Holt liked Jess's acceptance of Gina. If things did progress, they'd spend a lot of time with Jess and Clare.

"Are you sure? There were a couple times today, when she looked more than friendly at you." Jess's grin widened as he opened his door.

"That's the feeling I get, too. But she's adamant nothing will go any farther than friendship, which brings me back to something happening in her past."

Holt eased himself out of the truck. A door, several down from their motel room, opened and Gina peeked out.

"I've been listening the last hour for your truck." She hurried to his side. "Did you stay on? Did you land on your feet? How's the head?" She grasped his wrist, examining his pulse.

"I just want a hot shower and some sleep." He pulled his wrist from her grasp, placed his arm across her shoulder, and walked to the door in front of them.

Gina couldn't hide the happiness lightening her steps and fluttering her insides at the sight of Holt walking and his eyes not dilated. She spent the longest four hours of her life waiting for their return, hoping she didn't get a call saying they hauled him to the hospital.

"You're going to want to monitor him all night for that concussion aren't you?" Jess asked, opening the door.

"I thought you'd do that as his friend." She figured Jess could wake Holt up every two hours to make sure he didn't fall into a coma.

"I'm not losing sleep and possibly a spot in the money tomorrow playing nurse maid to him, even if he is my best friend." Jess turned to her. "Take him to your room. You've got two beds. Throw him in the shower, and you can get up every whatever and check him. It's what you do for a living."

His brusque comment side-swiped her. She barely knew Jess, but at this moment she didn't like him. And she sure as hell didn't want to spend a night alone with Holt.

"I'll bring his bag down in a minute," Jess said, disappearing into the room in front of the truck.

Holt was wobbly, and Jess shut the door in their faces. What choice did she have?

Holt led her to the room she'd sat in waiting for their return.

Gina glanced up at him. "I really think you should remain in your room." He no longer wore his heavy vest. His heat and scent clung to her, reeling her senses.

"I'll feel better knowing you're looking out for me."

His breathy comment increased her fear he had caused more damage. She pushed the door to her room the rest of the way open.

"Shower," he whispered.

She stared at his drawn face and pale color. "When was the last time you took a pain pill?"

"Too long ago."

"Where are the pills?"

"In the glove box."

Gina helped Holt into the bathroom. It was

small, so she quickly backed out, shutting the door.

She had a man in her motel room. Not just any man, but one that set off too many alarms. She moved to close the outside door. Jess stopped the motion with his hand and walked through carrying a duffle bag and a long-sleeved, western shirt on a hanger. The solid-colored shirt sported patches of various businesses.

"Here's Holt's things." He dumped the bag on the floor and hung the shirt in the closet.

A heavy thump shook the room then a frustrated, "*Shit*," reverberated from the bathroom.

Gina started to check, then stopped herself. She didn't need to walk in and see Holt naked. Just thinking about it spiked her blood pressure and rushed unwanted thoughts through her head. "Would you check on him, please?"

"Sure." Jess grinned and opened the bathroom door, leaving it wide. She scurried to the other side of the room to keep from seeing anything.

"What were you trying to do?" Jess's voice asked in an irritated tone.

She couldn't hear Holt's mumble. There was scuffling, and dirty clothes flew out of the door. Running water muffled anything else the two said.

Jess backed out of the room, leaving the bathroom door open. "Best to keep an ear out for him. I think he's getting muddled with being hit and all."

She didn't like the idea of having to help him when he was naked. Yet, once again Holt didn't seem to be giving her a choice. Gina swallowed a lump of dread in her throat.

"Would you bring in Holt's pain pills? He said they're in the glove box."

Jess saluted and ducked out the door, leaving her alone with a naked man in the shower.

Gina tried not to stare at the open door, her

fingers, twined together, ached from her twisting. Her heart thundered in her chest. What if he walked out naked? She wasn't a prude, in her job she'd seen many men naked, but this was Holt. A man who somehow knew her better than she knew herself. A man who was chinking the cracks in her heart. A man she should stay away from or fail at yet another one of her goals.

The outside door rattled. She hurried to it, keeping her gaze from roaming to the open bathroom door.

"Here's his pills. I'm in room one-o-four if you need anything." Jess smiled, tipped his hat, and disappeared.

Gina stared at the bottle in her hand and closed the door.

The water stopped. Gina froze, unsure what to do. Holt's clothes were in the bag on the floor at the end of the bed. She sniffed and scanned her dusty clothes. He was lucky to have clean clothes to change into. She'd have to wear these clothes to bed and again tomorrow. Not a comforting thought.

"Ah, my bag."

Holt stood in the bathroom doorway a mere arm's length from her with a small motel towel wrapped around his waist. His shoulders looked wider unclothed, his hips narrower, and his muscles more defined. He grinned and ducked his head in that way she found endearing, before heading to his bag. Droplets of water trickled down his chest, across his toned abs, absorbing into the towel hanging low on his hips and revealing thicker, curlier hair...

Gina snapped her gaze to the floor, stilling her breathing and rapidly beating heart. Just looking at him brought out urges and desires she refused to accept. Couldn't accept.

"Why don't you take a shower? It feels good to

cool off."

She heard a zipper and glanced up as he pulled a T-shirt out of his bag.

"I don't have any clean clothes to put on."

He flung the T shirt at her. She snatched it out of the air before it hit her in the face.

"Wear that."

She held the material up in front of her. It would just cover her bottom. "It's a little short don't you think?"

"Not really." He grinned and tossed her a pair of jogging shorts.

"Thanks."

She tossed his pills onto the bed and ducked into the bathroom, locking the door. A cold shower would help alleviate more than the dirt and sweat. But she opted for a hot spray to relax her muscles as she told herself she could get through this night. Holt was a good man who showed no dishonorable intentions. She snorted. For once, she found the perfect male to make a friend, and her body had become her enemy.

The shoulders of his shirt hung off her shoulders, the shorts hit her at her knees, and she puckered the waistband pulling the string tight enough to hold the garment on her hips. His spicy cologne lingered on the shirt. She breathed it in and couldn't stop the thrumming of her heart or the desire heating her body.

When she came out clean, calm, and ready for bed, she found Holt, wearing only a tight-fitting pair of boxers, sprawled across the bed closest to the bathroom. She stared at his body. The blond hair on his chest and legs sparkled in the lamp light. The muscles even at rest were easily defined. She smiled. With him asleep she could fully study him without him making something out of her perusal.

He murmured and shook his head, then moaned. His movements broke the spell. Gina crossed the room, set the clock for two hours, and crawled into the other bed. She assessed Holt with a professional eye, and then turned out the light.

Gina punched the pillow. She'd lied. It might have been to herself, but she was still a liar. She didn't accept Holt's offer to be his nurse completely because of her conscience. She was in this room, for one reason only—she couldn't deny the attraction she felt for Holt.

****

Gina slipped into a deep sleep and it came. The dream she spent every waking hour trying to forget.

"Rosie, lay still. Your mom's been sick a long time." His stinky, whiskey breath puffed on her face adding to her churning stomach as rough hands rubbed the spot between her legs that made her body feel funny.

"Why Daddy?" she choked, afraid of his actions and afraid to disobey.

She laid still, willing him to leave as tears burned down the sides of her face.

****

The buzz of an alarm clock woke Holt. Reaching toward the sound drew a moan from him as his ribs burned. His fingers found the clock and the sound ceased. He rubbed a hand over his face, gathering his wits, then moved his hand around on the bed. *Alone.* But the air was charged with fear and whimpering that tore at his heart.

Holt swung his legs over the side of the bed and cursed softly. If he thought his ribs hurt before, that was nothing. He ground his teeth and headed to the shadowed shape of another bed.

He sat on the mattress and turned the light on at the same time. Tears trickled down Gina's face, her body curled in a ball.

"Shhh, it's okay, you're all right," he said softly as he rubbed her back.

64

Her body stiffened under his hand.

"Don't touch me! Don't ever touch me, again." Gina shot to her knees, shoving away from him. She pushed long blonde hair from her face. Dilated, glassy eyes didn't quite fix on him as she crouched on the bed, ready to spring.

"Gina? Gina, wake up." Holt didn't know whether to reach out and provoke her or sit tight and wait to see what happened. He'd never dealt with someone not quite awake before.

When he didn't move, she slowly sank back down on the bed and fell into a fitful sleep. He listened to her mumbles for a while, but couldn't make any sense of them. He sat back on his bed and turned out the light.

Her actions further confirmed his suspicions. She had a past that was horrific. His hands fisted at his sides. The clenching of his muscles sliced pain through his ribs but he didn't care. Any physical pain he might endure would be minute to the emotional pain Gina endured. He glanced at her balled up form on the bed beside him. Whether she allowed him any closer or not, he'd find the bastard who hurt Gina and make them pay.

Chapter Eight

Gina woke as weary as if she'd been on a fourteen hour shift at the ER. She stretched, stared at the ceiling, and then scanned the room. This wasn't her apartment at the hospital.

Snoring drew her attention to the bed beside hers. *Holt.* The day before came back to her in frightening clarity. Her stomach dropped.

What will the hospital staff think of me?

Sheila wasn't a person out to cause harm, but she wouldn't be able to keep quiet about Gina staying the night with a cowboy. Even if it was for his health. One look at Holt and they'd all think...the obvious, that she'd spent the night with him. No one would believe they'd slept in different beds.

She groaned and glared at the alarm clock. Seven. She blinked her eyes. She'd set the clock for midnight. Why hadn't it gone off? Some nurse she was, sleeping through the night, never once checking on her patient. She glanced at the powerful form still stretched on top of the covers. If his snoring was any indication, he definitely wasn't in a coma.

Gina crawled out of bed and ducked into the bathroom. Her bra and panties hung from the shower rod where she'd draped them after her shower the night before. Her chest, back, and shoulders were red and tender from too much sun the day before. Touching her sunburned skin, she winced. Would Holt mind her wearing his shirt? Her face heated as scorching as her sunburn. Keeping his shirt would give her a reason to see him again. Just to return the garment. Gina slipped into her clothes, adding her bra underneath the over-sized T-shirt with a screen print of Holt riding a bucking horse.

A knock on the bathroom door, jolted her.

"You about done? I need to use the can."

Holt's scratchy voice sent shivers up her spine.

She grabbed up her socks, shoes, and shirt and unlocked the door. Holt leaned his tousled head against the wall next to the bathroom. The sight warmed her from her toes up and quivered her insides like jelly. His boyish qualities lowered her defenses. The disheveled appearance tugged at her mothering instincts.

"How are you feeling this morning?" She swept a hand through his curly locks before she registered the action.

Holt graced her with a crooked smile. "As good as can be expected, I expect."

He slipped into the room brushing past her, his bare skin igniting fires across her skin.

She scurried to the middle of the room to avoid any more contact. Holt didn't even know his actions tore at every wall she'd carefully placed around her. Freedom had crept into her soul since meeting him. He made her feel whole and untarnished.

Her chest squeezed with sickening dread. What if he found out about her past? How could he ever look at her as he did now? She was tarnished and broken. Nothing could ever change that.

Holt exited the bathroom as his phone rang. His slow gait prompted Gina to hand it to him. But she noted the name Trish before he took the phone.

He looked at the name and put it down, hunting through his bag.

"If that's a girlfriend you can talk to her." As she said the words, jealousy twisted like a tourniquet on her stomach.

"Not a girlfriend." He scowled and pulled a clean

undershirt over his head. "A pain in the rear."

The comment dripped with contempt. Obviously, that woman wasn't one of his conquests, or was she and he tossed her to the side? Gina stared at Holt. Was he a player? He hadn't acted like one. The longer she stared the thought of another woman vaporized. She wasn't sure which was more intoxicating, his bare chest or the white tank stretched across that chest with tan muscular arms bulging from the white arm holes. *Whoa.* Those were thoughts she didn't need.

She turned her back to him and combed her hair into a pony tail.

"What were you dreaming about last night?" he asked, walking to the closet, moving into her view.

Gina swallowed and stared at him. Where had that come from? "Nothing." She shoved her comb in her purse and yanked the drawstring tight.

"It wasn't nothing. You were whimpering, and when I tried to console you—"

"You what?" Her heart pumped. Did she dream about her childhood last night? It wouldn't surprise her. She'd learned to blank the dreams out as soon as she woke; otherwise, they destroyed her whole day. It was bad enough facing them at night; she didn't need them twenty-four hours a day.

"The alarm went off, and I heard you whimpering. When I turned on the light and sat on the bed, you told me not to touch you and sprang up like a frightened animal."

She gnawed on the side of her fingernail. No one, not even her brother, knew about her father's visits. She'd never even told her piano teacher the extent of her nightmares.

"I must have been dreaming some rodeo cowboy was after me." She tossed her pony tail over her shoulder trying to show him her dreams were nothing. Her face burned knowing he witnessed her childhood torment.

His phone rang again. This time, after he glanced at the number, Holt answered it. "What's the plan?"

Gina picked up her purse, but he stopped her from leaving the room by placing his body between her and the door.

"We'll be ready in thirty." He snapped the phone shut. "Jess is coming by to get us for breakfast in thirty minutes."

"We're ready now."

She welcomed the chance to be with other people; he wouldn't pry then. She didn't plan on telling him anything. Especially since he was the one person she could see herself unburdening her past. And then he'd no longer be a friend. He'd head for the hills.

"No, we're not. What were you dreaming about that made you whimper?" He pulled the purse off her shoulder and gently moved her back against the bed. "Sit."

The light caught the glimmer of golden stubble on his face.

"Don't you need to finish getting ready? Like shave or something?" She didn't want this conversation with him or anyone. She'd kept it tucked inside for twenty years. Letting it out now would only shatter the world of normalcy she'd built.

Holt sat on the bed beside her, not quite touching, but she felt the shift of his weight and heat of his thigh just inches from hers. His non-contact affected her stronger than his actual contact. That he respected her need for distance tugged at her resolve to stay aloof.

"I'm not going anywhere until you tell me what makes you behave like an abused animal."

She flinched and stared at him. How did he know? The concern in his eyes brought a lump to her throat. She swallowed and fidgeted with the hem of the shirt. How many times over the years had she longed to tell someone? But fear of contempt had kept her lips sealed.

"I promise whatever you tell me doesn't go beyond this room." He took her hand in his rough ones. "Gina, all I want to do is be your friend. But I can't help you if you don't let me in."

"I don't need a friend." Even as she said the words, her heart soared at the thought of finally having someone to share her painful childhood with and not be judged. Or would he? Yes, he donated to the child abuse auction, but did he really believe in the cause?

"Yes, you do. I could tell the night I met you that you keep yourself boxed up. Honey, that isn't healthy." His thumb moved back and forth across her hand. "Tell you what, we don't have to talk about this now. We'll talk when I'm driving you back to...wherever it is you came from." He laughed. "You haven't told me where I'm headed after the rodeo."

Change of subject. Her body uncoiled, and she shoved her fears in the trunk in her head.

"I'm working at the reservation southeast of here." Where Sheila was now. "I hope Sheila didn't tell everyone I spent the night with you."

"I'm sure the way you worded it, she'll know you only stayed on in a medical capacity."

Holt grinned that damn disarming lop-sided grin, and she grimaced. That sounded just as lame as anything she could have come up with. More than likely, they would suspect she and Holt were a couple.

She shook her head. "How am I going to work side-by-side with them when they think I spent the night with you?"

He squeezed her hand before raising it to his lips. "Just nod your head and agree."

"But—" she sputtered. Her heart raced—from the kiss or the comment? She wasn't quite sure.

"Hey, there's nothing wrong with people thinking we're involved, and what can it hurt?" One eyebrow rose as his dark eyes peered into hers.

"N-nothing I guess, but you... well, you know we're just friends, right?" The idea of being friends with Holt filled an empty part of her she hadn't realized was void. Friendship with anyone, male or female, was a luxury her tortured past couldn't accept. But could the adult she'd molded sustain a friendship? She stared into his brown eyes and wanted a friendship with him as deeply as she wanted to heal sexually abused children. In the short time she'd known him; Holt hadn't pushed his attentions and appeared to genuinely want to be friends and nothing more. Well, except for the kiss on the hand.

"Yes, we're just friends." He linked his fingers with hers. "But if I want to take it farther, you'll be the first to know."

Her breath caught, staring into his sincere eyes and feeling his warm, rough palm against hers. She trembled, in a good way. Well, not really a good way. She wanted to resist the attraction. Keep their relationship strictly on a friendship level. But could she?

Heavy pounding on the door, shot her to her feet.

"You two ready? I'm starving," Jess called.

"Yeah."

Holt released Gina's hand and shifted to stuff his dirty clothes in the end of his duffel bag. He was making progress. And she *would* spill about her fears on the drive back to the hospital. He couldn't get past the friendship stage if she didn't release the emotions bottled up. She may say differently, but the longing in her eyes to unburden herself had seared his heart.

Gina crossed to the door and let Jess in. The wide grin on his friend's face made Holt cringe. Hopefully Jess wouldn't say something to undo all the ground he'd gained this morning.

"Man, did I sleep like a baby last night." Jess turned to Gina. "I didn't have to hear *him* snore. Best night's sleep I've had on this junket."

Gina giggled and tipped her head towards his side of the room. "He was snoring when I woke up this morning."

"Hey, I don't snore that bad." Holt zipped his bag shut.

"You look rangy. Aren't you going to shave?" Jess grabbed the bag from him.

"Gina likes a rangy man." He laughed at her intake of breath and horror stricken look. "I'm kidding. I ran out of shave cream."

"I'll get mine. You can't ride a horse looking like a bum." Jess disappeared out the door.

Holt tipped his head to the open door. "He takes good care of me."

"Yes, he does. You're very lucky." The wistfulness in her tone had him stepping next to her. She may deny it, but she wanted a friend.

He put an arm around her shoulder. "And you have me. Remember that."

The corners of her lips slowly tipped into a smile. "That does sound kind of good."

At that moment, he wanted nothing more than to kiss her, but instincts told him to wait. Patience.

Jess walked back in and shoved the can of shaving cream at him before pulling Gina away. "Here, go shave. Gina and I'll be at the restaurant across the street."

"Wait a minute, Gina stays here." He wasn't sure what Jess had in mind, but he didn't want his friend mucking up the progress he'd made.

"Nope. You'll move faster if she's with me." Jess pushed Gina out the door ahead of him and glanced back.

Holt glared and lowered his voice for Jess's ears only. "Don't say or do anything stupid. I'm making progress."

"Don't worry so much," Jess tossed back as he closed the door.

But he did worry. He worried Jess would tell Gina that he was ready to settle down. A speech like that would have her running for the hills. Even if it was the truth. He hadn't really been looking all that hard for a wife, but he was at the stage in his career—and life—where he wanted to settle down, raise rough-stock and concentrate on his art.

He turned to the bathroom and hurried the best he could with a body that felt like a bull had danced on him all night. No good could come from leaving Jess alone too long with Gina.

****

Jess held the door open for Gina and directed her to a booth by a large plate glass window. She sat down, placing her purse in the sill.

"I see your patient survived the night. Is he okay to ride today?"

The concern in Jess's voice touched her. To have a friend or family member care that much for her had been one of her daily prayers after her mother died.

"He isn't any worse than he was before he made his second ride last night." She accepted the menu from a waitress. The older woman smiled and patted Jess's shoulder as she poured coffee in his cup.

"Fill one for Holt, too, Edith, he's on his way. Gina?" He indicated the upside down mug in front to her.

"I'll have green tea, please."

Edith filled the mug next to Gina and took the

other one with her.

"You know the waitress?" she asked.

"We always stay in that motel and eat at this restaurant. Edith has waitressed this shift every trip." He shrugged. "We've made friends all over, I guess."

"How long have you and Holt been traveling together?" Her fascination of the bond between the two men pushed her to ask questions she normally wouldn't. How could she pry into other peoples' lives when she didn't want them prying into hers. But, she'd never had a close friend. Her childhood didn't allow for it, and her own need for privacy secluded her as an adult. Still, she'd often dreamed what it would be like to have a friend to laugh with and share secrets, all of them.

Her infatuation with Holt also brought out her curiosity. Would they get to a friendship where she felt comfortable with him without crossing the line into intimate? Once they crossed the line, she would have to cut all ties with him. Her personal vow was her anchor.

"We started rodeoing in college. When Holt finished, he joined me on the PRCA circuit. We've been traveling the circuit together about five years I guess." He sipped his coffee. "Know a lot about each other."

Was that an innuendo or a warning?

"I would imagine you do." She didn't want to learn too many things about Holt. Not now, when she was feeling safe with him. "You mentioned Clare, is she your girlfriend?"

His gaze softened and a lazy smile tipped his lips. "No, she's my wife."

"So, why are you married and Holt isn't?" As soon as the words popped out she wished she'd not said them. It made her look interested in a commitment.

Jess smiled. "Simple. I found the one woman that would put up with me and I'd do anything for." He narrowed his eyes and studied her. "Holt hasn't. Yet."

"Hasn't what?" Holt slipped into the seat beside her, pushing her over with his hip and thigh.

The intimate act heated her cheeks and fluttered her heart. She also didn't miss the raised eyebrow of the man sitting across the table from them.

Edith returned with her tea. Her gaze lit on Holt and the older woman's smile raised her sagging cheeks. "Heard you got kicked yesterday. Didn't mar your pretty face any." The woman chuckled.

"That cuss caught me in the chest." Holt smiled and slid his arm around Gina's shoulders. "I'm headed back to win that buckle today, thanks to my nurse."

Embarrassment scorched Gina's cheeks. She wanted to pull out of his embrace, but realized that would make more of a spectacle than remaining in the warmth of his arm. The twinkle in his eyes said he knew her thoughts—again.

Edith gave her a big grin. "'Bout time you got someone to look after you." She winked. "There's been a few try to corral this cowboy. You must be something special, sweetie."

Gina started to open her mouth to correct her, but Holt jumped in with his order. "I'll have the cinnamon roll French toast." He squeezed her shoulder. "So will Gina."

How could she stay mad at him when he remembered her fondness for cinnamon rolls?

"That okay with you, sweetie?" Edith asked.

Gina smiled at Holt. "Yes. That sounds delicious."

When the waitress retreated, Jess gawked at them.

"You never seen happy people before?" Holt chided his friend.

"Just trying to figure out what went on in that motel room last night. You couldn't have—you know."

Gina choked on a sip of tea, and Holt patted her back.

"Just to get things straight. We didn't—*you know*. We're friends. Just friends."

Holt's stern tone held an edge of frustration. She studied him. Did he want more than friendship then? There were times she did, but she couldn't allow herself to think that way. She'd remained stoic too long to lose everything.

"Well, then friendship suits you both." Jess raised his coffee cup in a salute.

Holt grasped the hand she had resting on her leg and squeezed. Though the intimacy rattled her bones, the connection warmed her heart.

The food arrived, and the two men talked about the horses left to draw for the final round. Gina listened intently, trying to figure out the appeal of staying on a horse that didn't want you there.

Halfway through the meal, Sam and Timmy dragged themselves into the restaurant. Both had pale faces, deep creases around their eyes and mouths, and a disheveled appearance. She studied them closer. Still wearing yesterday's clothes, they grunted at Jess and Holt's greetings, pulling out chairs at the table across the aisle from the booth.

"Hell, Holt, you look better than these two and you were kicked by a horse yesterday." Jess laughed at the glares from the bedraggled twosome at the adjacent table.

Edith arrived to take their orders, and Holt called, "These two would like the greasiest bacon you got back there and runny eggs slathered in butter."

Timmy bolted out of his chair, hand over his

mouth, knocking people out of his way as he rushed to the restroom.

Gina whacked Holt on the shoulder. "That wasn't nice."

"But it sure was funny." Jess laughed and held up his cup. Edith re-filled it from the never empty pot she carried everywhere.

"You two are incorrigible." But Gina smiled behind her cup of tea. If Sam or Timmy stayed on a horse today it would be a miracle. "What time does today's performance start?"

"One." Holt pulled his phone out of his breast pocket, checked the time, and slid it back in, snapping the pocket flap shut. "Better take us to get a rental car and get the camper in place at the grounds." He pulled some bills out of his pocket and tossed them on the table. Gina pulled her purse onto her lap, digging for her wallet.

Holt's hand stilled hers. "This is on me."

She glanced up into eyes that brooked no argument. Fine, she'd buy the gas for the car.

He nodded to Jess and the others then grabbed her hand and slid from the bench seat, pulling her behind him. When she stood, he continued toward the door still holding her hand. She glanced around the room, conscious of being watched. The other cowboys and women in the establishment didn't hide their interest, giving her the impression Holt wasn't seen often with a woman.

She smiled inwardly then scolded herself. This was nothing more than friendship. He may not flaunt his women in public, but she was sure he had his number of conquests. He might seem sincere in his acceptance of their relationship, but she knew males had to have sex. Her father was proof.

A flash of her father's face hovering above hers strangled her heart. She shuddered.

Chapter Nine

"What's wrong?" Holt stopped in the middle of the street. "Why are you trembling?" A horn honked. The sound pulled Gina from her memories. She shook her head and marched toward the motel, trying to dislodge Holt's hand from hers. She'd dodged the flashbacks for years, working long hours and isolating herself from men. Since meeting Holt, she couldn't keep them locked up, they slipped out at awkward times and reminded her she wasn't worthy of a relationship—friendly or more.

Jess strode by them, digging keys out of his pocket.

At the truck, Holt stopped her from opening the door, wincing from the action. "What was that about back there?" He ran a hand up and down her arm as though trying to warm her up.

His actions and concern confused her. She didn't know how to respond to honest emotions. After her mother became sick, most males in her life used deceit to get what they wanted. Holt's honesty and sincerity baffled her. She'd learned how to deal with deception. Candor left her struggling to find her footing.

"Nothing. I just—" She couldn't tell him. She'd kept her secret too long to share it with anyone. "It was nothing."

He stared in her eyes. "We'll talk about it on our drive." His determination shone in his steely eyes. He wasn't going to give up.

"Why?" She wouldn't tell him anything. But it flattered and frustrated her he was so interested in her past.

"Because friends talk about things. Things that bother them." He stepped aside and, with slow movements, opened the door.

She hated watching him wince and do things that hurt but didn't say a word as she crawled up into the seat.

Jess gave her a curt nod. "I asked at the restaurant. The car rental place is on Beeline." He sat behind the wheel and inserted the key in the ignition. The truck rumbled to life.

Gina slid to the middle. She wanted to keep distance between her and Holt. It was the only way she'd get through this weekend without him learning the truth about her past. His concern and genuine interest filled her with hope she could find someone to not judge her for her past—something she'd only recently realized she did to herself.

Holt slid in, bumped their hips together, and smiled before he closed the door.

"What about Sam and Timmy?" She glanced in the rearview mirror but didn't see the two anywhere.

"I'll pick them up after I dump you two at the rental place." Jess put the truck in reverse and pulled onto the street.

"When you planning to catch back up with us?" Jess asked Holt.

"I'll meet you in Oklahoma. I should be back to normal by then." Holt slipped his arm along the back of the seat and grimaced.

"You'd heal faster if you didn't ride today." Gina couldn't help but get her thoughts out in the open.

He smiled at her and shook his head. "You aren't going to sway me, and I'm not going to sway you. Just keep your fingers crossed I hang on, spur, and don't get disqualified. If I can do all that, I should be in the money."

"I take it that means your ride last night was

good?" Her body started to lean into him, but she managed to snatch it back before contact was made.

"Almost as good as mine." Jess scowled at the road and pulled into the car rental lot.

"I've been telling you for years, I can ride better than you with my hands tied behind my back. What more proof do you need than my bruised ribs and banged up head?" Holt opened the door and gingerly slid his feet to the ground.

Jess tilted his head toward her. "I think it has more to do with showing off for a certain person."

Heat scorched her cheeks when she slid to the open door. Holt put his hands up as if to help her. Pain crossed his face from the effort, and she batted them away.

"You're in no shape to be helping me." She dropped out of the vehicle as a middle-aged, balding man hurried over.

"Looking for a rental today?" the salesman asked, eying the truck.

Holt shut the door, crossing his arms in front of him. The salesman wouldn't notice, but she saw the way he labored to breath and the dullness in his eyes from the pain. She wanted to tell him to get back in the truck and forget about it. But Jess revved off, and the stubborn cowboy had his mind set on seeing her back to the hospital.

"Yeah, I need to rent a convertible for two days," Holt said.

"Two days?" Gina studied him.

"I won't be in any shape to drive you to the reservation and get back here before they close tonight. Especially if we stop somewhere for dinner."

The twinkle in his eye skittered her heart; at the same time, she took a step back. *Dinner?* That meant conversation. He *was* determined to find out all he could about her.

"We have these two convertible models." The

bald headed man started walking to the front of the lot. Holt grasped her hand and followed.

A canary yellow Ford Mustang caught her eye. When she started her therapy camp, she was going to own a convertible just like that one. It projected fun and freedom. Two things she had yet to experience together.

Holt noted the yearning in Gina's eyes. She wanted the yellow Mustang. He grinned. "We'll take that yellow one." He pointed to the Mustang and watched happiness spread across her face. She was an eyeful to behold when she was somber, but joy transformed her into a beauty. It was like a sucker punch to witness the change and experience the attraction.

"Excellent choice! The weather should be perfect to drive around in this baby today." The salesman ushered them back into the office. He snatched a key off a board and settled himself behind a computer. "I need to see your driver's license, proof of insurance..."

Holt gave him all the pieces of information and answered all his questions, never taking his gaze from Gina. She seemed to listen intently to all his stats. She may keep saying they could only be friends, but she sure was nosey. He chuckled.

"What's so funny," she asked as the man left to have the car brought to the front of the building.

"You." Not that he'd tell her what he was thinking.

"Really? Why do you say that?" There it was, the slightest touch of humor laced in the words. One side of her mouth twitched as if she fought not to smile.

"You don't know how beautiful you are."

Her stricken expression washed away the humor.

"Don't. Please, don't call me beautiful." Her hands began to shake.

"I'm sorry I didn't—" He was at a loss for words. What could make her react so, to a word she should have heard a million times? Another puzzle to untangle about Gina.

"Your car is waiting for you outside, Mr. and Mrs. Reynolds."

Before she could round on the salesman or make a scene, Holt grasped her elbow, escorting her to the door. It hurt like hell to hold her, but he was determined to get her moving and not let anyone see how damaged his body really was.

"Thank you," he called over his shoulder as they exited the building.

"Why didn't you set him straight?" Her eyes narrowed, and her lips barely moved over clenched teeth.

Holt opened the passenger door for her. "Because it doesn't matter. You'll never see him again and it would waste time to explain." He slid into the driver's side and winced shoving the stick shift into first. Damn, he'd forgotten Mustangs came with manual shift. By the time they arrived at the hospital, his ribs would be killing him. Especially after riding a bronc.

He pushed his hat down tighter on his head and sped off to the rodeo grounds. Gina hunkered on her side, staring straight ahead. He'd give up finishing in the money to find out what had her preoccupied.

"Looks like we got more to talk about on our drive tonight," he said, watching her flinch.

"Maybe Sheila and Bud came back today, and I can catch a ride with them."

She didn't sound all that convinced. More like she wished that would be the case.

"I hope they didn't. I'm not ashamed to say, I like spending time with you." He reached across and grasped her hand. When she started to pull it away he simply said, "Don't."

Her gaze traveled over his face, hovering at his eyes a moment before she allowed him to pull her hand into his lap. A few minutes later, he released his hold to shift down and was pleased her hand remained on his thigh. He reclaimed it once he finished shifting.

"Do you want to take the car and do some shopping until the rodeo is over?" He glanced her way.

"Why would I want to do that?" Her expression turned perplexed.

"I don't know. I thought that was what women did. Shopped."

"Not when you're getting up on another horse." Her voice trembled with irritation.

"You don't have to watch. It won't hurt my feelings." Truthfully, he didn't want to think about her watching him while he rode. If she were off shopping, he could get her out of his head and concentrate on his job.

He pulled into the parking lot and eased through the gathering vehicles to park alongside Jess's truck and his camper.

A shrill whistle echoed around them as Sam stepped out of the camper.

"Shit, Holt, you trying to impress the lady?" Sam placed his hand on the trunk, ran it along the side and up to the hood.

"I happen to like airy vehicles. Get your hands off or I'll make you wax it." Holt didn't like Sam thinking he was trying to show off. It wasn't in his nature. He also didn't like the other cowboy making him look bad in Gina's eyes.

Gina hopped out of the car before he could pull himself out of the seat and stand. His ribs ached again.

"Gina, do you have any more of the ibuprofen the doc gave me yesterday?" He leaned his butt against the car door.

She hurried around the hood of the car, stopping in front of him. "Is it your head again?"

The worry wrinkles on her forehead made him smile.

"Naw, it's the ribs. Too much moving around, I guess."

She dug in her purse and handed him two small white pills. "Can you swallow them or do you want me to get you something to drink?"

"There's water inside the door of the camper," Sam offered, having finished his inspection of the car.

"Would you please get one for Holt?" She said it more as an order than a request.

It tickled Holt, and he couldn't hold the snicker. Sam scowled but headed to the back of the camper.

Gina leaned toward him. "He may be your buddy, but I don't care for him. I like Timmy because he's Timmy." She smiled affectionately. "And I like Jess because he cares about you. But Sam only cares about Sam."

"Wow, you saw that in him in the few times you've been around him?" He was impressed she had figured them all out so quickly.

"Working with patients who are in emergency situations you have to learn to size them up and categorize them quickly."

"Where do I fit in your categorizing?"

He arched an eyebrow and waited. But Sam returned with the water and their alone time ended. Then Jess showed up informing them of the horses they drew to ride. Timmy got the best horse, but he didn't look any better now than he had at the restaurant.

Holt wanted to shake some sense into Sam for taking Timmy out and getting him drunk, and Timmy for following the idiot Sam to the bar.

His own draw wasn't bad. He'd ridden Star Fire before. If the horse was having a good day, he could rack up some points. If it was one of the horse's bad days, when he was stubborn and didn't buck, he'd be lucky to get a score at all. That was the challenge of pinning your dreams on an animal. You never knew what they would do. He glanced at Gina. Kind of like the woman filling his thoughts.

"If you want to watch the rodeo, you better get in line, get a ticket, and find a seat." He heard Jess tell Gina.

"I'd feel funny sitting in the bleachers by myself. I'll just hang out here at the camper if you don't mind?"

She moved closer to Holt as if she feared the others would make her leave.

"You can stay here, but you're going to get bored." The medicine had thankfully started to kick in. He put a hand out to brush a stray strand of blonde hair away from her face. It pleased him she didn't pull away. He saw the resolve in her eyes. She had willed her body not to move. *Progress!*

"What do you do when you hang out waiting?" She watched only him as the others milled around preparing their rigging.

"I draw or read a book." Mentally, he tried to remember what books he'd brought along.

"Can I see your drawings?"

Her question stopped his thoughts. Of course she'd want to see his drawings. That was what brought them together.

"Timmy, will you get the drawing pad I keep above the table?"

The younger man slowly climbed into the camper. Holt smiled. *If you can't hold your liquor you shouldn't be drinking.*

Timmy returned with the pad he'd almost filled with sketches and some finished drawings. Holt took the tablet, running a hand over the outside cover. He had nearly a season's worth of sketches in the pad. Enough to keep him busy all winter refining and turning into paintings.

"You have to promise, you won't discuss these with me until after I ride?" Holt didn't offer the book. He also couldn't afford to think about her comments on his art while sitting on a bucking horse.

Gina stared into Holt's eyes and gave him a slight nod. She understood he needed to focus on his ride.

"Forget I'm here. Do what you usually do before a ride." She took the pad and placed it on the passenger seat of the Mustang. "I won't even look at it until you leave. And I don't want to interfere with your preparations. I'll wander down and get an ice tea and a snack."

"I don't want you wandering around by yourself." He put a hand on her arm. "Please."

Was that a spark of fear in his eyes? What kind of trouble could she possibly find standing in line for a snack?

"Holt, there are other women walking around this arena by themselves. I'll be fine." She placed her hand over his, squeezed his fingers, and removed her hand.

"She's a grown woman, Holt." Jess gave her a wink. "Besides, word's got out she's off limits. Don't worry."

"What do you mean?" Her stomach knotted. Did he mean what she thought?

"I kind of spilled that Holt had him a honey."

Jess smiled and Holt groaned. Was he upset his friend took him off the market?

Holt turned on his friend. "Why did you do something stupid like that?"

The anger darkening his features made her curious.

"So you wouldn't have to worry about her wandering around." Jess crossed his arms over his chest and took a solid stance.

"It's okay, Holt, as long as people don't ask me personal questions."

She stepped beside him. The last thing she wanted was for him to get in a fight with his best friend over her. She placed a hand on his arm, rubbing it up and down in a soothing motion.

He turned, his gaze sought hers. "Just be careful." His concern warmed and frightened her. Was there something he wasn't telling her? Did he have something in his past as well?

She studied his face, searched his brown eyes. Her pulse accelerated. He didn't turn away either. He held her gaze searching within her as well. Metal clanged against metal, and Gina shook free of their tangled gazes.

"How long till you head to the arena?" she asked, avoiding his gaze.

"About thirty minutes."

"I'll be back by then so you won't have to worry while you ride." She gave his muscle one last squeeze, flung her purse over her shoulder, and headed to the noisy throng of people gathered around the food tents. Getting lost in the crowd felt safer than losing herself in his gaze.

Gina had her drink and nachos balanced in her hands as she wove her way back through the growing crowd. How many of these people were here all day yesterday? Some of the western outfits were over the top in rhinestones and glitz, but the revealing outfits on young and old woman alike made her shudder. Why would a woman dress like that and go out in public? She wasn't a prude, but some of the shirts barely covered breasts and should have covered bulging stomachs.

Someone collided with her back, and she juggled

her purchase. Gina turned, expecting an apology, not the woman standing in front of her with a scowl on her thin, leathery face.

"I'm sorry, I was dodging people," Gina said to break the ice and possibly get an apology.

"Maybe you shouldn't be hanging around a rodeo if you can't walk and carry food at the same time." The emaciated woman's high-pitched voice caused a few heads to gawk their direction.

"Look here. You plowed into me, so don't go putting the blame on me." She sized up her antagonist. Why did this scrawny, dried up cowgirl pick a fight with her? Did she look like an easy target? If so, what was she after?

"Nice shirt." The woman's gaze traveled over the T-shirt she'd borrowed from Holt.

Gina glanced down at the likeness of Holt on the front with Jess's signature in red marker on one side. She studied the thin face in front of her. The leathery skin darkened, and the bloodshot eyes narrowed to a threatening glare before she whirled on her heel and stomped off through the crowd.

She stared at the retreating woman and caught a glimpse of letters etched on the back of her belt. TR-SH. The woman had been rude and downright spooky. She scanned the area. No one seemed to notice the ordeal or the strange behavior. Her attitude must be normal for what Sheila called buckle bunnies.

Gina put the scene out of her head and hurried back to the camper before Holt became worried. Everyone but Holt slung their gear over their shoulders and headed to the arena. The relief on his face told her he'd waited for her return.

"Sorry I took so long, there were long lines. I've never seen so many people gathered in one place to watch men behave like children." She smiled to soften her joke.

Holt took the jab with humor. He was just relieved she made it back, and he could concentrate on the ride. He had to be in the money since he'd dropped out of next weekend's competition to heal his ribs. He'd never kept a woman close to him during competitions. On one hand, he liked Gina's straight forward feelings about his occupation. It not only kept him humble, it made him see all the risks. On the down side, he found himself thinking of her and not the ride.

He touched her cheek with the back of his hand, and she smiled reassuringly. His body relaxed.

He gathered his rigging, wincing from the weight. "See you when the bareback riding's done," he said, wanting to kiss her cheek but resisting, for both their sakes.

"I'll be here." She set her drink and food on the aluminum table and headed to the Mustang. When she turned back around she had his sketch book in her hands. "Hang on and make some money." She smiled and waved a hand dismissively.

Holt turned, grinning like a fool. He couldn't help himself. There was something about Gina Montgomery that set real well with him.

Chapter Ten

Gina leaned her head against the leather seat of the Mustang. Stray strands of hair rippled across her face, clinging like spider webs. She brushed them away and watched Holt maneuver the vehicle smoothly through the mountain curves. He'd cleaned up at the motel after the rodeo. Her gaze roamed over his freshly shaved face. She'd looked up his stats on the computer right after their first encounter, and for thirty, he still had a boyish charm about him.

She'd been proud to stand by his side as the results were announced at the end of the rodeo. He placed behind Jess. Both men had been exuberant over their placings. So much so, Holt kissed her. Not a deep tongue clashing kiss—a brief brush of his lips against hers before he turned to talk to the announcer.

She placed a finger on her lips. The fleeting kiss had vibrated her body enough to make her wonder how a deeper kiss would affect her. She shook her head, dispelling any such thoughts. This relationship *had* to stay platonic.

"I wanted to tell you, I thought your drawings were wonderful." Gina turned in her seat to fully watch him.

"I'm glad you like my doodling." He smiled, but kept his eyes on the road.

"Those are more than doodles. The emotion you can put in a pencil drawing—it's magic." Each page she'd turned in his drawing pad had evoked visceral reactions.

He shrugged. "It's my way of showing what I see in the world."

"You see more than most people." That was why he was the first man to see beyond her icy reserve and look for the real woman underneath. And why she feared him getting closer. Sooner or later he'd discover her ugly past.

"Hungry?" He glanced at her and captured the hand closest to him.

"A little. You?"

His thumb moved slowly back and forth over the back of her hand. The sensation tingled every nerve in her body. She had to fight the attraction, but, at the same time, she wanted to wallow in the warmth. Until Holt, she hadn't realized physical contact in this simplest form could produce so much contentment.

"Another twenty minutes and we'll come to a place that doesn't look all that great, but has the best food." He glanced at her and smiled.

The winding road along the rim of a pine-covered mountain made a relaxing end to the day. The sun hovered just above the craggy slopes on their right. Her thoughts wandered to the perfectness of the moment. She'd had few moments in her life like this.

"So, tell me about that dream you had last night."

Perfection shattered with his words. She pulled in a deep breath of the cool mountain air. She reveled in the tang of pine and sweetness, before exhaling and bracing herself for the conversation.

"I don't understand why you want to know about my dreams—or my past." She pulled her hand from his.

He shifted down, maneuvered around a corner, and cast a glance her direction. "I want to be your friend. The one you tell all your secrets to."

"Why? You have Jess. You don't need a friend in me." Her stomach pitched. It was true. He didn't need her. But after having him in her life over the weekend, she was slowly realizing that she might just need him. Something she never believed before. Once she pulled herself out of her destructive behavior, she fully believed she would never need anyone but herself. This weekend proved her wrong.

"I have Jess, but he has Clare. Sure, we buddy around and know each other pretty well, but there are still things I don't tell Jess. Things about riding and such I don't feel right saying to him." He glanced at her. "But I can tell you. You won't judge me, but you'll tell it to me straight."

"Yeah, like what?" Now he had her attention. What could he not tell his best friend?

A sigh escaped his lips. "I haven't told Jess that after I win the title in December, I'm done. He thinks I've been hanging at home moping, looking for a wife, he doesn't know I'm sick of traveling."

She turned in the seat to watch him. "Really? You could walk away just like that?"

His lips formed a straight line, and he looked her in the eyes. "Yes. I've thought it over, and the best way to go out is to go out on a winning note."

His phone rang. He pulled it out of his pocket, frowned, and flipped it open.

"Penny, what's up? Okay. I'll call back as soon as I find a place to pull over." He snapped the phone shut and scanned the short stretch of road that could be seen before another curve.

Gina wanted to ask him about Penny. This was the second female to call him, and the first he talked to. The niggling in her stomach was more than curiosity; it made her hand clench and her mind frantically deny it upset her.

The car slowed, and she spotted a wide spot up ahead.

"Penny is ranch sitting for me. She checks in every day to let me know how things are," Holt said, stopping the car and shutting off the engine. "Let's stretch our legs while I talk to her." He slowly pulled his body from the low slung car seat and motioned for her to do the same.

There wasn't really anywhere to go; the road had been chiseled out of the side of the mountain. The pull out was just that—a short expanse of flat ground the length of two cars with a cliff only a few feet from where the car was parked.

Holt leaned his bottom against the hood of the car and snapped his phone open. "Okay, I can talk now." He paused to listen then smiled. "Yes and no."

He laughed affectionately. The sound warmed Gina as well as spiked a bit of jealousy. Where did that come from? He was giving her a ride. She had no claim on him.

"Yes, I'm with a woman, but not like you insinuated." He winked in her direction. "I'm giving her a ride back to her job." As he listened, his expression sobered. "Were you hurt? I'll be home tomorrow night if I can get a flight. No, I'm not coming back because of that. I'm sure it was just an accident." He rolled his eyes and smiled. "Yes, I'm coming back to mend. How did you—" His face formed into a scowl. "You really shouldn't spend so much time on the internet. There are people out there who prey on girls like you."

Gina walked farther away. The conversation was interesting and disturbing. Who was this *girl* staying at his ranch?

"I'll call you as soon as I get a flight. Don't worry about the barn. I'm sure my insurance will cover it." His words softened. "Don't fret. See ya tomorrow." The phone clapped closed, and his unhurried steps crunched in the gravel.

She didn't know whether to ask the questions

bouncing around in her head or pretend she didn't care.

"That girl reminds me of my sister." Holt chuckled. "You'd think after all this time of staying at my place, she'd remember where the barn sat and not run into it." He laughed.

Appalled he could laugh at something that could have hurt the girl, Gina turned on him. "Is she all right? How could she not miss a barn?"

"She's okay. She was driving the tractor with a bale on the forks in the front and miscalculated. Don't worry, she was going too slow to hurt herself, but sounds like there's a pretty good bite out of the side of the barn." He laughed again and shook his head slowly.

"Is Penny a friend of your sister?" She wanted answers without sounding like a snoop. But he'd brought the subject up.

"No." His eyes fogged over with pain.

"Do you want me to drive?" Gina stepped closer to him before realizing the pain was deeper than his physical injuries.

"My sister would have been twenty-two this year." Holt grasped her hand and leaned his bottom against the side of the car. "The drawing I donated to the auction was created after her death."

"I'm so sorry!" Gina leaned her head on his shoulder. The two had obviously been close for him to have captured her so well.

"She killed herself."

The pain and guilt in his voice tore at her heart. "You couldn't have known…" She knew all too well the desperation of wanting out of a situation out of your control. Music used to be the only thing that would drown her pain and let her leave the real world for hours at a time.

He stared into her eyes. "She begged me to take her along. I didn't want to watch after a teenage girl while I worked myself up the rankings." His eyes closed. "I sent her to her death."

"You couldn't have known she was that desperate," she whispered, putting her arm around him, offering comfort. She could feel his pain. And knew this was the pain she'd spared her brother by keeping the secrets of her shattered childhood from him.

"I should have asked questions. Found out what that bastard did to her." Anger shook his voice. His hand clenched hers.

She stiffened. Surely his sister... She gulped back the bile seeping into her throat from the realization. *That* was why she'd connected with the emotion in the drawing.

"I didn't find out until after the funeral that my stepfather had been molesting her ever since he moved into the house." Holt pulled away and stalked to the side of the cliff. "My mother knew, and didn't do a damn thing about it." He swung back around. "When Sherrie called me, all I thought of was myself. I didn't think to ask her *why* she wanted to spend the summer with me." Regret darkened his eyes. "I was so damn self-centered...I killed my sister."

"No! You didn't. It was that monster who used an innocent child that's to blame." The words came out with more force than she'd intended. "Don't ever blame yourself." It took her years to realize what her father did to her wasn't her fault, though, she still lapsed from time to time.

Holt's dark gaze sought hers. "You seem to know a lot about monsters preying on children."

His gentle tone didn't make her feel soiled. Her guard slipped, and his gaze softened, probed. A thousand pins of fear pricked her stomach. He'd figured out her childhood.

She bowed her head—couldn't look at him.

Couldn't witness the disgust or pity.

Strong arms encircled her, pulling her head to rest on his chest. The steady beat of his heart under her ear slowed her own racing heart. Warm breath tickled the hair on the top of her head before the light, moist pressure of a kiss. Unshed tears pooled in her eyes from the gentleness he showed over and over.

"No child should be mistreated by an adult." Holt's voice was low, but held conviction.

He understood. Gina had an overwhelming urge to tell him about her father. In her heart, she believed he'd understand, but the information had been bottled up for so long she didn't think she could let it out.

"Was it a stepfather, uncle, family friend?" he gently asked.

She shook her head and gulped back the sob. "It was the one person who should have protected me." She wrapped her arms around his solid body and clung, willing the images of her father's silhouette in her bedroom doorway to go away. "My father." A sob escaped.

"Shhh...I'm so sorry. What about your mother?" His rough hand snagged in her hair as he smoothed it. She didn't care. The tiny sting made her realize she wasn't dreaming. She stood in the arms of a man who cared about her feelings, urging her to reveal secrets she'd kept locked up for too long.

"S-she was ill. He...he came to me one night and said he needed me. Told me, *you're so beautiful, Rosie.*" She peered into his eyes, willing him to understand. Her stomach soured with bitterness. "I hate that word."

"Rosie? Was that your mother's name?" His eyes searched hers.

"No. My middle name is Rose. I hate being called beautiful." She burrowed back into his chest.

It was easier to confront her horrors clinging to his strong body and not looking into his eyes. "We lived in a small community. Everyone knew he was married and Momma was sick. He didn't want to ruin his reputation being seen with anyone other than his wife." She hiccupped and squeezed her eyes against the childhood emotions swelling in her chest. "At the time, I didn't know what he meant."

"How old were you?" His hand rubbed a circle on her back as the other one kept her tucked safe against him.

"Eight. He fondled me and..." She shuddered, remembering his groan of satisfaction.

"You didn't tell anyone?" There wasn't any censure in his voice, only the quiet question.

"He said it would kill Momma if I said anything." Anger and hatred rolled through her in a hot wave. Gina pushed against his chest to peer into his face. "Momma died anyway. Then he was free to date other women and left me alone. Sexually anyway." She couldn't hold back the hatred. A child shouldn't hate a parent, but she did.

"Did you tell anyone then?"

Gina stared at the snaps on his shirt. "You're the first person I've ever told. My piano instructor knew something was amiss, but I couldn't...I couldn't tell her...It just..."

Holt tipped her face up and peered into her eyes. "I'm glad you felt safe enough to tell me. I'm honored."

His head dipped. He was going to kiss her. She wanted his kiss as much as she wanted her next breath of air.

But she couldn't kiss him. Couldn't allow herself to fall into the old pattern. The one forced upon her by her father's actions and her naïve attempt to assuage the misguided needs he ripened in her body.

Shame washed through her, sending cold flashes

from her shoulders to her knees.

She turned her head, and his lips grazed her cheek.

Chapter Eleven

Holt understood why she turned from his kiss, but he had needed to show her he cared, and it was the only way he knew. He now had a better understanding of the haunted look in her eyes and sorrow in her music. He'd take it as slow as she wanted. She was worth it.

Her stomach growled, reminding him of the promised dinner down the road.

"We better get going." He gave Gina one more squeeze before letting her go. He liked holding her. Her fresh scent with a hint of flowers was a nice change from the buckle bunnies who slathered perfume on like lotion.

She stepped out of his arms and let him open the car door for her. It made him smile to see her in one of his National Finals T-shirts. The one Jess autographed after he won the title. It was a little big, but she looked adorable. He wanted to lean down and kiss her, but knew it wasn't a good idea.

Instead, he moved to his side of the car and gingerly lowered his body into the comfortable seat. With a twist of the key, the car roared to life, and he whipped back onto the road. Only a handful of cars had gone by as they talked. The remoteness of the area reminded him of his ranch located several hours from a large city. He liked his solitude.

A thought struck him. "When's your next break?"

"I have another month here, then I have a couple weeks before I head to my next assignment, why?"

The caution in her voice made him grin. "Where were you going to spend your break?" He glanced over and caught her nibbling on the side of her fingernail, again, a habit he found cute.

"My brother's. He lets me stay there when I'm between jobs." A scowl wrinkled her small forehead. "Why?"

"I thought you might like to hang out at my ranch. Do you like to ride horses?" He couldn't contain the eagerness in his voice.

"I don't know." The words were crisp and succinct.

Holt glanced in her direction again. Her lined brow and fidgeting hands worried him. "You don't know if you like to ride horses?"

Her nervous laugh tickled his ears.

"No. I'm not sure if I want to come to your ranch."

He wouldn't push. Not yet. One way or another, though, he'd get her to his ranch and show her his dreams for the future.

"You don't have to make a decision now. Think about it and let me know." He spotted the town where he planned to feed her and hopefully relax her enough to learn more about her past.

"Hope you're ready for the meal of your life."

He parked the car in front of a less than hospitable appearing wood shake building. Gina studied the establishment with eyebrows drawn together and her soft lips pursed in distaste.

"Believe me, you'll be happy we ate here." Holt got out of the car and stretched his tight, sore body, grimacing at the pain. A little thing like bruised ribs couldn't interfere with their last few hours together. He wanted her to enjoy their time, so she would welcome him when his hectic schedule allowed him to catch up with her.

He walked to the passenger side, opened the car

door, and watched her unfold from the seat. When would he get a chance to see those long legs bare?

She took his offered hand and waited as he opened the door and followed her into the dark interior of the restaurant. The atmosphere was bar-like, but if he'd told her that, he was sure she wouldn't have given the place a chance.

He placed a hand on her lower back, directing her to one of the booths closest to the door and farthest away from the bar and pool tables. The night was young, and the local crowd hadn't had enough to be wound up yet.

Gina slid into the booth, but not before she'd scoped out the restroom and the fact he'd brought her to a bar. Holt surprised her when he slid onto the seat beside her instead of sitting across the table.

A barmaid/waitress handed them a one-page list of items. Her attire made Gina think the woman had stepped out of the barn into the bar to do her shift. She was average size, a few years older than Gina, with weather-worn skin.

"Anything to drink?" the waitress asked in a raspy smoker's voice.

"I'll have a beer," Holt said, smiling.

Gina frowned. "That's not a good idea with the pills you're taking for pain and the fact we still have another hour to drive." She studied him. "Besides, weren't you the one talking about not putting alcohol in your athlete's body?"

He laughed. "Yes." Smiling at the waitress, he said, "Bring me an ice tea."

Her chest ached with happiness he'd listened to her, until the waitress made a comment under her breath.

"What did you say?" she asked, not believing she had the nerve to utter what Gina thought she'd heard.

"I said, another one caught by the balls." The waitress put her hands on her hips and shot a look at Holt, then at her.

"He made the choice. I just gave him the consequences. " Gina waved a hand toward the rowdy group playing pool. "I'm sure you've had half your customers walk out of here so soused they could barely stand up and climb into a car. I care about other people, can you say the same?" Man, she hated this type of person. All they thought of was the money in their hands, not the people.

"Ladies, please." Holt grasped her hand and pleaded with his eyes to back off.

She wanted to do as Holt asked, but the way the waitress smirked reminded her of her father. The way he looked every time after he'd get her to do what he wanted whether it was right for her or not. She'd learned to stand up to him, and wasn't about to cower to a stranger.

She opened her mouth to speak up, but Holt leaned over, covering her parted lips with his. Stunned, her fire sputtered out about two seconds before a different heat bubbled in her body and curled slowly to her extremities. Warmth and goodness filled her, lulling her into a cocoon of bliss the like she'd never experienced.

Holt pulled back, said something to the waitress, and grinned at her.

Gina shook herself mentally. What happened? One minute she was ready to do verbal battle with the barmaid and the next an overwhelming calm invaded her senses right before desire sparked. At least she believed it to be desire and not lust. She wouldn't go up that road again.

"Why did you do that?" Best to take a haughty stand rather than let him see how his kiss affected her.

"It seemed like the best way to defuse the

situation." He grinned like he had a secret. "The other option was throwing water on you, but there wasn't any available."

"Gee, guess I lucked out on that one." Her heart still fluttered in her chest as she gazed into his happy face.

The waitress returned with two ice teas. She placed them at the end of the table and pulled out a note pad. "What are you having?"

"We'll have two of the rib dinners," Holt said.

The woman spun on her heel and headed back to the kitchen before Gina could say she hadn't had a chance to look at the menu.

"How do you know I'll like the rib dinner? Maybe I'm a vegetarian?" She chuckled inwardly and watched him mentally search for that information.

"You ate the ribs Jess brought us yesterday." He waggled a finger at her.

Chuckling, she moved toward him, bumping her hip against his. Before the kiss, the touch intrigued her, now after having a flame lit that she'd snuffed for many years, the intimate contact nearly turned her limbs to mush. She shot a glance at Holt. Desire sparked in his eyes, but he slid away.

"I need to use the restroom," she whispered.

He stood and she squeezed out, walking toward the lit sign. Footsteps echoed behind her. She glanced over her shoulder and spotted Holt close behind. She didn't need an escort to the restroom. Stopping, she placed fisted hands on her hips.

"I'm a big girl. You don't need to escort me."

"Maybe not, but I need to use the men's room."

She bristled at her foolishness for thinking he followed to protect her and ducked into the room.

Holt stood by the pay phone between the restrooms waiting for Gina. This place didn't look like trouble, but after the emotional day she'd had, he didn't want her dealing with any horny drunks.

She finally emerged. The scowl on her face told him she didn't believe he'd just exited the restroom, too. He couldn't stop the smile curving his lips. Even though the kiss earlier had started out as a way to keep her from making the waitress mad, it had pumped his adrenaline as much as riding a crazed, bucking horse.

By her reaction, it shook her as well.

He'd played the field some as a rookie on the pro circuit, but after waking up with a hangover in Sam's fiancée's bed, he'd set his goal on a National title and danced away from any woman who tried to latch onto him.

Until this one.

He could see himself settled down, raising rough-stock, and loving this woman every day.

Gina slid into the booth, and he sat next to her. Two salads sat on the end of the table. He pushed one in front of her and pulled the other in front of him. His stomach growled, and he decided to eat and forget about talking. Maybe by the time her belly was full, she'd be more agreeable.

Their dinner arrived, and he dug in without saying a word. Halfway through the food on her plate, Gina groaned. One arm held her belly as she shoved her plate to the center of the table.

"It's delicious, but I can't eat another bite."

He waved at the waitress. When she arrived, he ordered a box for Gina's dinner.

Gina leaned back in the booth and sipped on her tea, watching him clean up his plate. His stomach protested the last bite, but the food tasted better than he remembered.

"I can't believe you ate all of that?" She stared at him in awe.

Holt laughed. "I've always been known as the cowboy with a hollow leg. I can eat just about anyone under the table."

"Are you sure that's something to boast about?" The playfulness in her voice and softness in her eyes made his heart skip a beat. She was actually flirting.

"Until I start showing it on my waist. Yeah."

Her sweet laughter filled the air. The carefree sound, her relaxed pose, and warmth radiating from her eyes gladdened his soul. He wished to see more of this side of her.

"Come on, as much as I don't want to take you back to the hospital, I do want to get you to myself."

Her laughter faded as brownish-green eyes assessed him.

"I don't mean it the way it came out. I just enjoy your company. Alone—without others interrupting." He tossed money on the table, grasped her hand, and slid out of the seat. Leading her out of the building, he realized the simple act of holding hands was a huge step in her accepting him.

They stepped out into a dusky gray evening. Stars popped one by one into the darkening sky.

"I love watching the stars come out and glitter in the sky." Gina sighed and stopped, peering into the heavens.

Holt studied her profile, his gaze skimming down her neck and back up. An innocent smile tipped her soft lips into a crescent much like the moon. He gently tugged on her hand, drawing her near. Every nerve and muscle in his body wanted to kiss her.

She fastened her gaze on him. Was she giving him permission?

A truck pulled up, sending dust around them and spoiling the moment.

"Let's hit the road."

He escorted her to the car, helping her in, and then moving to the driver's side. Before the night was over he would kiss her, there was no way he could walk away without tasting her lips, again.

They continued the drive with the car top still down, the cool night air whirling around them.

"You don't plan to turn around and head back tonight do you?"

Gina's worried tone gave him hope the relationship would build beyond friendship.

"No. I'll stay in a motel and head back in the morning. After that meal and the day I've had, I wouldn't be able to stay awake." He reached across the console, capturing her hand.

"Good. I wouldn't be able sleep, knowing you were driving." She squeezed his fingers.

The action said volumes. He meant something to her. How much, was still undetermined, but he planned to find a way to remain in her thoughts every day.

The lights of the town soon flickered in the darkness in front of them. All too soon, he pulled the car into the parking lot on the back side of the hospital. When she started to open the car door, he stopped her.

"Let me walk you to the door."

"There isn't anyone here to attack me." The teasing in her voice made him smile.

"Maybe I just don't want the day to end." Holt stepped out and walked around to the passenger side. Opening the door, he took both her hands in his and drew her to her feet.

"I'm going to miss you." He meant every word.

"You'll get over me as soon as you head back out to another rodeo." She bit her lower lip and looked away.

Did she really think that?

With their hands still linked, he nudged her face to look at him.

"No. I won't." Staring into her moonlit face, there was only one thing he could do to make her believe him.

He lowered his head and brushed his lips across hers.

She sighed; his invitation to deepen the kiss. His arms yearned to wrap around her, but he stood with their clasped hands held between them and poured his infatuation for her into the kiss. Her lips parted, and she kissed him back.

Her desire made him heady, her hesitancy made him cautious.

Slowly, he raised his head. "No, I'm not going to forget you." He released one hand and led her to the door of the building. "Are you working in the morning?" He had to see her one more time before leaving town.

"Yes. I start at seven."

"Do you mind if I come around and say good-bye?" He held his breath, hoping she'd agree.

She hesitated a moment then shook her head. "I don't mind. Come through the ER doors."

Holt pulled her to him and tipped his head for another kiss. If he didn't go, he'd never leave. Not since his high school sweetheart and teenage hormones raged had he found leaving a female so hard.

"Go on. Get in there before I take you back to the motel with me." He spun her to the door and waited until she unlocked it and stepped inside.

"Good night," she called when he was halfway back to the car.

"Good night."

Holt settled into the driver's seat and headed back up the road to find a motel and try to sleep. He couldn't wait to see her in the morning. Couldn't believe how in a short time her thoughts and feelings had become important to him. His goal, from here on out—show her how to enjoy life and smile more. A goal he hung right up alongside winning the National title.

Groaning, he downshifted and pulled into the first motel. He'd find a way to keep in touch. Otherwise, he'd never be able to concentrate on his rides.

Chapter Twelve

Gina spent the morning cleaning up two drunks with cuts and bruises from arguing over a bottle of whiskey. After that, the ER remained eerily quiet. She never wished for more work because that meant injured bodies. But today, she wanted to stay busy. It was almost ten, and Holt hadn't stopped in to say good-bye.

Had all those kisses been just a game to him? Her heart said, no, but her head, her disapproving head, said he could be toying with her. He hadn't demanded or forced the kisses on her. Every one had been sweet, slow, and melted her defenses. She'd spent an hour after he left debating with herself about letting him kiss her. But she couldn't shake how he, kisses or not, made her feel. Holt's friendship and understanding were treasures she didn't want to give up.

His kisses told her he wanted more out of the relationship. She'd spent half the night lying awake yearning for more, but her vow kept sliding into her thoughts. It was her pillar that held her together for so long. What would happen if she gave in to her desire?

She glanced at the sliding doors, wondering when she'd get to see Holt again after he left today.

"So, how was the night in Payson?" Sheila's voice penetrated her thoughts.

Gina faced her friend. "Oh, fine. Holt didn't have a concussion, thank goodness, but his ribs were badly bruised." She tried not to appear embarrassed and cursed the flaming tips of her ears. It would have been a miracle for Sheila not to have brought up the fact she spent the night with Holt.

"Heard he brought you back last night. In a convertible." Sheila sat down in the wheelchair and leaned forward. "Do tell. What's going on with you two?"

"Nothing. We're friends." Gina ducked behind the counter, busying herself with the charts.

"I'd say *more* than friends."

She glanced at Sheila, who now pointed to the door.

Holt stood inside, smiling, and holding a bouquet of daisies. Her heart skittered around in her chest. But she still wasn't ready to admit how he made her feel.

She placed the chart in the rack and waited for him to come to the counter.

He nodded to Sheila and turned his full attention on her. "How's your morning going?"

"Good." She stared into his handsome face and wanted to say much better now that he'd shown up. But she couldn't bring herself to let him know how his appearance in her life opened her eyes to the fact she didn't have to hide behind an icy façade.

His eyes glistened with humor. He set the flowers on the counter and dug into his pocket. "I bought you a cell phone. That way you can call me when you want or I can call you when I want."

She started to protest, then thought better of it. She didn't want their last conversation to be an argument when he was leaving, and she didn't want Sheila listening into the conversation.

He placed it in her hand, closing her fingers over it one by one. "My number is already loaded onto it. Press the number sign and one."

She laughed. "What makes you think you're number one?"

He grinned. "It's the first number in there, so it

automatically does that."

She smiled at his embarrassment, enjoying this new ability to banter with him. She'd kept all her conversations with males to this point all business and a bit frosty to keep them at a distance.

"Can you come outside a minute?" He shot a glance at Sheila.

Gina understood he wanted to talk in private. She shrugged, and casually sauntered out from behind the counter, even though her feet wanted to race out so they could be alone

"Sheila, I'll be back in a minute."

Holt instantly took her hand. The strength and warmth reminded her of the day before, snuggled in his embrace and unburdening her heart.

"Take more than a minute," Sheila said. "Make it ten."

When they were outside standing by the car, she bumped her shoulder against his arm. "Thank you for the flowers and the phone. You didn't have to give me either one."

"I wanted to give you the daisies to thank you for being my nurse over the weekend." He tugged her hand, drawing her to stand in front of him. "And I gave you the phone to call me. Please. I won't be able to concentrate on my rides if I don't hear your voice at least once a week."

Her heart fluttered in her chest. *He wants to stay in contact.* "I don't want to be a pest."

"You will never be a pest. Come here." He pulled her into an embrace. The parking lot, the cars, the people all disappeared as a safe cocoon enveloped her. She couldn't believe her luck, finding a friend in a man who was willing to take things slow.

"And I want an answer the week before you leave here, whether or not you plan to stay at my ranch." He tipped her chin up and gazed down into her eyes. "The rodeo season will be over other than nationals in December, but there's some things I'll need to have ready if you decide to visit."

Her panic-accelerated heart spun, making her lightheaded. Staying with him in an intimate setting—*his* place—set off alarms. She wasn't ready to take their relationship past platonic even though her body spoke otherwise. How could she go to his ranch and stay strong? One look or kiss and her body would overrule her head, and she'd be sorry when they both came up for air.

She leaned back to pull out of his embrace.

"Oh no, you don't. You're not running away. I'm not pressuring you. Just telling you the facts." His soft, undemanding lips pressed against her forehead. "But I am going to be highly disappointed if you turn me down."

Apprehension knotted her stomach. She could think of nothing better than spending time with Holt at his ranch. Away from demands and people. Then again, was she strong enough to be alone with him and remain faithful to herself? She'd have to think this one over.

"I'll think about it." She glanced into the car and spied his sketch pad sitting on the passenger seat. "Were you drawing last night?"

"Yeah. I couldn't sleep."

"Were you in pain?" She automatically captured his wrist and registered his pulse, scanning his face for traces of pain.

"Yeah." A wolfish grin lit up his eyes. "A certain woman wouldn't get out of my head."

He reached in and picked up the sketchbook, flipping through the pages. The papers stopped fluttering, and he turned the book to her.

"Oh!" A pencil sketch of her sitting in the convertible, the wind blowing her ponytail behind her graced the page. "This is wonderful! I can feel the wind just by looking at the drawing." She stared at the image of her. Happiness and wistfulness reflected in her face.

She peered into his eyes. "You captured the emotion. Just like every one of your sketches in that book moved me in different ways." Gina put her hands over his. "You have so much talent and such an eye for drawing emotion."

He tipped his head, shielding his eyes and avoiding her gaze.

"It's a wonderful gift. One that will keep your ranch running after you leave the rodeo circuit." She placed a hand on his smooth cheek. "A gift I understand." Holt's drawings were like her music. He put his feelings into the lines, shading, and composition just like she set her emotions free with sharps, flats, and chords on the piano.

Holt turned his head and kissed her palm. The contact with his lips jolted her to her toes.

He tossed the book into the car and wrapped his arms around her. "I'll call you as soon as I get to the ranch."

"You don't have to." She'd gone a lot of years without someone checking in with her. Would she get used to this intrusiveness? Then again, now that she knew the wondrousness of a friend like Holt, could she let a day pass without talking to him?

"Oh, yes, I do. I'll have to hear your voice or I won't be able to sleep." He dipped his head and kissed her. Not a quick, see-you-later kiss, but a deep, probing kiss that sucked the air from her lungs and sent her blood boiling.

She was light-headed and off kilter when he eased away. His hands remained on her arms. Her gaze traveled from his warm, firm hold, up his arms, to his face. His dark brown eyes watched her intently. The concern in their depths added to her befuddled emotions.

"Are you okay?" he asked, moving his hands up

and down her arms.

"Yes. Fine. Just—a bit stunned." Heat singed her cheeks and burned her ears as she replayed his kiss. She'd never received a kiss so staggering before. Happiness swamped her, sending the heady sensation of everything being all right to her nagging head.

Holt flashed his disarming smile and moved around to the driver's door. "I'll call you tonight."

He handed her the box the phone came in. She took it absentmindedly and clutched it to her chest, still enjoying the aftershocks of the kiss.

He turned the key in the ignition, grabbed his sketch book, and tore out a page, handing it to her.

"Take care."

She glanced at him as he pulled away and then down at the drawing. The pencil lines had formed her as well as a reflection in the mirror. Her finger hovered above the smiling mouth. Had she ever really looked this happy?

Gina stared at the retreating car. Holt made her feel special and desired. Two things she hadn't experienced in a very long time. Not since her mother's illness began.

She'd never been in a relationship. All the boys she'd slept with in high school had meant nothing to her. Looking back, they were all domineering and out for self-satisfaction. It wasn't until her senior year, when her music teacher started examining her male acquaintances and her looseness, she realized her father's incest had turned her into a slut. She'd thought that was what she was supposed to do. Allow any male who asked to use her body as they saw fit.

The day the realization hit, she'd vowed celibacy and kept all males at a cool distance. Until Holt Reynolds. Thinking his name warmed her. She'd never been in love, but at this moment, knowing she wouldn't see him for some time, her once stable world teetered. If this was love, she wasn't sure she could handle it.

Gina wandered back into the hospital, giddy from his kiss and stunned by her thoughts.

"Whoa, now that was some kiss your boyfriend laid on you out there," Sheila said, not even hiding the fact she'd stood at the door watching.

"He's not my boyfriend. That was just... a friend saying good-bye." Gina gathered up her phone and flowers. "I'm taking these to my room. I'll be right back." She ignored the smirk on Sheila's lips.

Holt's gifts were special, and she planned to keep them to herself. No one had ever given her flowers. She ruffled the white fringe petals with a finger and smiled at his choice. How did he know she preferred simple flowers to roses?

Today of all days, held few customers and the lack of work to focus on made the day drag out interminably. Gina didn't offer to stay on after her shift finished as she normally would. She said good night to the new shift coming in, which peaked a few eyebrows, and rushed to her small room. She showered, made a sandwich, and waited for Holt to call.

****

The flight hadn't been bad, but he was tired and his whole body ached, not just his ribs. Holt scanned the small airport parking lot for his truck. Instead, Penny pulled up in her compact car.

"You look like shit," she said, hopping out and opening the hatch in the back.

He shoved his duffel and rigging bag into the small area and winced. The pills he swallowed in Phoenix had worn off.

"How many times do I have to tell you, young ladies don't talk like that?" He lowered his aching body onto the passenger seat and tweaked his ribs buckling up.

"As many as you want. I just stated the truth." Penny was a true teenager. Rebellious and knew everything. That was everything except what she was going to do with the baby growing in her belly.

"What did the doctor say at the last appointment?" Holt took his hat off. The crown bumping the top of the car irritated and enhanced the cramped feeling of the small car.

"Everything is fine. I have a good strong baby." She shot him a grimace. "My mom called and said if I haven't had an abortion yet, to not plan on coming home—ever. They don't want to take care of a bastard grandchild. Loving parents, don't ya think?"

Holt still couldn't figure out how level-headed Penny came from the likes of the two who claimed to be her parents. Not to mention her mentally unhinged, older sister. "I'm sorry. You know you're welcome to stay at the ranch until you have the baby. If you put it up for adoption, I'll help, if you decide to keep it, same goes. I'm here if you need me."

"I know, and I really appreciate all you've done to help me out. God knows that creep who got me pregnant isn't helping." She swung the car out of town.

Leaving the illuminated city streets relaxed his muscles and allowed him to take a huge gulp of tangy juniper and sage air.

Twenty minutes and he'd be home.

Once he closed the door of his house on the outside world, he'd call Gina. During his layover, it took all his control not to dial her number. He knew she was working and shouldn't disturb her. The desire to hear her voice though made him too aggressive. He had to slow down, or she'd go running the other way as fast as she could. He'd do everything in his power not to have that happen.

Gina was the first woman to put him in his place one moment and show concern the next. The way she kissed him back revealed a deep desire lurking in her. He planned to wait her out and enjoy that side of her.

"So, who's the woman? I don't think you've been involved with anyone since I've known you." Penny turned the car down a gravel road.

"I met her at the charity auction I attended in Portland." Holt smiled, remembering how his curiosity had drawn him to her. Her music, her tough exterior. Her vulnerability.

"Did she follow you to the rodeo?" The awe in Penny's young voice made him laugh.

"No, she's anything but a buckle bunny. She was working at a hospital a couple hours from the rodeo. One of her co-workers urged her to go. She was as surprised to see me as I was to see her."

She smirked. "Sure you didn't plan getting kicked?"

Holt ruffled her hair and laughed. "You are something else, you know that? Of course I didn't plan getting kicked. I don't like missing rodeos to heal."

"But you got to spend time with your lady." Penny waggled her brows and parked the car in front of his ranch-style home.

The first time Holt toured the house and land, he knew this was home. He'd remodeled the entire 1940's ranch house making it more open and to his liking and even turned the small guest house into his studio. His latest renovations involved the barn, fences, and sectioning the two hundred acres into usable pastures and fields. With good irrigation habits, the land would produce hay and grass for his growing rough-stock herd.

Before Holt made it out of the small car, Penny had his bags sitting on the ground by the steps. "You

Paty Jager

shouldn't lug those around." He bent, groaned at the motion and hoisted the bags over his shoulders. "Get the door."

Penny hurried ahead of him. Zip, his border collie, was true to his name, zipping out the door and circling his feet like a black and white whirlwind.

"He missed you real bad," Penny said, grabbing the dog's collar and tugging him away from Holt's feet.

That wasn't good. "How bad did he miss me?"

"He chewed up a pair of your boots. They're ones you don't wear very often. I don't think. They had pretty new soles."

Shit. "Are you talking about the dark brown pair with the blue stitching?" He imagined his six-hundred-dollar dress boots tattered and discolored. His gut twinged at the wasted money.

"Yeah. That's the pair."

Double shit. "Zip what am I going to do with you? You're lucky Penny was here to watch you this time and you didn't have to go to a kennel." He knelt, scratching the dog behind the ears and trying to make up for lost time. Stupidity hit him when he brought home a dog. He was gone too much. But until Penny moved in the house, he'd been lonely, and coming home to Zip was like coming home to someone.

"How'd he get in my room? I thought I left the door shut?"

"That's what I can't figure out, either. I'd gone to town for some groceries, and when I got back, he was lying in your closet, chew marks and slobber all over those boots." Penny scrunched her face in thought. "I didn't even put the clothes away I'd washed for you. They were stacked on the table outside your door."

How could a dog open not only his bedroom door but the closet as well? He didn't like the idea forming in his head.

His growling stomach interrupted his thoughts. "Do you mind fixing me a sandwich? I'm going to call Gina." Holt dropped his bags in the entry and moved to the leather couch in the living room. Zip hopped on, flopping across his lap.

"You missed me that bad, boy?" He scratched the dog's ears and dialed Gina's number. The mantel clock above the fireplace struck eleven. Would she be asleep? He'd forgotten about the time change.

After three rings, his hand clenched and his gut roiled. He may have given her the phone, but that didn't mean she would use it.

"Hello?" Her soft voice started his heart racing.

"Hello, yourself," he growled into the phone.

"You're home? Did you have any troubles? How are you feeling?"

Her anxious questions tipped the corners of his mouth. She cared more than she let on.

"Yes. No. Better, now that I'm talking to you."

Her soft throaty chuckle floated through the phone.

"How was your day?" he asked, just wanting to hear her voice. She regaled him with a boring day other than two drunks she patched up. Penny placed his food on the table next to him and motioned she was headed to bed. Holt waved her off, listening intently to Gina's sweet voice on the other end of the phone.

How had he gone so long with no one in his life to share things? Sure, Jess had been there when he needed to vent and had kept him sane after Sherrie's death. But, having a woman care and share—was a whole different level of intimacy.

"Are you still there?" Her voice quivered.

"Yes, just enjoying the sound of your voice." Was that a sigh on her end?

"You're tired, I should let you go."

Her softly spoken words rushed a knot of

disappointment to his throat. The regret in her words made him wonder how they would both function until they were together again. "I'm more hungry than tired."

"You should go eat." Again, though her words were supportive, she sounded reluctant to hang up.

"I'll eat. You tell me something about you I don't know." He picked up half of the sandwich and took a bite.

"Do you need to go make something?"

"No. Penny brought me a sandwich."

"Oh." The one word spoke volumes. Jealousy and uncertainty rang in her tone.

He softened his pitch. "Honey, you don't have to worry about her. She's a kid who needed a place to stay. She takes care of the animals, and me when I'm home, as payment for staying here. She's like a little sister and that's all she'll ever be. I promise. You know, if you come visit my ranch, you'll get to meet her and see for yourself."

"What do her parents think of her staying with you?"

"They kicked her out. That's why she's here." Holt didn't miss the fact she bypassed his invitation to come to the ranch.

"I'd let you talk to her, but she went to bed right after we started talking." He heard Gina yawn and glanced at the clock. It was nearly midnight in Arizona.

"I should let you get some sleep." She started to protest, but he quickly continued on. "No, you need to sleep and so do I. If you want to talk, give me a call anytime. Like I said, I keep the phone on me all the time. And if you don't call me—expect a call from me tomorrow night."

Her laughter tickled his ear. "You're going to run your cell bill up if you call that much."

"I have you on my friend plan. We can talk all

we want. So don't let a phone bill keep you from calling whenever *you* want." He knew they should hang up, but he wasn't ready to let her go.

"Okay. Good night." The sadness in her voice made him think she didn't want to hang up either.

"Sweet dreams." Holt left the line open until he finally heard it click on the other end. They acted like two teenagers.

He shook his head, took a bite of his sandwich, and stared at the clock. It was going to be a long twenty-four hours.

Chapter Thirteen

Gina stared at the magnetic calendar on the apartment-sized fridge. The month had flown by. Looking forward to her chats with Holt every night had a lot to do with it. Even on the road, he called her the same time every night. Some calls she heard his buddies kidding in the background, but he never hung up early. One night, they talked until three in the morning.

The more she conversed with Holt, the more she found herself falling for him and wondering how to continue their relationship as just friends.

The phone jangled a country tune, and she glanced at the clock. Right on time. Her chest expanded as she inhaled, stalling her thumping heart. Every night she experienced the same thrill and excitement. She resisted the urge to snatch up the phone and picked up a mug of chamomile tea before flipping the phone open.

"Hello?" she said, holding her breath to hear his voice.

"Hey."

The deep, sexy timbre of the one word warmed her to her core.

"How was your ride tonight?" Even though she feared the details, the pride in his voice when he retold the ride made her ask every time.

"I had a good draw. It was an ornery piebald that's known for his twisting. He threw in a couple new hops, but I stayed on and had a fair score."

"Did you place where you wanted?" She wandered from the kitchen area to the Murphy bed in the sitting room.

"Jess beat me, but I ended up third, in the money. I'm getting to the top third of the standings. That's better than this time last year." Satisfaction rang in his words.

"That's wonderful!" Excitement for his success overrode her fears of his riding.

"Yeah, it's looking good. I have one more rodeo next weekend, then nothing until finals in December. I'd like to entertain you at the ranch." The air waves buzzed, and he blew out a sigh. "What do you say? Come for a visit when you're done there next week."

The soft plea, tugged at her conscience. Gina chewed on the side of her finger. She missed him miserably. Which was laughable, considering she'd never needed or missed anyone before.

"I'll beg if I have to. I miss you, Gina, come see my ranch."

The huskiness of his voice jolted her heart and sent it racing.

"I've missed you, too." A tear trickled down her cheek. She longed to feel his strong arms wrapped around her.

"Then meet me in Phoenix next Sunday, and we'll fly to the ranch together."

Her heart wanted to say yes, revel in his warmth. Her darn conscious warned, *Don't go, you'll only get in deeper.*

She squeezed her eyes shut as her head and heart battled. Her head told her taking that step would push her vow to the limits, and possibly hurl her back to her past.

Her heart thudded thinking of his smile and laughing eyes. She plain missed him.

"Yes," she whispered.

"Yes? You said, yes?"

"Yes, I said, yes."

She pulled the phone from her ear as he whooped like a liquored cowboy, and she laughed at his exuberance. When he started listing all the things they could do, however, she sobered.

"But that doesn't mean I'll climb into your bed." Over the course of their nightly talks, they'd discussed her vow of celibacy several times, but she'd yet to tell him exactly why she'd made it. He understood her vow, or so he said. But he also argued that was ten years ago, and she was now a grown woman who had her life under control. True. However, her vow played a large role in getting her to where she was now.

"I'm not expecting you to. I understand your commitment, I just don't happen to agree with it at this time of your life, but I won't hold it against you."

His softly spoken words only imbedded even more trust in him.

"You do know you are the only man I've ever met who not only knows everything about me, but hasn't tried to make me a conquest in bed. That's one of the reasons I care about your friendship so much."

"I just can't wait to see you and hold you." His tone deepened, became sexier.

She heard pages riffling on the other end of the line. "What are you doing?"

"I'm looking up the airline number. When we get done talking I'll book our flights."

"I'll pay for mine." If he paid, Holt may think she owed him. He'd yet to use that with her, but going to his place took their relationship to another level. A scary level.

"You can pay me back when we get to the ranch. Unless you want to rack up some flyer miles on your account?" He always looked for ways to scrimp and save, too.

"My tickets to and from the jobs are taken care

of by the company. You can use my ticket to rack up your miles, or I can go through the company and get a ticket."

"No. I'll get it. I want to make sure we sit together. Once I see you, I'm not letting anything get between us. And that includes the armrest!"

His humor always made her smile. Including her in his jokes was the same as being wrapped in his arms. Before she knew it, they'd talked for two hours.

"I'll see you in a week and call you with the details tomorrow." Holt's tone didn't allow her to think about backing out.

"All right. Good night." Gina closed the phone and turned out the light.

One week and she'd see Holt. She moaned and turned her face into her pillow. This week was going to drag, she just knew it.

****

Holt stood at the security screening gate waiting for Gina. He tugged his phone out of his pocket, again, checking the time.

"She'll be here on time." Jess slapped him on the back and pointed a thumb toward the line of travelers passing through inspection. "I'm going. See you on the other side."

Holt nodded and stared down the wide corridor. Even though she confirmed last night she found a ride to Phoenix from the reservation, he worried she'd over think her acceptance to visit the ranch and run the other way. Gina wasn't one to back out of a commitment, but he realized this was a huge step for her to put her past behind and trust he wouldn't hurt her.

The minute Gina emerged in the crowd, his nerves untangled and his feet started toward her. He enfolded her into his arms, inhaling her floral scent.

"You made it." He kissed her silky hair. Relief ebbed through every pore. Until he saw her smiling face, fear had overrode his excitement. Here she stood, smiling and hugging him tight. The light in her eyes spread waves of happiness through his body like rays of summer sunshine.

Her hands stroking his back proved she had more than friendly feelings. She'd missed him physically as well. His heart raced with thoughts of cozy nights in front of the fire, possibly making love if he could get to the heart of her vow.

"Come on, we need to get in line." He captured her hand and led her through the zigzag maze to the screeners. Within minutes, they hurried hand-in-hand to their gate.

Jess waved as they neared the waiting area, and Holt steered them over to his friend.

"Good to see you again, Gina." Jess tipped his hat, smiling a little too smugly for Holt's liking.

In fact, Jess was downright pleased Gina had agreed to go to the ranch. Holt wasn't sure why his friend liked the idea of her visiting, but he appreciated that Jess approved.

"Hi, Jess. I didn't think I was going to make it on time. A truck spilled something nasty smelling on the highway between Phoenix and the reservation. We sat on the highway for over an hour waiting for them to clear the road." She clutched Holt's hand as if she were afraid he'd run away.

He pushed a strand of her hair behind her ear. She had it down, thick and straight, falling to just below her shoulders. The style showed a younger more carefree woman. He wanted to kiss her so bad his heart banged around in his chest. "The important thing is you made it."

"Yes. I made it." Her gaze slid from his eyes to his lips and back to his eyes.

Hot dang! She wanted to kiss him, too. He

glanced at the departure time on the digital sign above the ticket agent. A nasally, static-laden voice announced their flight was ready to board.

He'd kiss her sweet lips once they were seated And not stop until they changed planes three hours later.

Gina followed behind Holt. She still couldn't believe she'd be at his ranch in less than eight hours. Living in the same house with him for two weeks. He squeezed her hand and glanced over his shoulder. She wanted to kiss those lips curved in his disarming smile so bad her toes gripped her sandals.

She'd played devil's advocate all week, telling herself why she shouldn't be here. Every time, her heart and desire to be with him won out over her head. Now, holding his hand and seeing his excitement, she was glad her heart won.

He led her down the aisle of the plane. "Window or aisle?"

"It doesn't matter."

His eyes twinkled with mischief. "Then I'll take the window so you have to lean on me if you want to see out."

"I like that idea." She followed him to their row. The minute her bottom hit the seat, he flipped up the armrest and pulled her into his arms.

"I've been waiting a month for this."

His head dipped, her eyes fluttered closed, and the warmth of his lips covered hers.

Relief and desire rippled under her skin as she returned the kiss. The long, sultry, glad-to-see-you greeting uncurled her toes and melted her body to his.

Holt pulled back, kissing her temple. "I have never missed anyone as badly as I missed you this past month."

Staring into his eyes, she believed him. "I've felt the same." She leaned back to gaze into his face. "It's scary the way I've missed you." Gina glanced down at the snaps on his shirt and played with one of them. "After my mother died, I missed her horribly. Slowly, the emptiness filled with other things. School, piano, work. I learned to ignore the loneliness. I haven't missed or needed a single person since. I was content to be alone and work toward my goal." She sighed and gazed into his desire lit eyes. "After meeting you, all I can think about is the next time I'll hear your voice or see you."

Holt's luscious mouth quirked that devastating smile before he leaned down to kiss her.

She placed a finger on his lips. "It scares me, a lot."

"Buckle up, please." A stewardess stood beside their seats smiling down at them.

"Can I buckle her in with me?" Holt asked, grinning like a boy with a pocket full of treasures.

The stewardess laughed. "No, I'm afraid that's against regulations. Once we get in the air, you can," she motioned to the two of them, "continue."

Gina playfully pushed away from him. "I can't believe you asked her that." She settled into her seat and buckled up.

"Honey, I'm not letting you out of my reach for the next two weeks." Holt took her hand in his.

Gina lowered her voice. "You will at night."

He smiled and raised her hand to his lips. "I think you need to relax and enjoy our time together."

That's what frightened her. The way her body reacted to Holt, would she be able to remain celibate once they were alone at the ranch? Holt made her teenage vow seem foolish. But to give up on her vow was weakness. Most important, after the gratuitous sex of her past, how would she know if what she had with Holt was real?

She had no knowledge of a true relationship. She only knew what her father had taught her.

Alleviate a male's urges.

Her hand on the armrest clenched the plastic. Holt soothed the other hand balled in his palm. When would she be able to live one day and not have her childhood encroach?

"Hey, what has you looking so stormy?" He slid an arm around her, drawing her head to his shoulder, and pressed a kiss to the top of her head. "You can tell me anything, you know."

"Not here." His acceptance of her childhood and her feelings about sex still stunned her. Could she tell him what caused her to make her vow?

"That's fair. We have two weeks—fourteen days—to spend together. You can spill anything you want in that time." He tipped her chin, making her look at him. "And nothing you say will make me think any different about you than I do right now."

The sincerity in his voice and approval in his gaze spread hope over her heart like a shimmery, satin pillow case. No one had ever believed in her the way this cowboy did. His acceptance, touch, and caring made her feel untainted. She didn't have to keep a barrier between them; he was the first person since her eighth birthday she trusted.

"Just hold me and let me feel content," she whispered, snuggling deeper into embrace and closing her eyes.

Holt held Gina in his arms all the way to Portland. Her warm body cuddled against him made him a happy man.

After exiting the plane, they met up with Jess.

"Stay in touch." His friend nodded toward Gina who'd wandered off in search of chocolate.

"I'll keep you posted." Holt's gaze followed Gina, watching her inspect a display of magazines. He glanced back at Jess. "Did you fall in love with Clare before or after you slept with her?"

Jess had turned to leave when Holt asked the

question. His friend spun around, questioning him with his eyes before he glanced at Gina and then back. "You mean you two haven't?" He shook his head and slapped Holt on the back. "Then I guess this is the real thing for you and not infatuation."

"You didn't answer my question." Holt started walking toward the shop. Gina had disappeared. He spotted her and turned his attention back to Jess.

"Shoot, I fell in love with Clare the first time I laid eyes on her and she told me to get lost." A lopsided, love-struck grin spread across Jess's face.

Holt knew what his friend was talking about. He swung his gaze to Gina at the counter buying a handful of candy. The sight tickled him. So, she had a sweet tooth.

"That's the same with me," he admitted. "The first night I met her, I had an inkling I was in love. But after spending time with her in Payson—I knew I was hooked."

"Have you told her?" Concern wrinkled his friend's brow.

"No. She's still talking 'friends.' It's a cover for something she hasn't told me yet." He watched her sashay back towards them, fighting with a candy bar wrapper. "I plan to find out while we're at the ranch and tell her my feelings, too."

Jess slapped him on the back. "I wish you luck."

"Luck with what?" Gina stopped beside Holt.

"Nationals. That's when we'll see each other next." Holt pulled her hand toward his mouth and took a bite of the candy.

"That's mine!" she squealed and playfully tugged it out of his grasp.

This was the side of her he hoped to see more of at the ranch.

"I'll see you two later. Clare and the kids should be waiting for me." Jess slapped Holt on the back and smiled at Gina. "Make sure he behaves himself."

"I will." Gina slipped her arm through Holt's.

The action spoke as clear as her getting on the plane with him. His heart expanded twofold. She'd grown attached to him. With luck, after this weekend, he could think about a future with Gina.

"Shall we find the gate for our last flight?" Holt didn't wait for an answer, just walked at a leisurely pace down the concourse. He grinned at the open stares she collected. Her happiness put a sparkle in her eyes and her skin glowed. Why some man hadn't taken the time to get to know her was their loss, and his gain.

He stopped.

"What?" She faced him, her gaze scanning his face while her lips slowly curved into a smile.

He leaned in, kissing her with the sweet happiness he felt clear to the soles of his feet.

"Hmm... you can stop any time if that's what you have in mind."

She smiled dreamily, and he couldn't contain the happiness bubbling.

"I can't wait to get you to the ranch. We're going to have so much fun." He grinned again at her raised brow. "I don't mean what you're thinking. I can't believe your mind is in the manure pile."

She smacked him playfully. "I can't believe you said that so loud in public because you know what all of them are thinking."

Holt played innocent. "No, what?"

"There's our gate, and look, you almost made us late." Gina disengaged from his arm and marched into line.

Shaking his head, he followed, not allowing anyone to get between them.

They settled into the smaller prop jet and, in less than an hour, landed in central Oregon.

"I told Penny to pick us up in my truck. It has more room than her Matchbox car." Holt reached back to claim Gina's hand. She'd stopped halfway between the building and the plane.

"I thought we would be alone at the ranch?"

Was that fear dulling her eyes? Why would she fear Penny?

"Penny has nowhere else to go. She won't intrude. That's one thing nice about her. She knows when to stay out of sight. Guess it comes from being raised by her loony parents." He walked back and captured her hand. "Give her a chance. You're going to love her. She's like a kid sister to me."

Gina tried to remember what he'd said about the girl in their phone calls. He'd only mentioned her a few times. She couldn't explain it, but whenever he said the name her stomach squeezed.

They entered the revolving door into the small airport. Her gaze flicked over an older couple, a woman with a toddler, and hovered on a beautiful woman openly ogling Holt. Was this Penny? She looked a little old to be thought of as a 'younger sister.'

A teenage girl with a round, pregnant belly hurried forward, grinning and waving wildly. Gina's clenched teeth dropped open. *That* was Penny?

Chapter Fourteen

"Wow, you're as gorgeous as Holt said." The pregnant teenager pumped Gina's hand and smiled at Holt.

"Gina, this big-mouthed, young *lady* is Penny Landers." Holt ruffled the girl's brown curls and smiled like a doting parent.

Gina pasted a smile on her face. Why hadn't Holt told her Penny was pregnant? How did her parents feel about her living at Holt's ranch unchaperoned? Why did *he* take her in? Was he the father? That thought sickened her.

She studied Holt as he and Penny conversed. Her feelings for him had grown with every touch and conversation. She'd given him her trust. Gina watched Penny. The girl didn't act like a smitten teenager around Holt.

Gina shook the thought away. If anything untoward was going on he wouldn't have invited her. Right? Or had he invited her as a smokescreen, knowing she wouldn't fall into his bed? She stepped away when Holt reached out to take her hand. Visions of her father doting on her in public and demoralizing her in private surfaced. She shook her head, not wanting to think she'd fallen into the same trap. Had she attached herself to a man just like her father? Her body trembled. She searched her heart and stared at Holt.

"Penny, why don't you bring the truck around to the front," Holt said. His brown eyes held Gina's, the conviction staring back at her shrunk her self-assurance even more.

Holt escorted Gina to a corner away from everyone. "What's going on inside that pretty head of yours? You knew Penny lives at the ranch. Does her condition bother you? I'd think someone with your compassion would understand her situation." He took a seat and drew her down in the padded chair beside him. "Come on. We have no secrets from one another. What's going on?"

"I don't know. I thought it would be just you and me. I find out Penny will be around, and she's living at your house in her condition—I just... I don't know. It felt like..." She didn't know how to say aloud, *I'm jealous, now I'll have to be guarded all the time*, and worse, *I doubt you.*

Holt took her trembling hand. "You know her parents tossed her out. I can't turn my back on her. Not in her condition. If you don't want to see Penny, I promise she'll be out of sight and out of mind. She's a likable kid who knows how to be invisible."

Gina didn't know what to say. Her emotions twisted in a knot. She didn't like herself for believing the worst, and she did feel sympathy for the young, pregnant teen.

"I told you she reminds me of Sherrie. I figure this is my way of making up for that mistake. Don't make me take sides on this. I can help Penny, and be your friend."

His last statement knocked sense into her. She had no right to come into his life and expect him to change, after all, she didn't plan to change her beliefs or vow for him.

"I'm sorry. I would never ask you to change who you are. I just—I'm not used to the feelings I have when I'm around you."

He kissed her hand, and the twinkle returned in his eyes. "I'll never tire of hearing you say that." He stood and pulled her to her feet. "Let's get the luggage and get home. I have someone else I'm dying for you to meet."

"I hope it isn't another wayward girl." She tried to make the comment lighthearted, but didn't know what she would do if there *was* another pretty young girl at his house.

His laughter echoed in the waiting area. "Zip is definitely not a girl. Wayward, yes!"

"Oh, you mentioned him in your phone calls." She'd never had a dog, but had always longed for one. Her adult life wasn't spent in one place long enough to give a dog a home.

"He's going to like you." Holt grabbed his two bags off the moving belt and placed them at her feet. "Which one is yours?"

"Actually it's two." She sent him a nervous glance. "That one," she pointed to a bag with a bright orange ribbon. He moved to claim it and she added, "That smaller one with the orange ribbon as well."

He grinned and set the bags at her feet. "You take the small one. I'll get the rest."

She started to object, then thought better of it. Holt loaded his duffel on top of her larger, wheeled case and looped the handles of his other bag over his shoulder. She fell in step beside him and out the automated door.

A tall, maroon truck rumbled at the curbside. Penny slid off the seat and onto the sidewalk. A dog leaped out the back window of the vehicle and ran circles around Holt's feet in a black and white blur.

"Hi, boy!" He knelt down. The swirl of color stopped and whining commenced. "Yeah, I know. But I'm back now. We'll go for runs and hang out together a lot." After a good scratching behind the ears, Zip riveted his attention to sniffing Gina.

His whiskers tickled her hand. She giggled and stroked the soft hair on his back. Holt secured the luggage in the back of the truck and stood beside her.

"Zip, this is Gina. She's going to stay with us a while, and I want you to be nice."

Penny scuffed her shoe on the sidewalk. "Well, he hasn't been nice."

"What did he do this time?" Holt asked, glaring at the dog.

"He got in your closet again. I swear I don't know how he's doing it. But he chewed up a pair of sneakers this time." Penny also sent the dog a scathing look.

The dog cocked his head to one side as if listening. Gina could swear the animal smiled.

Holt roughed his head and captured Gina's hand, leading her to the driver's side. "Load up. Let's get home." Zip leaped into the back of the truck as Penny pulled herself onto the passenger seat.

Gina put a hand on the handle Holt indicated and placed a foot on the running board. "Why is this thing so high in the air? Are you compensating for something else?"

Her comment got a giggle out of Penny and a swat on the bottom from Holt.

"No, it's set high because I like it that way." He climbed up behind her, cupping her body in his.

She ignored the racing of her heart and slid under the steering wheel to the middle of the seat, straddling the gear shift.

"I'm not sure I like this spot," she said, trying to move her legs.

"It's just fine," Holt said, placing his hand on her knee, stilling her movements. He slid his hand to the gear shift knob, resting his arm across her thigh.

The heat of his arm scorched a path up her leg to her pelvis and took her breath away. Each time he shifted, his arm moved across her thigh, upping the heat and vibrations. She flicked a glance at Penny, worrying the girl would notice her flaming cheeks. But Penny was more concerned with the position of her seatbelt over her protruding belly.

The vehicle rumbled down the road, vibrating the seat and causing Holt and Penny to talk loud.

"Did the work crew get the barn finished?" Holt asked, resting his hand on Gina's knee once he'd stopped shifting and they cruised down the highway.

"Mr. Walker said they were done with the majority of it, but there were things you requested after your last visit they're still working on." Penny shrugged her shoulders. "It will be nice to get those men gone. All they do is stare at me when I go out to do chores."

Holt's hand resting on Gina's leg balled into a fist. She watched him. His anger hardened his features and darkened his eyes.

"Why didn't you say something before? I'd have had a word with Walker." Holt's voice held a note of censure.

"I know how much you wanted to get this project done and didn't want anything to mess it up. Besides, most of the time I did the chores before they came or after they left."

Gina glanced at the girl. And realized that was what she was—a frightened girl. She reached out, squeezing the hand Penny rested on her belly. "I know what it's like to hide away to keep people from staring or bothering you." She glanced at the child's swollen abdomen. "Don't let your past mistakes take over your life."

Holt squeezed her knee gently, and she turned to him.

"Have I told you lately how wonderful you are?" The desire in his eyes told her more than his words.

Penny giggled, reminding Gina they weren't alone.

Holt shifted down, turning onto a bumpy gravel road that crunched under the wide tires. Within minutes, she spotted a two-story, ranch style home with a wraparound porch. It was the house of her dreams.

"How can you leave this?"

"Knowing I'll soon only leave because I want to. Not because I have to." Holt stopped the truck in front of a small green patch of lawn. A thin row of marigolds bobbed their blossoms in the early afternoon breeze.

Holt helped her out of the truck, holding her in his arms, and kissing her a quick peck on the lips. Her feet found the ground, and she moved out of his embrace as he closed the door and faced the house.

"When'd you plant the flowers?"

"A week ago. I thought it could use some color." Penny walked up the steps to the porch.

"It looks homey," Gina said, again wondering at the odd relationship between the two.

Holt lugged the bags to the front door. She took control of her luggage and followed him into the great room. A wonderful combination of male and old farm captured her attention. A leather couch and chair sat in front of a big screen TV. Haphazard piles of DVD's lined the shelves beneath the television. Log tables enhanced the outdoorsy theme along with the wood floor and scatter rugs. A shiny, black, baby grand piano stood in the corner. The instrument completed the inviting nuance. Her fingers itched to slip across the ivories and fill the room with her happiness.

"My room is at the end of the hall. Penny sleeps upstairs in the room to the left. You're welcome to join me in my room or take the room to the right at the top of the stairs."

Was he joking or did he really expect her to jump into his bed? She caught the sparkle of mirth in his dark brown eyes and smacked him, then grabbed her bags, one in each hand, and headed to the stairs.

"Here, let me help you." Holt grabbed her suitcases and banged up the stairs behind her.

The hallway held a collection of his drawings grouped on the walls between four doors. Gina stalled at each grouping, again entranced by the emotions his renderings oozed. Holt eased her away from the artwork and into a room at the top of the stairs. The colorful quilt on a queen size bed gave the room a homey appeal. A bedside table and lamp stood to one side. Soothing baby blue washed over the walls. Lace curtains encased a window framing a new wood building and a green pasture beyond.

"The closet has hangers and shelves for your things." He tucked his hands in his back pockets. "The walls are kind of bare. Maybe you can help me pick out pictures to put on them while you're here. I've only been fixing up rooms when they're needed."

"How long have you lived here?" Gina tossed her purse on the bed and opened the closet.

"About three years. Just me the first year, then Zip came along and Penny about three months ago." Holt crossed the room and embraced her. "I'm so happy you're here." He nuzzled her hair.

Her cravings couldn't be ignored any longer. She wrapped her arms around his neck, meshing her body with his and sought his mouth. Her mind shut down, and she let her body take over. She knocked his hat away, skimming her fingers through his curly hair.

His hands slid under her shirt. The scratchy texture and gentle movements caused her to moan. They stopped and he raised his head.

"How far are you willing to go?" he asked. She knew what he meant. At the moment, her body screamed all the way, but her mind began an incessant chant of denial.

"Not that far...yet."

Hope shimmered in his eyes. "I like that word."

139

His hands moved under her shirt again, tracing her backbone. "Do you want to unpack, eat, or just laze around the rest of the afternoon?"

"What are you going to do?" His hands roaming her body felt like sinking into a warm bath.

He kissed her chin, her cheek, her temple, her forehead, and down around the other side of her face. "Sample you, eat, unpack, and see how far the workers have gotten."

"Ummm... I like all of that. Can I do it with you?"

A deep throaty chuckle warmed her ear. "I would hope you'd be with me when I sample you."

She shook her head and grinned. "No, I mean can I see what the workers have done?"

"I'm not sure how much we'll see with you along, but it sounds interesting."

Holt commandeered her mouth and kissed her dizzy. Her body melted in his arms. Gina reveled in the giddiness of his kiss, yet, became frustrated at how easily her body gave in to him. He had the capacity to make her weak. Something she'd worked long and hard at overcoming.

Without stopping the kiss, he moved to the bed, reclining them side-by-side on the colorful quilt.

Fear stiffened her. She wasn't ready. Not now, not with the door open, and Penny lurking somewhere.

"It's okay. I'm not forcing anything. I'm resting." Holt kicked off his boots. Two heavy thumps were muffled in the carpet at the end of the bed. His stocking-clad feet slid the length of her calf, pushing her sandals off her feet and over the end of the bed. They slapped together, landing on the floor. He snuggled Gina into his arms and held her.

She inhaled his scent; spicy, earthy cologne, starched shirt, and a touch of musty animal. A combination she remembered from the first night they met.

Squirming, she rolled to study his face. His seductive charms, kisses, patience, and acceptance wore through her protective armor. His arms tightened, drawing her against him. The sensation of his hard body against her breasts and his hand splayed across her lower back aroused feelings in her she didn't know how to express—wasn't even sure she should harbor for this or any man.

"Go to sleep," he pleaded between clenched teeth.

"I'm trying, but I can't get comfortable."

He drew his arm out from under her, grazing her breast in the motion. Her breath caught as he released her. He kissed the tip of her nose and turned his back to her.

His arm hadn't been the problem. She wasn't tired. Pent up emotions and uncertainties plagued her. His breathing took on a heavy cadence. He could sleep, she'd check out the rest of the house.

After ensuring he was asleep, she slowly rolled to the edge of the bed, trying not to disturb him and tiptoed from the room.

Gina found Penny humming in the kitchen as she spread peanut butter on bread.

"Is there enough for two?" she asked, causing the girl to jump. "I'm sorry. I didn't mean to startle you."

"It's okay. I'm so use to it just being me in this place, I forgot you were here." Penny slid the bread and peanut butter across the counter. "Help yourself. Did macho cowboy crash?"

Gina snickered. "Yes, he did."

"He always does after being on the road a few weeks." Penny checked the clock. "You should have about three to four hours to do whatever you want."

"Thanks." Gina spread peanut butter on a slice of bread. "What does your family think of you staying with Holt?" She knew Holt's answer, but wondered what the girl would have to say.

"They kicked me out. Holt took me in. If they don't like it, I don't really care." Penny stared at her. "He's like a big brother I always wished I'd had. My older sister is strung out most of the time and following cowboys the other half. She couldn't help me if someone paid her all the dope she wanted." The teenager's voice rang with disgust.

"How do you handle people thinking—you know, that, Holt has you here because that's his child?" She glanced at Penny's protruding belly.

"I ignore any comments. Not sure what Holt does, since he's never around." Penny set her sandwich down. "You don't think this is his, do you?"

Gina started to speak, and the girl slammed a glass of milk on the counter.

"If you think that, you aren't the woman for him. So you might as well pack up and get out before he wakes up."

"I didn't say I thought that. I asked if others thought that. When Holt speaks of you there is respect and big brotherly love. However, there are people who only see him as a cowboy out to ride horses and knock up women." She held up her hand when Penny opened her mouth. "I'm just stating what I'm sure many have said."

"Are you always this blunt?" Penny narrowed her eyes.

"Yes, she always is." Holt's deep voice jolted them both. "Unless you ask her questions about herself. Then her jaw needs oiled."

Gina swung around to refute his claim. His tousled hair and laugh lines accenting his eyes accelerated her heart beat to an allegro tempo. "I thought you were sleeping."

"So you snuck out to harass my ranch help." He crossed the floor and grabbed up the sandwich she'd made. He took a bite, chewed, and winked. The intimacy of the action along with all the other small things he'd done similar to this dispersed warm contentment through her. This was the connection—the cozy security of her dreams.

"I wasn't harassing"—she stole a peek at Penny—"was I?"

Penny smiled, waggled her fingers, and sauntered out of the room.

"Did I hurt her feelings? I didn't mean to, I was just—"

"Digging for answers." He leaned his backside against the edge of the counter, his arm brushing hers. "There's nothing going on here that isn't moral other than my thoughts about you." He arched an eyebrow and slid his gaze slowly up and down her.

Gina raised the peanut butter covered knife and pointed it at him. "I told you, I'd come to your ranch, but I wouldn't slip into your bed."

"I understand your belief in celibacy. I don't understand why you made it. Just because your dad sexually molested you doesn't taint you. It also doesn't mean you shouldn't experience having love made to you." His voice dropped a seductive octave. Desire flared and darkened his brown eyes.

The gleam in them reminded her of a cougar she came eye to eye with at a zoo. With startling clarity, she realized Holt was stalking her. And he wouldn't give up until he caught her. A shiver of anticipation and fear slinked up her spine.

She gulped, unable to move. Holt leaned over and covered her lips with his, devouring her mouth like a starved animal. His firm lips brushed back and forth against hers, then opened, gaining entry. He tasted of peanut butter and desire.

He cupped the back of her head, deepening the kiss. Her body throbbed and hummed. She wrapped her arms around his neck to keep from sliding to the floor and fought the heady sensation. This was what he wanted. To make her so emotionally needy she'd follow him to his bed.

She pushed away, breaking the kiss, and forcing her body to separate from his.

"Don't do that again." She wiped a hand across her mouth and gripped the counter. Her mind cried out to save herself, while her body swayed toward the man shifting his legs and readjusting his jeans.

She glanced down and saw the reason for his repositioning. The sight of his desire made her ache for him. For what she couldn't give him.

"I need to leave." She spun away from him.

"Not yet!" The firmness of the words stopped her. "You aren't leaving here until you tell me why you can kiss me like you can't get enough, and then walk away when my desire for you shows." Holt put a hand on her shoulder. Gently, he twisted her to look at him. "I've never wanted anyone like I want you. I don't need anyone else. I need you. And I'd walk away if I thought that was best for you. But I'll be damned for you to kiss me like that and then walk away without more of an explanation."

"I-I—"

She didn't know what to do. His desire and confusion radiated from his eyes. She couldn't look at him. Burrowing her face in her hands, she hid from his stricken expression. He wasn't the only one confused. Her emotions rocketed out of control. She was so mixed up. She hadn't wanted anyone, ever, the way she wanted Holt. Giving into her body's needs would be weakness. *Like her father.* Tears trickled down her face. Shame and fear battled in her head and her heart.

"Come on." Holt hugged Gina's shaking, sobbing body against his. "Shhh, I don't ever want to hurt you, but we need to talk." He led her down the hall to his office. He had to get to the root of her damn vow for both their sakes. The most secluded spot in the house for her to feel safe to talk would be this room.

He lowered her onto the desk chair, closed the door, and parked his backside on the desk. Straggling tears trickled down her flushed cheeks. He hated having that affect on her.

"You can't go on pulling back every time things get hot and heavy." He smiled, softening his words. "And that isn't going to chase me away. I spent two years getting flung off Duece's Folly, but I kept climbing on that horse's back every time I drew his name. When I want something bad enough, I work to figure out how to fix it." He leaned down, capturing her hands in his. "Last year, I rode Deuce for eight seconds and garnered a fair score." His thumbs rubbed back and forth over her hands. "You don't deserve to be head shy. Tell me why you made the vow, so I can help you overcome your fear."

Gina's wide, hazel eyes peered at him, void of emotion. She slowly shook her head.

"What could have been so bad that you vowed not to make love with someone you care about and who cares about you?" He had to coax the information out of her. Not knowing ate at him. If she needed therapy, he'd find the best therapist he could. Gina didn't deserve to go through life missing out on intimacy because of something out of her control.

He stroked her cheek, wiping away the tears dotting her hot face. "I won't judge you or anyone else. But, the more I'm around you, the more I think you make too strict of rules for yourself."

She shook her head. "Rules are there for a reason."

"Only if they're justifiable."

Chapter Fifteen

Holt raised her hand to his lips. "Does your father's actions make you think you don't deserve being with a man?"

Gina stared into his eyes. So far she'd been able to hide her tawdry teen lifestyle from him. Why did he have to push all the time for answers?

Once she'd matured and fully understood her adolescent lifestyle, her actions mortified and shamed her. How could any man of good character want her after that? Some things were better left unknown.

"Have you had any counseling?"

His words were spoken softly, but they stung. She wasn't a lost cause that needed another person to help her find her way. She'd learned the hard way the best person she could depend on was herself. There was no way she'd sit in a room with a stranger and have him judge her. She'd dealt with her past so far. It was bad enough Holt dug so much out of her.

She glared at him. "I've worked out my problems on my own."

His sarcastic chuckle prickled the hair on the back of her neck.

"You obviously haven't if you can kiss me like you just did then fly into a fit when it gets too hot for you to handle."

Gina yanked her hands from his and pierced him with a glare. *How dare he start analyzing her!* He was a cowboy, not a psychologist. He didn't know what she'd gone through, how her father's actions tainted her thoughts and actions. He could never understand the full scope of her out of control life.

The part of her working so desperately to stay unattached to him, reared up. *Tell him the truth and he'll back off.* Her heart didn't want to let him go, didn't want to tell him. The part of her so used to taking control and holding back her emotions urged her to tell him.

"You really want to know why I vowed celibacy?" She stared at his calm demeanor and encouraging eyes, ready to spit out the words, yet her lips trembled. Did she want this man to know all her sordid past? Would his knowing everything change how he viewed her as a friend? Desperation clawed at her throat. Now that she had his friendship, she didn't want to do anything to lose it.

Realization zapped her. He was the first person since her mother she wanted to rely on. Wanted to tell the truth to and be absolved. But could he take the full truth? Her stomach knotted with fear. Fear he wouldn't understand. The chasm of despair opened up, and she clung to the edge hoping she didn't fall in.

Holt nodded, "Yes, I want to know everything that's made you who you are." He skimmed a finger down her jawline, lighting a fire of hope and desire. "No matter how unpleasant." Concern softened his eyes.

His touch and tone spoke more than his words. *Please, let him truly care.*

"It's because as a teenager"—Gina took a deep breath—"I allowed any boy who asked me out to use my body." She hurried through the first confession, then waited for him to comment. When he didn't she cringed and continued. "I thought that's what a good girl did. Allowed men access to whatever they wanted." She hated she'd been so stupid and vulnerable. Shame for how promiscuous she'd been dug into her conscience like salt in an open wound

147

and twisted her stomach. The person who should have protected her, told her, her behavior was destructive, had put the restlessness and immoral notions in her head. Gina couldn't look at Holt. If he showed any emotion, she wouldn't be able to hold herself together.

She drew another fortifying breath. "I knew what my father had done was wrong, but I didn't fully realize the sick perversion until my senior year of high school. I read about it in a psychology book." She sat up straighter. "By then, my piano teacher had put me straight about what was appropriate with boys. But I realized what my father's actions had turned me into, and I made the vow to never allow a man to take my body again."

Holt cleared his throat. "I appreciate your courage...and trust in me." He picked up her hand and laced his fingers with hers. "Your vow was to never allow a man to *take* your body. But if you *give* your body because you want to, you haven't broken your vow. You're still the one in control."

Gina stared at him. There wasn't any censure in his expression. His voice hadn't hummed with disrespect or disgust. She wanted to weep with gratitude that he didn't consider her soiled. She searched his face, questioning. Was there truth in what he said? Could she be the one in control when it came to sex?

Holt leaned in, kissed her softly on the lips, and stood. "I'm going to check things over. Do you want to come, or stay here and unpack?"

"I think I'll stay here. How long will you be gone?" She stood, but took a step back to avoid getting too close. She had a lot to think about. His reaction and his words.

"Two hours max." He grasped the handle to the closed door and glanced over his shoulder. His gaze swept from her head to her toe, leaving her with a feeling she'd been wrapped in a warm blanket. He flashed that disarming smile and disappeared down the hall. She stared at the opening long after he whistled for Zip and a door clicked shut somewhere in the house.

****

Holt sauntered through the barn, his face ached he grinned so large. Pride swelled his chest as he scanned the size and convenient set up of the building. On his last trip home, he'd added areas for doctoring and breeding his stock. The squeeze panels and chutes had been ordered and once in place the barn would be fully functional. He turned slowly, taking it all in. The only thing to make this moment better would be if Gina stood by his side.

He still reeled from her confession of past promiscuity. He was far from a saint and had no call to hold it against her. Considering the actions which propelled her in that direction, he could only marvel at the strong woman she'd become. Still, his mind needed time to wrap around what she'd said. He now better understood her vow. It gave her stability and control. Something she'd lacked until her revelation.

Thinking of Gina and walking, he found himself at the corral staring at his four saddle horses. He'd ride out and see how the grass held up in the south pasture. If the cattle needed to be moved, he'd take Gina on her first cattle drive. A smile tugged at his lips. Maybe another first he could give her would be unconditional love. If she thought about his words, about giving rather than being taken, they just might break through her forced celibacy together.

****

Gina moved about the room enjoying the act of cooking in a real kitchen with ample utensils and supplies. The refrigerator and pantry overflowed with fruits, vegetables, whole grains, and white meat. Was that Penny's choice or Holt's?

She thought of all the phone calls the last month and a half and the moments she'd spent in Holt's arms. Her heart raced, and her blood heated. He'd shown her with the late night calls and the flight here he was into her and no one else.

Penny was his crusade to make up for his sister. The guilt he harbored over Sherrie had come up many times in their nightly conversations. She frowned. He opened up so easily to her, yet, she'd held back until hours ago when he'd finally chipped away the last secret from her sealed and battered heart.

Holt had put their relationship into her hands, completely, and his words had made sense. It was her body. She could decide if and when she gave it to a man. She was no longer a victim.

Heat curled in the pit of her belly and spread, simmering up to her face and out to her extremities. There was no doubt her body desired Holt's. He had a magnetic force that drew her closer and enfolded her in security. She craved that security. Needed to appease the throbbing in her center. But did she dare give herself to him? It would mean throwing her safety net vow to the side and risking—her heart and dignity.

Gina stirred the finely sliced chicken and added more garlic to the vegetables sautéing in a large wok. She glanced at the clock. Holt was an hour late. Dinner would be overcooked if he didn't show soon.

Even though he acted like her past didn't faze him, was he really dealing with it? He was the only person she'd ever told about her father and her promiscuity. The only one she'd felt safe enough to unburden to. After all she said had sunk in, did he find it hard to face her? Her stomach knotted. *Please, let him be as open and loving as he'd proven so far.*

Zip barked, drawing her attention back to the

kitchen. She turned the heat off under the food and headed to the back door to see why he barked. Holt walked from a newly built building toward the house, Zip circling his legs. Contentment expanded her chest and eased her restless thoughts. Holt stopped and scratched the dog's ears, giving the animal the attention he craved. The way he made sure Penny had a home, Zip received attention, and steadfastly waiting her out, he seemed to live to make others happy.

He straightened and spied her standing in the door. That darn charmer smile of his slid into place, and his eyes lit up. His warmth was infectious. She couldn't help but smile back as her heart took up a staccato beat. He made her feel special. A heady feeling. One she didn't want to ever lose.

"You were gone longer than two hours." She stepped away from the door so he could enter.

"I couldn't find all the yearlings. A couple hid out in the scrub brush." He placed his hat on the hook by the back door and sniffed the air. "What smells so good?"

"Dinner. Go wash up and find Penny. It's getting overcooked." She moved to the stove to start dishing up. The kiss he planted on the back of her neck wasn't unexpected, but his quick retreat surprised her. Had she been right in thinking he questioned her past and their involvement?

Within minutes, Holt returned, alone.

"Where's Penny?" Gina set the last dish on the table as he pulled a bottle of beer out of the refrigerator.

"Said she wasn't hungry and would grab something later." He flicked the lid into the trash can by the end of the counter and took a seat at the table. His gaze scanned her face.

What was he looking for? His scrutiny set worry and anxiety banging about in her chest.

"I see." Sitting through a meal with just the two of them after their discussion earlier twisted her stomach. Would he dig deeper or worse, retreat?

Gina stood by her chair, chewing on the cuticle of her thumb. Did Holt have wine stashed somewhere? She hadn't come across any when acquainting herself with the kitchen. She could use a little to help her relax.

"You need something?" he asked, watching her.

"Wine. Do you have any?"

A slow smile tipped the corner of his mouth in a sexy smirk. "What kind do you want?"

"White. Sweet."

He studied her, his gaze resting on her lips. He pushed away from the table and stood. Pausing beside her, he pulled out her chair. "Sit and I'll get the wine."

His warm breath fluttered across her cheek. His closeness zinged electricity through her body. She sat to put space between them.

He disappeared into the pantry. Scuffling noises, a clank, and a muffled curse seeped out the pantry door. The sounds could have been dubbed into an old Charlie Chan black and white. She giggled at the comparison. Holt reappeared clasping a bottle of white wine and wearing a triumphant grin. It nearly bested the grin she witnessed when he came up with money at the Doin's.

He crossed to the bank of drawers. Rattling and scraping ensued as he dug in a drawer and came up with a cork screw. He snatched a wine glass from the cupboard and stood beside her chair.

His face scrunched in concentration as he worked the cork screw into the bottle. The wrinkles enhanced his looks, giving him a more mature profile. He uncorked the bottle and poured the golden liquid into her glass.

Gina read the label and peered into his eyes.

"That's a pretty fancy wine. I didn't think cowboys drank from the grape."

He grinned and placed the bottle on the table within her reach. "I bought a case of it at a charity auction last year." He took his seat, holding her gaze. "I sat next to the vineyard owner. He told me no woman could resist a good, white wine."

She raised an eyebrow. "So you're going to get me tipsy and take advantage of me?"

"Hey, you're the one who asked for wine. I figured you need to relax. If you want, you can take the bottle and go to your room and lock the door." He winked and picked up his beer, saluting her.

After a sip of his beer, Holt stared at the food growing cold on the table. "Wow, you didn't tell me you could cook." He spooned some of the stir-fry onto her plate and then his.

"I worked in a restaurant the last two years of college and picked up a few pointers from the chef." She added rice to her plate. Her nerves buzzed, waiting for Holt to take his first bite.

He chewed slowly and smiled. "This is as good as it looks!"

"Thank you." The buzzing subsided, and she took a bite.

"Something about you has been bugging me," Holt said, glancing up from his plate.

Her throat constricted around the bite she'd swallowed. What could he possibly want to know now? He knew every sordid detail of her life. How much deeper could he dig? And why?

"The way you play the piano, you should have been a concert pianist. Why are you a nurse?" He stabbed at the steamed vegetables and watched her.

He'd hit on a subject as sour as her ruined childhood. Gina took a swig of wine. The taste didn't sweeten her mood.

"Because my father didn't believe I could make a

153

living playing the piano." Her father's fury the day she told him about the letter still brought chills to her arms. "My piano teacher helped me apply to Julliard. I was accepted."

"Was there any doubt with the way you play?" His eyes sparkled with sincerity.

Why couldn't her father have felt that way? Her heart expanded, encompassing him even more for believing in her talent.

"My father threw a fit and said he'd already enrolled me in the nursing program at Oregon Health Sciences University. There was a future and money to be made in the medical profession." Another wrong by her father she would not forgive. Her anger and disillusion still flamed hot remembering how her father took away the thing she loved most, and she'd allowed it. If only she had been as strong as Penny and walked away or run away and joined Julliard.

"You couldn't defy him. He still had a hold over you."

His quiet, nonjudgmental comment soothed her soul.

"Yes." Gina choked back a sob. "He still controlled me. It wasn't until my second year in college I broke free of his hold." She swallowed some wine and stared into his eyes. Eyes that saw more than she even understood. Eyes that gave her strength and comfort. "That's when I began planning my future. I'd learned of the company I work for now and applied as soon as I graduated." He may have forced her into the nursing profession, but she had won by using it to help others like her against men like her father. "I haven't seen or talked to my father since the day I took control of my future."

"But you still stay in contact with your brother?" Holt slid his empty plate to the center of the table. He could have eaten more, but he wanted to concentrate on Gina. He leaned back, taking his beer with him and studied the woman across the table. She was strong to have gone through all she did alone and come out a stable individual.

"Yes. I shouldn't though." She tapped the side of her wine glass with a finger. "He's the reason our father set up my college without my knowledge. Jerry defied my father by taking off and becoming a ski bum-slash-instructor. He wanted Jerry to go to college and become an accountant." She laughed a full-bodied laughed. "You should have seen the look on our father's face when he received a postcard from Jerry in Aspen. My brother was supposed to be ensconced in classes at Oregon State." She frowned. "After the postcard, our father became fanatical about my going into the medical profession. Even though he told me to stop taking piano lessons, I worked Saturdays for the piano teacher and took lessons after school three times a week."

Holt leaned forward, reaching across the table. "Come play the piano for me." She glanced at his hand, then searched his eyes. Did she see his sincerity? Her eyes lost the dullness of memories and she smiled. Gina refilled her wine glass and placed her palm in his.

The rush of her acceptance warmed Holt better than a fire in the middle of winter. He'd ordered the piano when she'd agreed to visit. Their first meeting, he understood the piano and music were her pillars and comfort, and he wanted her to feel comfortable in his home. He squeezed her hand, leading her out of the kitchen and into the great room. At the piano, he kissed the top of her head, savoring her sweet floral scent, and retreated to the couch.

Gina placed a magazine on the piano and set her glass on top. "When did you get this piano?" she asked, settling her backside on the bench.

His answer might scare her, but he prided

himself on telling the truth. "When you agreed to come spend time at the ranch."

Her eyes glistened with unshed tears above a glorious smile. "Thank you," she whispered and ran her fingers up and down the scale.

After limbering her fingers, she dove into a piece Holt had heard before. Not being a classical music lover, he hadn't a clue what it was called. He did know he loved watching her play and hearing the instrument sing under her hands. She was so gifted, how could her father not see a future for her in music? It only added to his list of reasons to have it out with the man.

She swayed to the strains and nodded to the chords, revealing the power the music held for her.

The tune became spritely. One hand worked magic with the keys while the other picked up her glass of wine. She sipped, returned the glass, and both hands took up the melody again.

Holt reclined into the couch cushion. He closed his eyes and dreamed of Gina sitting at the piano, playing just for him with nothing on. Her hair loose around her bare shoulders, a seductive smile on her lips...

The couch bounced. He opened one eye. Penny sat on the other end, mesmerized with the music. He smiled and leaned his head back. Every night on the road he dreamed of nights like this. Being home. Relaxing, working on his art, raising good rough-stock. Gina in his life. Tomorrow he'd clean up the studio and get to work. Turn some of his road drawings into paintings. The first one he'd start on would be of Gina. He smiled, pondering the tones of her skin and the silky texture of her hair.

The music faded, easing the room into silence. The couch moved slightly, he opened his eyes and found Gina kneeling beside him, desire heating her gaze. He glanced over her shoulder. Relief dispersed on an exhale, Penny had disappeared.

He trailed a finger down Gina's face. "Your music is enchanting, just like you."

Her eyes sparkled, and her luscious lips formed a seductive smile. Better than the one he'd dreamed of moments before. She leaned forward, her breasts grazing his arm. Her warm breath tickled his ear.

"I want to spend the night in your arms."

The declaration was so soft, at first he thought he made it up.

He twisted to peer in her eyes. He caught a glimpse of green in their brown depths moments before her mouth covered his, and she slid her knee over his legs, straddling him.

Chapter Sixteen

Gina kissed Holt with all the pent-up desire she'd harbored since their first encounter.

His confession he'd bought the piano after she agreed to come to the ranch, told her he would never lie to her or hurt her. All his actions proved he would always tell her straight and not push her into anything. He had earned her trust, and her heart.

The coarseness of his fingers skimming across her skin under her shirt sent tremors of delight skidding out to her extremities.

While playing the piano, she'd glanced over at his sexy body sprawled on the couch; his closed eyes, mouth curved in a sultry smile. Every nerve had wanted him. That's when she decided to take control tonight. He'd said it was her move. She'd spent the afternoon dissecting her life, her reasons for her celibacy, and his words.

Her body longed for his, and her heart wanted more of him. It was time to put the past where it belonged and join the living. He'd taught her that.

Straddling his lap, she slid her fingers through his silky, curly hair, drawing him closer. Her mouth moved over his from every angle, playing tag with his tongue, and heightening her own arousal.

Her hands roamed down his muscular neck and inside his shirt, popping the snaps open on her downward trek. His muscles flexed under the tight-fitting, tank-shirt. Gina inhaled the clean scent of his deodorant and aftershave. The familiar combination flared her nostrils and excited her body.

Holt pulled away from the kiss only long enough

to peel her shirt over her head. He pressed her against his hard, hot chest, his hands working at the back of her bra. She yearned for his touch on every inch of her skin.

Zip barked, slapping her out of her dream and back into the great room.

"Shouldn't we, you know, go somewhere else?" Gina held her bra to her breasts since he'd managed to unhook it as the dog barked.

Without a word, he stood, cupping her bottom with his hands. She wrapped her legs around his waist and her arms around his neck, pressing her breasts against the soft cotton of his undershirt. The motion of his gait rubbed her nipples on the ribs of the cloth, igniting a fire in her center.

At the bedroom, he kicked the door shut and moved to the bed. She refused to let him go. The strength of his rippled muscles moving against her reeled her senses. His hands moved from her bottom to her hair. He pulled the band from her ponytail, cascading the strands around her face and over her shoulders.

"I like your hair down."

He kissed her until her legs weakened, no longer able to cling to his upright body. She melted onto the bed, and her bra slid down her arms. Holt grasped the lacy undergarment and dropped it on the floor at his feet. His eyes appraised her naked breasts. The nipples tightened and tingled under his earnest approval. She'd never been viewed like this before. Never bared her whole body to a male. A feral light sparked in his dark eyes. His perusal heightened her desire and cemented his need for her.

Holt knelt in front of her and rubbed her already ripe nipples between his forefinger and thumb. The sensation nearly shot her off the bed.

Gina hissed through clenched teeth. She didn't want to think back to the years of her promiscuity, but she knew for certain she'd never experienced anything like this. As a teen, it had all been motions, never feeling. Holt ignited every nerve and woke up passions she couldn't fathom. Her heart hovered in her chest, weightless, and soaking in a new emotion—Love.

His calloused hands splayed across her abdomen, and he gently pressed her down on the bed. She couldn't stop panting. Her body was scorched and wanting. He popped the snap on her jeans and drew the zipper down. His hands worked their way between her skin and her panties, removing the last of her clothes. She lay on the bed naked, watching his gaze leisurely take in the length of her.

"You. Are. Gorgeous," he said, ripping his shirts off and unbuckling his belt.

Feeling confident from his actions and compliment, she purred, "Come show me how gorgeous." She held her hands up, offering him an invitation. If he didn't touch her again—and soon— she would die of starvation.

He shucked out of his jeans and shorts, and she saw how gorgeous he thought. He knelt over her on the bed, his growing length resting on her belly like a hot torch. She reached down to touch him, but he grasped her hands, raising them above her head and teasing her with light and deep kisses as he grew, heating and hardening.

Gina spread her legs and begged, "Please."

Holt released her hands, sliding down her body and tasting her breasts. He nipped and sucked. Her body rocked, and her hips pushed toward his. The ripples of sensations lighting her body on fire had her biting her lip to keep from moaning.

He rolled off.

Throwing a cold towel over her would have had the same effect as his leaving her hot and wanting.

"Where are you going?" Gina couldn't believe he walked away, just like that. She wanted him. Her body ached to have the growing fire sated. Did her past all of a sudden haunt him?

"I'll be back. I-" Holt grinned sheepishly and shook his head. "I don't entertain here. My covers are in my travel bag."

Watching him walk to the closet, she wondered how often he had sex. Did her actions even mean anything to him, if he could stop just like that? Past memories swirled in her head. Her father replete, walking out of her room, leaving her young body confused. Then teenage males getting what they wanted and leaving her needy and restless.

What had she done?

Gina rolled to her side, curled in a ball, and drew the spread up over her. Flushed with ardor moments before, she now shook with cold and uncertainty. What was she doing? She'd fallen in love, but did Holt feel the same? Or was she just another conquest? And was getting her to be unfaithful to her vow a sick game he planned to win? Was he just another perverted male? Her stomach clenched and sobs burned the back of her throat. She trembled and tried to think of a way to get out of the mess she'd made.

Holt returned ready to finish what Gina had started. One glance at the bed and his desire slipped down several notches. She had the bedspread drawn around her like a cocoon, her body curled tight in a ball. He walked to the bed. It vibrated from her trembling.

"Honey, what's wrong? I just wanted to make sure you were safe." He rested a hand on her shoulder, and she pulled away. What happened while he hunted up a condom? Did she have relapse memories of her childhood?

"Hey," he lowered his body onto the bed and put

an arm over her, spooning against her back. "What's wrong?"

"How often do you have sex?" The way she said the word, sounded offensive.

"Not as often as you seem to think."

She believed she was another one night stand. He thought he'd shown her she meant more than that to him. Holt kissed her temple and rolled her to her back. Her arms were clasped across her wonderful peach tinted breasts. They'd been just as sweet as the fruit when he'd sampled them.

He kissed her cheek, but her eyes remained closed. One tear slipped out from under her eyelid.

"I can count on one hand how many times I've bedded a woman in the last three years. And never..." He turned her head and kissed her lips. "Never, have I asked a woman to my ranch before you." Holt kissed her again, urging her lips to respond. "You are the only one I want here or"—he kissed her deeper, longer, with all the emotion she brought to him—"anywhere."

Her arms slid away from her breasts. He cupped one and played with the nipple.

"I only want *you* here, now and forever." He nipped her neck and worked his way down to her breasts. His hand slid to the golden curls at the junction of her legs. He cupped her and she stiffened. Just as deftly, he slid his hand back up, fondled a breast. He captured her luscious mouth with his and seduced her with his tongue until she moaned and grasped his head in her hands. Her legs spread, and her hips pushed toward him.

His desire strained in the restrictive cover. Holt slid his hands under her bottom, raised her hips, and entered. Her eyes widened at the entry, and a breathy sigh whispered through her parted lips.

He started a slow rhythm, watching her desire soften her face and flare in her eyes. Her hands fisted on the covers. Her eyes glazed over. He paced himself, bringing her to completion several times before he picked up the pace and exploded with a hard, deep thrust. Gina licked her lips and rubbed against him as he fell on top of her, sinking his face into her soft, floral-laced hair.

When he could breathe normal and push his body off, he rolled to his side. He'd never experienced love making like this before. Her body was a perfect fit and reacted to his touch like a well-trained reining horse. He pulled her into his arms and kissed her temple. If he hadn't fallen in love with her the first time they met, her faith in him tonight would have clenched it.

"Are you okay?" Holt hugged her tight. He never wanted to let her go.

"Yes. I didn't..." She paused and took a deep breath. "I've never experienced those sensations before." Rolling, she reclined on his chest. Her sparkling eyes stared into his. "If it's like this every time, I could get used to making love to you."

His heart galloped in his chest. She said, 'love' not sex. He wanted to shout and crow. He didn't want anyone but her.

Drawing her head down, he kissed her warm inviting mouth.

Gina slipped to his side and snuggled against his body, her arm draped across his chest. He tucked her tighter against him and smiled. *She came to him.* They'd conquered one of her barriers. He nuzzled the top of her head. Once he had the National Title, he'd settle down, and he'd ask her to settle with him.

****

Gina squinted at the slash of light blinding her. The sun peeked through the slightly parted curtains in Holt's room. She stretched and reached a hand out. The other side of the bed was empty. Where was

Holt?

She sat up. The effect of the several glasses of wine last night thrummed in her head. The whooshing stopped, and the sound of a shower running soothed both her nerves and the thud in her head. A door on a side wall was ajar. Steam curled out the opening.

Memories of last night flashed in her mind. Her body heated, and her heart expanded with newfound love. Holt's tenderness and patience had helped her through the flashbacks. He'd proved she meant more to him than a one night fling. And she learned she wasn't too broken to love, and be loved. The revelation lifted a heavy curtain from her mind and unchained the loneliness from her heart.

Slipping from the bed, she crossed the room and entered the bathroom. Mmmm. She'd always been partial to glass doors on showers. Watching Holt slide a bar of soap up and down his muscled torso aroused her as much as touching his exquisite body. Her body tingled with anticipation. She opened the door and stepped in.

"Good morning," she said, nipping his shoulder and wrapping her arms around his waist.

"Hey, you." Holt's soapy body slid sensually against hers as he turned in her arms. His mouth covered hers in a molten kiss. Gliding her hands over his soapy back, she skimmed down and grasped his tight bottom.

He groaned and stepped back.

"Let me help you." Holt lathered up the soap and ran his hands over every inch of her skin. She'd never thought of being clean as erotic. The way he left no area of her body untouched had her panting, hot and needy.

He held her against him, her back to his front, massaging her breasts and teasing her folds with his hardness. He entered and she climaxed immediately.

If not for his arm around her middle, she would have slid to the floor. Gina stood, feet spread, his hands still clasping her breasts as he spun her senses into another explosion. She blinked the fireworks away and slumped in his arms, realizing he was spent as well.

"You're going to wear me out," he huffed just before kissing her ear.

"A cowboy like you should have more stamina," she joked. He swatted her bottom and stepped out of the shower, leaving her alone with the cooling spray and heated thoughts. Where did they go from here? *She'd just made love in a shower!* Her body hummed with energy.

Her chest swelled, aching in a pleasant way. Rimsky-Korsakov's *Scheherazade*, the young prince and princess, played in her head. If this was what it felt like to be in love—she never wanted to lose the feeling.

The thought made her giddy and fearful. She'd fallen for him the very night she met him. His insistence to get to know her, his charm, and his ability to make her feel completely at ease. She just hadn't wanted to admit she'd found a man to break through her fears.

But where did they go from here? She could ask, but had a feeling he wouldn't commit to anything until after Nationals. Could she hide her true feelings till then?

Chapter Seventeen

Holt whistled and walked into his closet to get dressed for his run and workout. He hadn't been this relaxed and happy in years. And it all had to do with the vixen in his shower. He smiled, reflecting on the night's activities and their latest romp in the shower. One thing for certain, he would never tire of Gina. Her lustiness in bed was a paradox to her public demeanor.

He'd fallen for her that first night watching her play the piano. But he'd known it would take time and gentleness to get her to come around to care for him. And she did care for him. Otherwise she would never have come to his bed. The thought of her caring for him as much as he cared for her made his belly quiver like it did before he climbed on a bucking bronc. Excitement, anticipation, praying the outcome was what he wanted.

He pulled out the drawer where he kept his workout sweats. The corner of a paper caught his eye. What was a paper doing in here? Grabbing the corner, he tugged it out and studied the scrawled print.

If you don't get rid of her, I will.

Anger spiked the hair on his arms. Who put this in his drawer?

His thoughts went to Gina's distrust of Penny. After last night, she should have no doubts about his affections. And the only time she could have had access to his closet was this morning. He knew she slept all night. He'd awaken several times hardly believing the warm body in his bed was Gina. No, she was too forthcoming. She'd say something if Penny bothered her that much.

The only other person who had access to this room was Penny. He backed out of the closet and sat on the bed. Why would Penny want to get rid of Gina? She barely knew her and had been taken with her from the beginning.

"What's wrong?"

Gina crossed the room. Her long legs captured his attention, drawing his gaze up to the blonde tuft of hair at the edge of the towel wrapped around her body.

He wanted to pull her down on his lap, kiss her, and forget about the message. But he couldn't put this off as a joke. The one sentence and where he found it made the note much more than a prank. His gut clenched. If his actions put her in danger, he'd never forgive himself.

"Get dressed." Holt stood, kissed her cheek, and went back in the closet to pull on his running clothes. He had to think, and he couldn't do it with Gina distracting him. He re-read the note, slid the paper into the pocket of his sweats along with his cell phone, and stepped into the empty bedroom.

Where was Gina? He hadn't meant to sound so harsh. It took a moment to remember her clothes were upstairs. He'd remedy that after he got to the bottom of the note.

In the kitchen, he started coffee brewing and pulled ingredients from the fridge for omelets. Penny straggled in, poured a cup of coffee, and sat at the table. He studied her. She appeared her usual disheveled, innocent self.

"Did you have a good time last night?" she asked, smiling with a funny smirk on her lips.

"Yes. Thank you for cleaning up the dishes." He wasn't sure how to act around the girl. Her question didn't sound snide. Her tone had teased. Either she was a good actor or she wasn't the one who slipped the note in his drawer.

"It looked like you two were preoccupied." Again, she gave him a sly smile. "So is she moving in permanently?"

"No." Gina's firm response startled both of them. She'd stopped just outside the kitchen door to listen. The question made her wonder what the two had been discussing, but it sounded like her. Penny looked away. The girl's red face, gave Gina even more reason to believe she was the topic.

Holt strolled across the room, put a hand behind her head, and seduced her mouth as if he planned to take her there in the kitchen. At first her fingers fisted in the front of his T-shirt, but she fought the urge to succumb, and pushed away, leaving space between them.

"Good morning, again," he said and sauntered back to the stove.

Penny shot out of her chair, gathering dishes from the dishwasher and placing them on the table. Unsure what to do, Gina searched the cupboards for a teapot.

"What're you looking for?" Penny asked, seated back at the table sipping from a mug.

"Tea pot." Gina closed another cabinet door.

"Don't have one." Holt filled a mug with water and handed it to her. "Pop that in the microwave. Teabags are in that cupboard." He pointed to the cupboard above the coffeemaker and glanced over his shoulder at Penny. "Put teapot on the list."

"Why, if she isn't staying?" The teenager sat like a statue, staring expectantly at Gina.

Her mind whipped through several responses, unsure what Penny insinuated.

Holt put an arm around her shoulders. "Because Gina may not be staying permanent, but she will be visiting." He flashed her with that darn heart-stopping smile. "Until we make it permanent."

"I'm—"

"I know you're not ready to talk about it, neither am I." He dropped his arm from her shoulders and stepped back to the stove. "But we *will* talk about it."

The finality of his words rocked Gina back on her heels. Holt wanted to talk about a future. Her stomach fluttered. Even after knowing all her sordid past and her fears, he wanted her to become a part of his life. It scared and excited her.

The microwave dinged. Gina grabbed the mug, and Holt handed her a teabag. She stood at the counter dunking the bag and contemplated Holt's words. He wanted something permanent. The thought made her heart race. But what about her plans? She didn't have enough funds to start the camp, and what about her job?

"You gonna dunk that thing all day?"

She spun toward his voice and found Holt and Penny waiting patiently at the table.

"Sorry." She slid onto a seat, and Holt passed a platter with cheese omelets and fruit. "You didn't tell me you could cook."

"You didn't ask."

"Guess I need to ask more questions." Was it her imagination or did he shoot a glance at Penny?

"Penny, when did you say Zip chewed up my boots and then my sneakers?" The underlying stiffness and accusation in Holt's voice surprised Gina.

"I don't know. With the construction going on, I went to town a little more than I should have." Penny stared at the picture on the wall as if the cows on it had come to life.

"Well, the first time was before I'd returned from Payson. Did it happen a few days before, or longer? Then the sneakers. How long before I came

home did that happen?" Holt stood and pulled the
calendar off the wall.

"Why is it so important?" Gina asked.

His dark eyes met hers. Was that indecision in
their depths? He pulled a paper the size of a
photograph out of his pocket and unfolded it.

"The reason Zip was in my closet chewing my
footwear is because someone has been visiting here
when Penny goes to town." He set the note on the
table. "And they left this the last time."

Gina reached for it first, read the line, and
handed it to Penny with trembling fingers. Who
would want to cause the teenager harm?

Penny's intake of breath made them both stare
at her.

"Do you know who put it there?"

Holt's scrutiny of the girl rivaled anything Gina
witnessed in nursing school by the instructors when
a procedure wasn't carried out in detail.

"No, but it looks like Trish's handwriting."
Penny dropped the note on the table.

"Has your sister been around here?" Holt's deep
voice growled like a surly dog.

"No. She's called a couple times. Asked what
you're doing." Her young eyes widened. "I don't tell
her a thing. I promise."

The fear in Penny's eyes and the anger radiating
from Holt sent shivers down Gina's arms. "Why do I
get the feeling your sister isn't welcome here?"

"She's overstepped her welcome." Holt shoved
his unfinished food away from him.

"Why?" The set of Holt's jaw told her she
wouldn't like the reason.

"I met Trish at a time in my life when I wasn't
under control. We got drunk, ended up in bed, then
her fiancé showed up." His gaze hardened, and his
hand clenched into a fist. "I stopped partying and
picking up women after that. I didn't need anything

getting in the way of my goal."

"Okay, I get you aren't mutual friends." Gina glanced at Penny. "So how did you two"—she waved her fingers between Holt and Penny—"meet up?"

"Trish wouldn't stop calling me." His gaze flicked to hers. "Still does as you've seen. I've ignored her since Penny came here to stay. But before that, she called and said she was overdosing and needed help. I went to the house and found her threatening Penny with a knife."

Penny jumped in. "Because there wasn't any chocolate in the house, she was going to attack me. Said it was my fault. Of course, she was strung out."

The fear in Penny's eyes and disgust in her voice tugged at Gina's heart.

"I got Penny out and gave her my phone number in case she ever needed help." Holt ran a hand over his face. "You know the rest. She called when her parents kicked her out."

"But Trish—why is she still bothering you?" Gina had dealt with drug addicts in the ER rooms. They could be a threat to themselves and others, using or not.

"She's become obsessed with me. I guess that's the word to use." Holt stared at the note. "But I don't understand how she knows about you." His gaze locked onto hers.

Me? She witnessed guilt flickering in his eyes.

"She must've put the note in there when Zip chewed up your sneakers, otherwise you would have found it sooner. You were home right after Payson." She didn't like the idea of the woman having easy access to Holt's home. There was no telling what Trish might do when high.

Holt shook his head. "I don't know why she'd sneak in here in the first place, but this note—she knows I'm interested in you." He grasped her cold hand in his large, warm one.

171

Gina stared into his caring eyes. She'd given this man more of herself than she'd ever dreamed possible. He accepted her flaws and all. There was no way she'd let a drug-crazed woman come between them.

"Damn, Jess. At Payson, he blabbed it all over that I had a woman." He slammed his fist on the table.

Gina's stomach soured. "And I wore your shirt— Oh! When I went to get food that day, a woman shoved me in the back. When I turned for her to apologize, she made a comment about the shirt I wore and walked away." She stared at Holt. The vision of the letters on the woman's belt came to her mind. "There were letters on her belt. T-R then a belt loop and an S-H."

Holt slammed a fist on the table. "Damn! I had a gut feeling something wasn't right."

"We should call the cops," Penny said, nodding her head.

"We don't have enough proof. It's all just our speculation it's Trish." Holt rubbed a hand over his stubble.

The strain on his face called to Gina's inner strength. She wasn't going to let some lunatic ruin Holt's chance at his dream. Together they'd figure out what to do.

"And she hasn't really hurt anyone." He picked up the note.

"Is there a way to prove she was here?" Gina couldn't believe there wasn't a way to prove Trish was a threat.

Three hard-knuckled raps on the front door echoed through the house. Zip barked at the intrusion. Penny started to rise, but Holt stopped her with a hand on her arm.

"Neither one of you open the door."

Gina started to protest.

"I won't have something happen to either of you." Holt placed a kiss on her head and left the room.

"Stubborn man." Gina stood, grabbed dishes from the table, and carried them to the sink. She expected Penny to do the same, but she didn't move or say a word. Gina glanced at her.

Penny stared at the note.

"Do you really think your sister would go so far as to hurt me?" Gina pulled out the chair next to Penny, settling in it, and taking the note from her young hands.

"That's the thing. Between my controlling parents and the drugs, I don't know her any more. The time Holt saved me, I really believed she would have killed me over the damn lack of chocolate."

A shiver slithered down Gina's back. The vicious shove she'd received at the rodeo from the woman swirled curls of fear in her belly. She wrapped her arms around Penny for comfort and to ward off her own misgivings.

"Holt's going to tell you to leave." Penny's statement did little to squelch the growing dread.

"Why?" She pulled away from the teenager.

"Because he'll think that by pretending he doesn't care for you, Trish will stop. But if she knows you're here. I doubt she'll back off."

Gina stared out the window. She finally allowed a man into her heart, making her life more worth living, and had possibly put herself in danger. She shook her head. This only happened to people on television or in books.

Holt strode into the room. "It was Walker. I'm going to the barn and see what changes he thinks need made."

"Can I come with you?" She didn't want to stay cooped up in the house on such a beautiful day.

"Grab a jacket. It's nippy out there this

morning." He followed her to the stairs. "Which, reminds me. We need to gather your stuff."

"Why?" Disappointment rumbled in her belly. Was Penny right? Did he plan to push her out of his life? She'd go kicking and screaming. She'd never find another to unconditionally care for her like Holt.

"Because you need to put it in my room." He stopped her at the top of the stairs, placing a hand on her waist. She curved into his arm, and his lips brushed across hers. "Now that we've crossed the friendship barrier, I don't plan to let anything else get in our way." His arms molded her to him, and he kissed her with a desire that heated her insides and turned her limbs to gel.

He came up for air, and she asked, "So you won't make me leave for my own good?"

"No. You're the woman I want, and I'm not going to let some drugged-up psycho keep me from what I want." He linked their hands, and they walked to her room where her suitcases stood in front of the open, empty closet.

"You didn't unpack?" Disappointment clouded his eyes.

This brief glimpse of a crestfallen cowboy tickled her. "It makes moving into your room easier." She kissed his cheek and bent to pull a jacket out of the closest suitcase.

"Is that why you didn't unpack? You already had plans to get in my bed?"

An arrogant smile spread across his handsome face. The contrast of that and the disappointment moments before struck a humorous note. She laughed until tears blurred her vision. Holt stood gazing at her. His head tipped to the side, looking full of himself.

"No. I figured if I lost nerve, I could make a quick exit." She exhaled. There she told him the truth.

"Even if you couldn't have slept with me, I wouldn't have let you go." In one quick move, he swept her into his arms and laid her on the bed under him. He cradled her head in his hands, resting his body on his elbows. His eyes took on a serious gleam, lowering closer and closer, making her heart palpitate so fast she thought she'd faint.

Gina closed her eyes to steady her heart, and his lips caught hers. The soft caress of his mouth on hers, his hands holding her like a cherished treasure unleashed her desire. Her body throbbed for his touch. She wiggled seating her body closer, needing to embrace his solidness and strength.

Vibration at her hip stilled her movements and registered the hard object.

Holt reached in his pocket and pulled out his cell phone. He glanced at the number before placing the phone on the bedside table. "Where were we?"

"It wasn't Trish, was it?" She shouldn't let the woman affect her. However, she couldn't help but shiver at the coincidence.

Chapter Eighteen

"No, it was Jess. He can wait." Holt planned to do everything in his power to make Gina forget Trish's threat and enjoy her two weeks. He believed Penny's sister capable of anything, but he wasn't going to scare Gina. Not when she'd finally opened up. He smiled and drew back to study her face. "Jess wants to know if we're still only friends."

Humiliation shrouded her eyes. "He what?"

She started to shove away, but Holt wouldn't relinquish his hold. He snuggled closer, dipping his head and tasting the soft sweet skin under her ear. Holding his lips barely against her skin, he said, "Jess figured out you and I had more than friendly feelings for one another."

"How?" She relaxed, allowing his hands to sneak under her shirt.

His fingers skimmed the silky skin along her sides. "He said he could tell by the way we looked at each other." Holt took her mouth captive and came up for air, aching to get his hands on more of her.

Gina came to life under him, nipping his chin and squirming, matching his hot desire. He wanted her *now*. He gripped the bottom of her shirt to pull it over her head. Incessant knocking invaded his centered thoughts. He ignored the intrusion.

"Ahem," echoed through the room clear and loud.

Gina stiffened under him, and his hands fell to the bed.

He hadn't shut the door.

Compassion filled him at Gina's stricken

expression. "Sorry," he whispered against her ear and kissed her. He pushed off her and sat on the edge of the bed, crossing one leg over his knee.

"Yes?" he asked, giving Penny a stern glare.

"Mr. Walker said he needs to head out. So if you wanted a rundown on the progress you need to get out there right away."

Holt stood and held a hand out to Gina. "We'll gather your things later. Come on." When they passed through the door, he ruffled Penny's hair. "We'll remember to close the door from now on."

She giggled and headed to her room.

"That was embarrassing," Gina said as they descended the stairs.

Yeah. He'd been about to seduce her without regard for anything else. He had to tame his desire before he compromised her so badly she wouldn't forgive him.

He opened the back door, escorting her across the yard.

"Sorry. Now that I can touch you it's hard to stop." He kissed the knuckles on the hand he held. Her luscious lips tipped into a thoughtful smile.

"I like how you make me feel. Safe, cherished. You're the first male who hasn't *used* me." She leaned her head on his shoulder. "You're helping me slay my demons."

"I'll be your knight—"

"Sorry to cut into your day." Mr. Walker stepped in their path. Gina pulled her head from Holt's shoulder and put more space between them.

"I need to go oversee a new job that another crew started today."

Anger swirled in the pit of Holt's belly. Gina deserved respect, and this man stared at her like a street walker standing on a corner.

"Mr. Walker," he said with authority and controlled rage. Walker's gaze jerked from Gina to

Holt. Holt didn't mask his feelings. "This is Gina Montgomery. She's staying with me for a couple weeks."

Walker nodded and averted his eyes. At least the man had a bit of shame in him. Since he had the man's attention, he'd deal with another problem.

"Penny's uncomfortable coming outside and doing the chores when your men are around. You need to tell them to keep their mouths shut and their eyes on their work. She's got enough problems without your men causing her more." He glared at the man. Gina's hand rubbed his back, but her gentle touch didn't sooth the mounting tension he fought to control.

"Hey, I can't tell my men what to think." The man's gaze rested too long on Gina, again.

"I can find another contractor." Holt narrowed his eyes. "And I will if I see or hear any more derogatory remarks made to or about Penny. She's just a lost teenager."

Gina squeezed his hand. He was a bona-fide hero with her by his side.

Walker snorted and nodded his head. "This is what we've accomplished so far."

Still holding Gina's hand, Holt followed the contractor into the barn. The whir of saws and hammering echoed through the building as they discussed the changes that had taken place since he was home a few weeks earlier. It wouldn't be long and he could bring all the stock he'd purchased over the last year to the ranch.

When that day came, he wanted Gina by his side. There was no one else he wished to share in the moment. His mom never believed in his art or his rodeo career, she sure as hell wouldn't care about a bucking stock ranch.

Astounded by the progress, he said, "You must have added more employees. The job looks almost complete."

"We'd finished another job, so I brought extra workers here for about a week." Walker pushed open the large, barn door on the far end of the building. It slid easily on new, shiny rollers.

The smell of fresh lumber greeted them as they walked into the new corrals. A hundred feet beyond the last corral stood a half-sized rodeo arena complete with chutes and gates. He pulled Gina over to the arena. Excited to share this project, he climbed up the fence and leaned his arms over the top rail, taking in the whole area. She climbed up beside him, hanging her arms over as he did.

"I thought you were giving up riding?"

The sorrow in her question drew his gaze from the freshly disked ground to her worried face.

"This isn't for me to practice. This is to test the bucking stock and to teach young bareback riders."

"Who's going to ride the stock?"

Her worried gaze told Holt she hoped it wasn't him.

"I'll have bronc riders come practice here on the off season. That's the best way to see how the animals will perform." He stepped down and grasped her about the waist, holding her against him a moment before sliding her feet to the ground. He wanted to kiss her, but figured she wouldn't want the workers to see their newly discovered attraction.

Instead, he took her hand and headed back into the barn. "We'll go for a ride this afternoon." He stopped in the middle of the barn and stared. That person couldn't be... Holt squeezed Gina's hand and hoped he pasted on a sincere smile.

"Go on in the house. I'll be there in just a few minutes."

She studied him a moment.

"Really, I just need to speak to someone. I'll be there before you miss me." He kissed her cheek and escorted her to the door. She walked slowly to the house, glancing back once. He smiled and waited until she entered the door. His breath rushed out on a curse as he pivoted on his heel and stalked back into the barn.

What the hell did that man think he was doing here? He stopped in the middle of a stall three men were constructing.

Holt didn't try to control his outrage, just grasped the man by the shoulder and spun him. "What the hell are you doing here?"

Penny's father stared venomously back. "Making sure my little girl isn't taken advantage of."

"You son-of-a—" Holt grabbed the man by the front of his work shirt. "*Now* you're worried about her? That's hilarious. What did you think would happen to her when you kicked her out?" The other workers had stopped to listen. If it weren't for Penny and whatever lies her father might spout, he'd let them know what kind of a man worked by their side.

Holt pulled the hammer out of the man's clenched hand and motioned for him to follow.

He fumed and stomped to the finished tack room. Mr. Landers took his time. Holt wondered if it was because he didn't want to battle with anyone other than his weak daughters. He tapped the hammer against a nail on the bench, impatiently waiting for Landers to arrive. Penny said she avoided the workers, was that because she knew her father was here?

Mr. Landers sidestepped into the room. Hatred shone from his eyes. "If you hadn't taken my girl in, she would have done what was right and come home."

"Done what was right? You mean had an abortion?" Holt couldn't believe this man. "Do you know the mental anguish a lot of girls go through after having an abortion?"

"Trish had one and she's fine." The man shrugged his shoulders.

Holt scoffed. "Trish isn't running on all cylinders. Did she start the drugs before or after you made her get an abortion? And doesn't it make you wonder why both your girls became pregnant? Like maybe they weren't getting the love and acceptance they needed at home?"

"So, cowboy, are you giving her love?" The lecherous lift of Landers's lip couldn't be ignored.

Holt connected with the worker's jaw in a good upper cut. Landers staggered back, collected himself, and charged. Arms wrapped around Holt, carrying him backward and slamming him against a saddle rack, jarring his still healing ribs and shoving air from his lungs. The man had a good thirty pounds over him and a whole lot more anger.

Holt didn't believe in fighting unfair, but Landers lived by wrong values, not him. He brought up a knee connecting with Lander's crotch. His arms released. Holt shoved out from under Landers and glimpsed two workers dashing through the doorway.

"I don't want him working here anymore. I want to talk to the person in charge when Walker isn't around."

"That's me." The older of the two men stepped forward, crossing his arms.

"This man is not to come on my property again. You send him somewhere else to work." Holt picked up his cap and winced. Damn, the fight had bruised him up again.

Landers struggled to his feet, clutching his crotch. "You're gonna be sorry for taking in Penny."

"I'm only sorry you can't see the pain you've created for your children." Holt spun away and stomped out of the tack room. If he stayed around the man, he couldn't be accountable for his actions. He'd never been thrown in jail for fighting, but damn if he'd stand around and let that jackass spout off. And the threat—he now had another suspect for the note.

****

Holt slammed the back door and stomped across the kitchen. Gina hurried to his side. She'd witnessed the hatred in his eyes the moment he dismissed her in the barn. She didn't have a clue what happened, but planned to find out.

He pulled her into an embrace and stiffened when her arms wrapped around him. "What's wrong?"

"I got in a little fight." His disarming smile flashed, but his eyes didn't light up. "Where's Penny?"

"Taking a nap. Did this fight have to do with her and what the men have been saying?" If only her big brother had known to stand up for her like Holt did for Penny. Her life might have been different.

"Yes and no. Could you bring her down to the great room?" He kissed the top of her head. "It's days like this I wonder how anyone turns out normal."

She didn't understand and didn't have time to question. Holt patted her on her rear, sending her off to wake the girl.

Penny lay curled on the bed, her legs drawn up and arms holding her protruding stomach. The sight hit Gina. *She could have been this girl.* Her actions as a teenager could have easily given her a child. What would she have done? Kept it or done the unthinkable? It was rare she went back to that time in her memories, but the startling fact was, if she hadn't come to her senses, she could have ended up like Penny. A child carrying a child.

What were Penny's plans? Keep the baby or give it up for adoption? What she'd witnessed of Penny so far, she was bright and could have a successful future. A child would make that future tougher. She should have asked Penny what her plans were after the baby arrived, but having met her the night before it wasn't her place to interfere.

"Penny? Penny. Holt wants to talk to you downstairs."

The girl's eyes popped open. "Did he find out more about my sister?" Her voice wobbled with worry.

"I don't know. We'll have to go down and see." She watched Penny uncurl and sit on the edge of the bed.

"I'd say you're about six months along," Gina said, making conversation.

"I'm due after the first of the year. Which is good. I wouldn't want Holt worrying about me while he's at Nationals."

Even though innocence coated each word, it stung. Holt treated the girl like a sister, and Penny looked up to him like a big brother. Still, a little niggling bit of jealousy at how he cared for the teenager ate at her. She was a nurse. She cared for others and shouldn't harbor ill feelings.

"Have you started any Lamaze classes?" she asked, descending the stairs together.

Penny's shoulders slumped. "I attended one and felt stupid because I didn't have anyone to help me. I know Holt would go if I asked, but I feel kind of funny attending a class with him..."

"You don't have any friends who could go with you?"

"I've never had many friends. With Trish and my parents, I could never really get close to anyone." Her young shoulders shrugged.

Gina could relate to the loneliness. She'd never had a best friend. She'd been too ashamed to tell anyone about her problems. Until Holt.

"How about I be your partner? If you can get enrolled in classes the first of December. I'll take the month off, and we can attend together." Benevolence lightened Gina's heart, and she smiled at Penny.

"Don't you already know all of that stuff?" Her eyes widened and glistened with trust.

Gina couldn't douse the girl's hopes. "I know it from a nurse's side. It might be interesting to learn it from the patient side."

"Oh, thank you!" At the last step, Penny wrapped her arms around Gina.

Her round belly pushed against Gina. The sensation thrilled her. Many times over the years she'd wondered if she would have a child. She knew she would be a better parent than her father. She would protect her children, love and nurture them.

"Hey, what's all the hugging about?" Holt stepped out of the great room.

"Gina's going to take the month of December off and be my Lamaze partner." Penny wrapped an arm around Holt's waist hugging him.

Holt's eyes shone with gratitude and something—she didn't want to think about that something.

He pulled Gina into his arms. "I like that idea." He kissed her head and whispered. "Very much."

She did, too, experiencing his reaction. December and Christmases in the past had been spent on duty at the hospital where she was employed. Since her mother's death, the holiday had been just another day. To spend it with someone she loved and actually celebrate the day, raised goose bumps of anticipation.

Holt kept his arm around her and took Penny's hand, drawing them both into the great room. He sat on the leather couch and pulled them down, one on either side of him.

Gina didn't like the way his jaw twitched when he peered at Penny. She wanted to be on the other side of the young woman to buffer her.

"Penny, you said you stayed away from the workers. Was there a reason?"

The strong accusation in his voice prickled her skin. She watched Penny's eyes widen in fear.

"Nothing other than I didn't like the way they looked at me and the things they said. Why?"

"Because your father was one of the workers. We had a little go round." He rubbed his ribs, and Gina moved closer to him, placing a hand on his shoulder for support.

"Dad? Was here?"

The fear in her eyes brought Gina to her feet. She moved to sit beside Penny and took her hand.

"Yes. Here. I was surprised when I saw him. I confronted him." Holt's eyes locked on Gina's a moment before he glanced back to Penny. "He's pissed at me for taking you in. He believes if I hadn't, you'd have gotten an abortion like Trish."

Gina stiffened. Was that why Trish took drugs? But why was she stalking Holt? Was the aborted child his?

Penny stared at Holt. "S-she was pregnant? I've never heard of it."

"Apparently your parents took care of it." Holt's derision for Penny and Trish's parents shone clear.

Gina studied his drawn features. Did he wonder if the baby was his? Would it make a difference in how he felt about the woman?

She didn't believe in abortions. Plenty of childless couples searched for babies. But she did believe in abortion when a life was at stake, or in the case of incest or rape. Trauma was trauma and it was hard enough to get over without having a reminder.

"What did her father say when you confronted him? Could he have slipped the note in here?" Gina didn't like the idea. That made the threat targeted at Penny.

"Not much. He believes I've ruined her life by allowing her to have the baby. He gives us another suspect." He studied Penny. "Does your father's writing look like Trish's or could he have tried to copy her writing?"

"I don't know. I guess." Her voice wavered. "He can get pretty mean."

Gina didn't like the way Holt nodded his head. Had the man threatened him? How could he concentrate on his riding with all of this looming over his head?

"I'm glad I'll be here from now until finals." He smiled at Gina. "And Gina will be here in December." He pulled Penny into a hug. "Don't worry. You'll be fine. We aren't going to let your family drag you down."

The unconditional support Holt gave Penny showed a natural ability to soothe distressed people. His sincerity shone through, proving he would give his all to help those in need.

A thought had simmered since he showed her the barn and arena. Now was a good time to tell him about her goal of a camp for abused children. And maybe, just maybe...

Chapter Nineteen

The two weeks with Gina passed too quickly. Holt spent their last night showing her the depth of his emotions. Sleeping then waking and showing her all over again. He loaded her suitcases into the truck, missing her already. Penny hugged her and grasped Zip's collar. The dog had remained Gina's constant shadow since the first day.

Gina walked down the brick walk to him. The smile on her lips didn't hide the sorrow in her eyes. One day he hoped to peer into her eyes and not witness a trace of sorrow, loneliness, or hurt. One consolation, this new sorrow rimming her eyes was because she didn't want to leave him. He'd tried to talk her out of going. But she'd signed a contract for the next job and needed the money.

She'd told him about her dream to build a place with music therapy for sexually abused children to heal. He believed in her dream, but it didn't make her leaving any easier. The long, lonely six weeks until her return would be a true test to their commitment.

Holt took her hand and led her to the driver's side. He wasn't going to let her slip in the passenger door. Gina would remain by his side until she had to pass through security at the airport.

Gina climbed in and slid to her spot straddling the gear shift. He'd never drive this truck again without thinking of her. Getting her out of his mind to stay focused at rodeos would be practice for December. They'd have five days together before he headed to the finals.

They'd discussed how he'd rather she stay at the ranch with Penny. He had to concentrate on the rides and knowing how Gina felt about his riding would be a distraction. They'd celebrate when he returned home. She agreed.

Holt took his place behind the wheel, jabbed the key in the ignition, and halted. "I don't want you to go." He pulled Gina into his arms and kissed her.

Tears glistened in her eyes. "I know. But I can't back out of this. I'll be back before you know it."

"Not when I already miss you and you haven't even left." He kissed her again.

She pushed away. "Don't do this. I'm not dying, and I'm not running away. We'll talk every night." A deeper hue graced her cheeks. "I like our phone conversations."

Holt smiled. Now that they'd been intimate, he could say a whole lot more about what they could explore together. Just thinking about it revved his heart rate. "I do, too. Make sure you keep that phone charged."

He started the truck and pulled down the drive. "You told the agency not to give out any information about where you work?"

"No one has tried to hurt me in the last two weeks. I think you need to concentrate on Penny. I believe it's her deranged father after her." Gina shuddered. "And I thought my childhood was bad."

Holt captured her hand resting on his thigh and kissed the knuckles. "It takes a strong person to live through what you and Penny have. You're a good role model for her."

"You're not too bad as a big brother either."

Like hell he was. Sherrie would still be here if he hadn't brushed her off.

"You're thinking about your sister aren't you? You can't help people if you don't know what's happening. You taught me that. Sherrie's death isn't your fault." Gina rubbed a hand up and down his leg.

She was right. Sherrie's death wasn't his fault anymore than Gina's promiscuity was hers. That didn't change the fact guilt sat like a thousand pound bronc in the pit of his stomach.

"Let's talk about when you come back." Gina's return would be a happy occasion. That's what they both should focus on.

"What about when I come back?" She ran her fingers up the inside seam of his jeans.

"Don't do that. I might run off the road."

A sultry laugh tickled his ears, and his heart sung with happiness. He'd chipped away the ice and found this playful woman underneath. She was worth every minute of the effort. The last couple of weeks they'd poured their fears, dreams, and hopes out to one another. There wasn't a thing about the woman he could find fault with.

He didn't know if she felt the same about him. He knew he had some quirks she tolerated. Like getting up in the middle of the night to watch videos of his rides. When he couldn't sleep, he plugged in a video of one of his worst rides and critiqued it. When he had things clear in his mind about what he should have done, he'd fall back asleep.

The airport arrived all too soon. Holt pulled her bags out of the back of the truck and stood at the tailgate, staring at the luggage. He didn't want her to leave. Pulling Gina into his arms, he hugged her, breathing in her scent. Soap, something floral and spicy, and her pheromones drove him crazy.

She rubbed her hands up and down his back. "Do you want to just say good-bye here?"

"No. I want to sit with you until you have to go through security." He placed her small bag on top of the larger one with rollers and claimed her hand. They walked into the building. Holt twirled his hat in his hands as he waited for her to check in and take her baggage to be inspected. Then they sat, with his arm draped over her shoulders, and waited until the last possible minute before she had to go through security.

He didn't like the feeling of loss that nagged at his constricted chest. It was ridiculous the way his body responded to her leaving.

Holt pulled her into his arms and kissed her. Her knees wobbled, and she sagged in his arms. He drew out of the kiss, holding her until she steadied. "I'll see you in six weeks and talk to you tonight."

She nodded her head. He spun away before he changed his mind and pulled her back in his arms, begging her not to go. She'd captured his heart and soul in the last two weeks.

Gina made it through security on wobbly knees. She should be mad at Holt for kissing her senseless when she needed her wits about her, but she couldn't. Six weeks without his arms and security loomed like a lifetime. She'd managed on her own for twenty years. How was it in the space of two weeks she'd come to rely on one person's strength so heavily? Her heart palpitated irregularly. Because she'd never been in love before. The headiness of knowing she could love after all she'd gone through and be loved unconditionally made her light-headed.

She sat a moment on the other side of the security machines waiting for her head to clear. When it did, euphoria and freedom she'd only witnessed in others filled her like helium inflating a balloon, and she floated to her gate.

At the Portland airport, she sat in the waiting area between flights, watching people. Her phone buzzed. Only one person would call her on this phone. She didn't even glance at the number before answering.

"I miss you already," Holt's deep voice said.

"Me, too. But you're just torturing both of us by mooning." She laughed at his snort.

"That's the same thing Jess said. He told me to come on over and watch some videos of the horses that will be at Nationals. So I'm taking Penny and heading up there tomorrow."

"That sounds like a good idea, but doesn't Penny need to stay and take care of the animals?" She didn't mind his taking Penny. She just didn't want the animals, especially Zip to suffer.

He didn't answer. Panic squeezed her chest. "What's happened? Is she all right?"

"She's fine. Just, Trish called her all high and made threats. I'd just feel better if Penny went with me."

"Oh, that woman. I wish there was a way to get her out of Penny's life."

"Me, too."

A static voice announced her flight. "I have to go. Talk to you tonight."

"Count on it." The huskiness in his voice made her insides quiver.

****

Gina prided herself on keeping a low profile at work. But for some reason this time all the eligible males talked to her and asked her out to dinner. All week, she'd been the center of attention among the male staff. Holt had softened her. Giving her the aura of availability.

Snuggled into her room for the night, Gina cursed at the knock on her door. "Holt, just a second, I have to answer the door. They might need me in the ER." Holt groaned and she smiled. He'd just called. They still had an hour and fifty minutes left.

She opened the door. An intern stood in front of her holding flowers and wearing a big, sappy grin.

"I figured you couldn't turn me down if I showed up with flowers."

"I told you *no* and I meant *no*. I'm sure Lucille would love to go out with you." Why couldn't this guy pick on the younger, plump girl who longed to go on a date with him?

"I want to go out with you."

His scowl said he didn't like her suggesting the other woman.

"Well, I'm already taken so beat it." She shoved on the door, and he stuck his foot in the opening.

"If you're taken where's the ring?" He nodded to her left hand.

"I don't like to wear it when I work." She didn't have a clue if Holt had plans to get engaged. She'd use any means to get rid of the man.

"You aren't working now." He eyed her suspiciously.

"One second." She walked to the couch and grabbed the cell phone. "Holt, there's an intern here who wants to take me out to dinner. Would you please tell him I'm not interested?" Whew. She held the phone from her ear. Now she knew how a cowboy cussed.

"Ummm..." She handed the intern the phone. "You might want to hold it away from your ear."

The intern held the phone like it dripped bodily fluids.

"Who's this?" he asked. Then listened. "Well, if she's taken, where's the ring?" His face brightened like a ripe tomato, and he handed the phone back to her. "I'm sorry, I thought you were just playing hard to get."

Gina collapsed on the couch laughing and pointed to the door. "Let yourself out."

"Gina, Gina?" Holt's voice drew her to the phone. "Yes?"

"Why didn't you tell me he'd been hitting on you?" His voice held a note of wariness.

"Because it didn't matter. I don't want to go out

with him or anyone else." She sighed. "Until you, men rarely approached me because I would freeze them out. But now, I can't seem to get as cold."

He laughed. "I thawed the ice princess. I'll send you a ring tomorrow. And you just flash that under their noses."

"Oh, no, I don't want—" She wanted to be his forever, but not if he didn't.

"What, you don't want to marry me?" His forced question revealed his hurt.

Her heart dropped to her stomach.

A knot bobbed in her throat. "No. I mean yes, I want to marry you, but I don't want you jumping into something you aren't ready for just because some intern thinks I should have a ring."

"I already have one."

Words caught in her throat. Her heart raced and goose bumps of excitement tingled her arms. Gina whispered, "A ring?"

"Yes. I planned to give it to you when you came back in December. I'll send it to you certified mail."

"No. I want to see your face when you give it to me." She had to make sure the gesture came from his heart. And she wanted the moment locked away as a good memory.

"Then I'll fly down this weekend."

"I'm on shift." Her heart raced. She wanted to see him, kiss him.

"Can you switch?"

"I'll try. I miss you." She couldn't keep the emotion from warbling her words.

"I'll be there Friday night. Book us a room for Friday and Saturday night somewhere nice." The determination in his voice made her smile.

"What if I have to work?"

"We'll figure it out when I get there. I'll let you know the flight and time."

They hung up an hour later. She couldn't sleep.

In two days, she'd be able to stare into his eyes, drink in his irresistible smile, taste his ardent kisses, and breathe in his scent of horse, spicy aftershave, and desire.

She lay in bed, thinking of all the wonderful times they'd spent together. But neither had said the three words. She'd kept them to herself, lost in the belief he would tire of her. She didn't want to give her heart away and have it flung back at her. But a ring? And he'd purchased it before the buffoon intern made a spectacle of himself. That meant commitment. That meant he loved her, too.

Could her life finally have turned round? She hoped so. She'd spent many years believing she'd never have a family, and now, the idea of home and family warmed her heart like a fireplace on a cold winter day. She loved Holt. His concern and interest in her and his acceptance of her past solidified her emotion.

The ringing of the cell jolted her from her thoughts. Gina smiled and flipped the phone open.

"What did you forget?"

Silence. She strained to hear anything. The line was open.

"Hello?" she asked. Did she hear breathing?

Gina snapped the phone closed, glancing at the display. Unknown caller.

Since only her brother and Holt had this number, someone must have dialed wrong.

Chapter Twenty

Holt's legs couldn't move fast enough from the plane to the area beyond the security kiosk. He couldn't wait to see Gina. She'd managed to get the whole weekend off and promised to meet his flight.

He spotted her the minute he cleared the security gate. Her smiling face, dancing eyes, and honey hair swaying with her steps, hastened his heart. He strode toward her, drinking in her confidence and beauty. Their toes touched. He dropped his duffel bag and folded her into his arms.

He nuzzled her hair, breathed in her floral scent, and reveled in the way she fit in his arms. He was complete once again.

"I've missed you." He kissed her soft and reverent.

Gina's arms tightened around his neck, and she melted against him. Holt drew back his head, peering into her glistening eyes. "Shhh, don't cry. I'm here." He kissed her eyelids.

"I'm just happy to see you. I didn't realize I could miss a person as much as I missed you."

Her confession zinged to his heart. He wanted to fling his hat in the air and whoop like after a great ride, but refrained.

"Let's get out of here so I can show you how much I missed you," he said, hugging her and wishing they were in privacy already.

She nodded and he picked up his duffel, tucking her under his arm, next to his heart. They exited the terminal, and she led him to a hard-top Ford Mustang.

"I think your wedding present should be a Mustang." He opened the driver's side door for her.

Gina stopped, her mouth gapping. She shook her head. "That is way too extravagant and unnecessary." She slid behind the wheel.

Holt deposited the duffel in the back seat and dropped down into the passenger seat.

She put the car in gear and pulled out of the parking lot.

Holt reached across the seats, sifting her hair between his fingers. "Have I told you, I really like your hair when you wear it down?" He raised the curtain of hair, to reveal her long, slender neck. His knuckles brushed against her soft skin.

Gina shivered and smiled. "Yes, several times. That's why I wore it this way."

The car swerved into the parking lot of a first class hotel. He raised his eyebrow. "For turning down a wedding gift you picked a pretty upscale hotel."

Her head tilted, and a provocative smile turned his guts to mush. Not since grade school had love sickness jumbled his brain.

"They're the only place in this town that has room service."

His blood pressure shot up and a part of his anatomy aching for her came to attention. "You little vixen. I take it you don't plan on spending much time out of the room."

She parked the car, pulled the keys out of the ignition, unbuckled her seatbelt, and leaned toward him. "I plan on making up for lost time."

He liked the sound of that and slipped a hand behind her head, drawing her lips to his. He took his time sampling, arousing her, and bringing his blood to the boiling point. Gina pulled away and opened the door at the same time. He wanted her worse than the first time.

Holt jumped out of the car, grabbed his bag, and followed her into an elevator in the parking area. The clunk of closed doors signaled their solitude. He dropped the duffel and wrapped his arms around her, kissing her breathless. His desire for her went beyond physical. The elevator dinged, and the doors opened.

He came up for air, and she slipped from his arms, exiting. The sway of her hips and the chaste glance over her shoulder rang in his head like the clang of a chute opening. Adrenaline coursed through his body. He grabbed his bag and hurried after her. Gina slid a card in the contraption behind the door latch. It clicked and she swung the door open.

A Jacuzzi tub, king size bed, and fireplace took up the spacious room. She not only got them a room, she'd sprung for a honeymoon suite.

"Honey, this is—" Holt stared at the extravagant room.

"I figured if you were proposing, we should have a nice room to celebrate." Her eyes sparkled.

"I agree." He tossed his bag in a corner and moved toward her. He'd dreamed of holding her in his arms, naked, while they discussed their future.

Holt stopped in front of her and captured her left hand in his. He dug around in his breast pocket and pulled out the ring he'd purchased on his last visit to Jess and Clare in Mollala.

"Gina, I can't live without you. Will you marry me?"

She studied his face, peered at the ring between his fingers, then at their clasped hands. Her eyes dulled with disappointment.

His heart stopped beating. "Did I say something wrong?" Confused, he ran the words back over in his mind. On the phone she'd sounded ready to be engaged and make plans to marry.

"You didn't say—" She glanced away, disappointment ringing in her voice.

Holt skimmed through what he'd said and wondered what she'd expected. He placed a finger under her chin and kissed her tenderly.

"What didn't I say?"

She put a hand over his heart. "What you feel."

How stupid could he be? He wrapped her in his arms and kissed her, pouring his love into the kiss. He drew back and stared into her eyes. "I love you. Have since the first night I watched you play the piano."

She sighed and relaxed in his arms. Those were the words she wanted to hear. He planned to make sure she never had reason to doubt his love.

"I love you, too." She held up her hand, wiggling her fingers.

Her eyes shone with an inner glimmer he hadn't witnessed before.

He slid the band on her finger. The significance as strong for him as branding cattle. The ring he slid on her finger branded Gina as his, and no one could take her away. The ring settled on her finger perfectly.

"It's beautiful!" Gina touched the twinkling stones.

"I bought the band figuring it would be less likely to cause problems when you work. The diamond in the middle is for our love. The pale green stones on either side of that—the month we met."

"You put a lot of thought into this." Gina threw her arms around his neck. "I love it!"

"I can't take all the credit. Clare kind of helped me decide." He bowed his head.

"I still love it and you." She kissed him with ardor and worked her hands down the front of his shirt, popping the snaps open.

"You're a wild woman," he said, liking her

unreserved actions. Holt undressed her in kind. The rest of the afternoon blurred into talking, making love, and delighting in each other's company.

"I want to celebrate by taking you out to a nice dinner." Holt laughed at the playful pout Gina flashed. He loved this playful side and marveled he was the one able to bring it out in her. "We'll use room service tomorrow."

"Promise?" She twirled a finger in the curls on his chest.

He grasped her hand, kissing her fingers. "I promise we'll use room service and I promise I love you."

Her eyes went dreamy a moment before she whipped the covers back.

"Hey, what's the hurry?" He grabbed for her, but she moved away.

"Do you want to shower now and use the tub"— she nodded toward the Jacuzzi and a sultry smile tipped her luscious lips—"later?"

"Let's shower now and spend the evening after dinner in the tub." Excitement at covering her body with bubbles and re-exploring her hastened his shower.

They dressed, flipped through the listings of fine restaurants in the area, and decided on a fancy, Italian place.

****

The restaurant lived up to its advertisement. Gina gawked at the replicas of famous Italian painters and sculptures, twisted the ring on her finger. She hadn't dreamed of such a thoughtful, beautiful ring. She peered across the table at the wonderful man she would marry. His disarming smile warmed her heart.

"Is it too big? We can get it re-sized tomorrow somewhere." He took her hand, placing a kiss on the ring and then her palm. "You're gorgeous tonight.

Glowing." His brown eyes sparkled with his love and admiration.

"Thank you. You're pretty dashing yourself." The cut of his western shirt set off his wide shoulders and trim waist. His dark blue jeans hugged his legs, revealing the muscle she'd earlier traced with her tongue. They'd wrestled, loved, and played naked all afternoon. The wonder of her new found freedom both in herself and with him still astounded her. She'd only known him a few months, yet he felt like an old friend and lover. Someone she'd spent years growing to know and love.

"I can't wait for you to return to the ranch."

His excitement reminded her of a child. The wistfulness and search for approval.

"You'll only be there a few days." She'd checked on the internet and National Finals lasted ten days. That would be less time apart than they'd just endured.

"I started a painting for you." Holt's cheeks reddened and the uncertainty in his eyes caught her attention.

Her heart stuttered. "You have?" Was there no end to what this man would give her?

"It's got a ways to go, but it has been the best way to take my mind off missing you."

"I can't wait to see what you've created." She glanced at her plate and over at his. "Can we order dessert to the room?"

His eyes lit up. "I think that's a wonderful idea." They hastily finished their meals and paid. Holt drove them back to the hotel.

Gina scurried into the room ahead of him and started water running in the Jacuzzi. She couldn't believe how she craved Holt. Not just his body and the sensations he gave her, but his companionship. She relished the time they spent together, just the two of them, locked away conversing, touching.

Warmth rippled the length of her, settling in her heart, warm and bright.

They slipped into the hot tub and talked about everything, from the cranky head nurse at the hospital, to using part of the ranch for the camp for abused children, to the bronc stud list he'd been studying.

Her cell phone rang, jolting them both.

Holt stopped his administrations to her breast. "Who else has your number?"

"Just my brother and it's not him. He's at some patrol gathering." Gina hadn't told him about the calls she now received every night. She'd put them off as someone dialing the wrong number.

"Then who is it?" Holt surged out of the tub, dropping blobs of bubbles across the carpet in hunt for her phone. His muscles bunched and flexed as he stalked about the room, drawing her attention to his naked body.

The ringing stopped. He shoved aside a garment and snatched the phone.

"I've been getting a call a night from an unknown number. The first couple of times it happen just after you hung up. I thought it was you calling back. But there wouldn't be anyone there. So I've just stopped answering."

"Have you tried calling them back?" His face deepened color, and his eyes sparked with anger.

"No. It's probably just someone who punched in a wrong number."

"Not every night." He punched buttons. Listened, then said, "Who is this?" Holt's face clouded over. "How did you get this number?" He paused. "If you call this again, I'll place a restraining order on you." He snapped the phone shut and stalked to his shirt and his phone.

"Who was it?" His twitching jaw and narrowed eyes said she wasn't going to like his answer.

"Trish." Holt flipped his phone open, hit some numbers and waited. "Penny, did you give Gina's number to Trish?"

He listened and Gina's heart raced with concern for Penny and fear of what her sister may be capable of.

"Then how the hell did she get it?"

The frustration in his voice made Gina's skin crawl. It hadn't dawned on her it could be someone harassing her. As a child, she remembered getting lots of wrong calls on their land line. She assumed cell phones were the same.

Gina stepped out of the tub, pulled on the fluffy hotel robe, and curled up on the couch, waiting for Holt to end his interrogation of Penny. She didn't like the idea of Penny's crazy sister calling her every night. Not knowing who the caller was had made it easy to ignore. Now—her body shivered even though her skin was flushed from the hot water—knowing it was Trish, she couldn't push the niggling fears away.

Holt finally snapped the phone closed and paced the room. His naked muscles flexed, revealing his honed body. The determined clamp of his jaw exposed his dangerous side.

"Holt?"

He continued pacing, lost in his thoughts. His agitation sent the hair on her arms prickling.

Gina uncurled from the couch and stood, stopping his momentum with a hand on his bare chest. "Talk to me."

Holt wrapped his arms around her. "I'm so sorry to have dragged you into this nest of weirdoes that have staked a claim on me." He pressed his lips against her hair.

"What did Trish say?" Fear dissolved with Holt holding her. He was her security. His love would keep her from harm.

"Believe me. You don't want to know what she said." He held her tight. "At least she doesn't know where you are. Trish said she didn't like me bringing you to the ranch. That tells me she thinks that's where we are." He nuzzled her hair. "Which means you're safe as long as you stay away from the ranch."

Gina pulled back. "Is this your way of saying I'm not to go to the ranch in December? What about Penny? She needs my help."

"I'm not sure." He drew her against him. "We'll worry about that after we celebrate."

His head lowered, and his lips sent all her worries away and heated her need for him.

Chapter Twenty-One

The next day, Holt insisted on purchasing a new phone and number. Gina agreed and watched him wrestle with indecision while they purchased the phone. Back at the hotel, his indecision turned to excruciating gentleness and passion. His actions showed her he blamed himself for Trish's unpleasantness. She tried to tell him differently, but he found inventive ways to take her mind off anything but him.

Sunday morning came too soon. Gina tried not to cling. She didn't want him to leave, ever. He'd become an integral part of her. However, until after National Finals they both still had separate lives to lead.

They drove to the airport in silence. She couldn't let her loneliness dampen the wonderful weekend and promise he'd made by giving her the ring that glittered on her finger.

"I'm glad it worked out you could come." Gina held Holt's hand, waiting for his turn to go through security.

"I don't want anyone thinking they can horn in on my woman." He rubbed his finger over the ring on her finger and kissed her.

"I don't give in to anyone's charms but yours."

Holt laid his charmer smile on her. "Same here. I know we haven't said much about my past, you know, with women."

Gina shifted and stared at an old woman passing by. Even though he knew her sordid past, she didn't want to hear about his prior relationships.

Holt placed a finger under her chin, bringing her gaze back to his. "Other than a few buckle bunnies, I really never played the field."

Just thinking of him with anyone else put a sour taste in her mouth.

"You're the one and only woman for me." He kissed her again. A static-riddled voice announced the last chance to get through security and board his plane. "I'll call you tonight." He squeezed her hand and let go, stepping in line to pass through the metal detector. On the other side of all the security equipment, he spun around. "I love you."

Gina watched him until he disappeared in a sea of bodies. A heavy heart and leaden feet hindered her progress back to the rental car. Three weeks and she could see him again. Where, she didn't know. He was still formulating a plan.

It angered her some strung out woman could dictate how they lived. They'd argued about calling the police. Holt said there wasn't enough evidence. Their word against hers. A druggie's word against theirs didn't balance in her mind.

She returned the rental car, took a taxi to the hospital, and couldn't wait to wave her ring under the nose of the obnoxious intern.

****

Holt arrived at the ranch late. He checked on Penny and found her curled up asleep in her room. Zip followed him into his room, sniffing the duffle bag and whining.

"I know boy. I miss her, too." He stripped to his briefs, climbed into bed, and dialed Gina's number, waiting to hear her voice. He'd thought about their problem all the way home and was still unsure how to stop Trish—short of throwing her in jail. As resourceful as she had proven to be, he wasn't sure that would work.

Gina's sleepy hello shot heat to his loins.

"Hey, gorgeous. Sorry to wake you, but I can't go to sleep if I don't hear your voice."

"I was reading a book, waiting, and fell asleep."

"That doesn't say much for the book." He chuckled.

"I talked to Jerry." She rarely talked about her brother. "He's the one who gave out my number. He said some lady called, said she was with my employer and needed to get in touch with me. He said he wondered why they didn't already have my number, but told her anyway. I told him not to give it to anyone, that I've had some problems with prank calls."

"Trish is turning out to be more inventive than we give her credit for." Holt didn't like the premeditation.

"How did she find out where I work and my brother? There has to be lots of Jerry Montgomerys in the world, and he has a cell phone, too. How did she get his number?"

He heard the unease in her voice.

"Don't worry. I'm still working up a plan to stop her harassment." He pushed the scowl off his face. "Show your ring off to anyone yet?" He didn't want her falling asleep worrying.

Gina's warm laugh filled his senses. "A couple of the nurses."

"Well, flash it under the loco's nose who brought you flowers." He still didn't like the idea of someone wooing his woman.

"I will, first chance I get."

"Good. I'll let you go and give you a call tomorrow night." He hated hanging up, but her yawns and sluggish speech proved Gina needed her sleep.

"Okay. I'll be here, waiting."

"I love you." Just saying the words filled him with euphoria.

She sighed. "I love you, too. Good night."

"Sleep tight." Holt waited for her phone to click, and he shut his. The case barely touched the bedside table, and the phone rang. He glanced at the number. *Trish.*

He flipped open the phone. "What do you want?"

"I don't like you talking to that woman." Trish's speech slurred, her loud voice pierced, jangling all his nerve endings.

"Are you high?" He didn't feel like playing counselor in her drugged state, but he had to find out her motives.

"What does it matter to you? You don't even see me. You come rescue my baby sister and then take up with that nurse." Her voice became muffled by sniffs and sobs. "Why can't you see me? I love you, and you don't even answer the phone when I call."

Holt sat up in bed. This could be a long call; one he hoped shed some light on their problem.

"Trish, I do see you, but you deserve someone better than a bronc rider." How could he make her expose her deeds and keep her from harassing Gina?

"You don't see me. No one sees me." Her voice climbed to a high pitch. "You'll all see me soon!" The phone went dead.

The hair on his head quivered as a shiver of dread ran down his back. How the hell did he keep the woman he loved safe from a wacked out druggie?

****

Gina had one more week on her latest job, and Holt still hadn't come up with a plan for her and Penny. No way would he let a deranged woman tear Gina out of his life. He needed help and there was only one person he trusted. *Jess.* He could use another man's opinion.

The phone buzzed twice, and Jess answered in a less than jovial response. Holt didn't waste time. He jumped right into the whole Trish mess.

"I'm driving to Nationals with Clare and the kids. Why don't you, Gina, and Penny do the same? Besides, if we all stay in the same place and hang out together that doesn't leave Gina and Penny alone."

Holt rationalized the set up. Logic told him the more people surrounding them who knew the problem the better, but did he dare bring another man's wife and family into it?

"I'm not sure I want Clare and the kids involved?" He couldn't jeopardize innocent children.

"Hey, once I tell Clare what's going on, and you know I will, she'll be the first to say we go as a group." The conviction in Jess's voice made Holt smile. Clare was one spitfire, and she had army training.

"Okay, but I still don't like it, and I'm not sure Gina will be excited in possibly endangering children either. But they're your kids."

A half-hour later, he had the road atlas spread out on the kitchen table tracking the route Jess mentioned.

"Planning your honeymoon around rodeos?" Penny entered the kitchen with Zip on her heels.

"I didn't know pregnant females had such smart mouths." He glanced at the conflicting sight. A teenager wearing faded Winnie the Pooh pajamas stretched to distortion by a belly swollen with child. A heartbreaking sight.

"So, is this your honeymoon route?" She sat down, scanning the pages in front of him.

"No, our route to Nationals."

Disbelief furrowed her brow. "You're taking me? What about Gina?"

"I'm taking both of you. We're caravanning with Jess and Clare. That way I don't have to worry about the two of you alone here, and you'll always have people around you who can intercept any trouble from Trish." The more he thought about the plan, the more he liked it. He'd involve the whole Nevada National Guard if that was what it took to keep Gina and Penny safe.

"Does Gina know this?" The skepticism in the girl's voice yanked him out of his thoughts.

"Not yet. Why?"

"She told me staying here with me was good for your riding. She didn't want to distract you at Nationals."

"Well, we'll have to figure that one out. You're both coming to Nationals and that's final." He closed the atlas and stalked out of the room.

Would Gina pitch a fit and refuse to go to Nationals with him? And if she did, what would it take to persuade her? They were engaged, but she was still her own woman and could do what she wanted. Fear pricked his scalp. He hoped she didn't insist on staying at the ranch with Penny. The isolation here made it easy for Trish to harm them.

****

Gina tipped her head from side to side, loosening the tension in her neck. *So many injured children.* She'd spent the better part of her shift and half way into the next, caring for a busload of students whose driver had a heart attack on a field trip.

She couldn't shut out the pain on the faces of the parents asking for a list of survivors, or the devastated parent's of the deceased. She'd stayed on after her shift assisting the children still untreated.

One small girl, Lissa, had remained in the hallway all day. Only her teacher asked about her. Gina sat with the child several hours, waiting for the overworked doctors to get to her. She'd learned Lissa was a foster child. Gina asked if she could call someone and Lissa became frightened and agitated.

The staff nurse ordered Gina to leave, but she

promised Lissa she'd check on her in the morning. The relief in the girl's eyes said it all, she needed a friend. Even though Gina would only be in the area another week, she'd make sure she learned all she could about Lissa and help her the best she could.

The shrill ring of the cell phone stilled the hand massaging her neck and pulled her thoughts to the present. Holt's loving voice would help ease the tension. She picked up the phone and flipped it open. "Hello?"

"I'm missing you." The loneliness deepening his voice freed the tears burning behind her eyes to slip down her cheek.

"Hey? Is that a sniffle I hear?" His concerned tone doubled the flow of tears.

"I'm sorry, it's—it's been a long, ugly day. A bus load of children..." She pulled a tissue from the box and dabbed at her eyes.

"Gina, honey, I wish I could hold you and..." A rush of frustrated air hissed in the phone. "Damn, I hate not being there for you."

"I know. I thought of you so many times today and how your strength would help not only me, but the parents."

Bits of white noise hummed in the phone.

"Holt? Are you still there?" She didn't want to lose connection tonight like had sometimes happened when he'd called from the road.

"I'm here. You just stunned me."

The uncertainty in his voice confused her. "How?"

"By saying I could help the parents. I'm no psychologist." His tone reflected disbelief in himself.

"No, but you're a caring person who knows what it feels like to lose a family member, a child." He had to see how much he had to give people. She planned to suggest they use the ranch for a camp, not only for abused children, but for those who have lost a loved one. Between their combined pasts, they would be able to help children and families mend. Tonight though, wasn't the night to bring it up.

"I don't know. What if I said the wrong thing?" Holt couldn't believe she was serious. Sure, he helped her out of her ice armor, but he'd felt an immediate attraction to her and wanted her to see how much really living could inspire a person. Their connection had made it easy to want to help her. And Penny—how could a person turn away from someone so young who had so much to give others?

"You wouldn't say the wrong thing. You'd size them up and say what they need to hear."

Her confidence in him brought a smile to his face.

"Well, you need to hear I love you and can't wait to meet you at the plane." He'd planned to tell her they were headed to Nationals when she arrived, but with the traumatic day she'd had, he didn't want to add to it.

"I can't wait to help Penny with Lamaze. I've been reading up on it from the brochures they hand out here." The excitement in her voice forced a knot of shame into his throat. Damn, he better tell her tonight or she'd be even madder.

"I'm glad you have the brochures and have been studying. There's been a change of plans. Jess and I decided we'd all drive to Nationals. You, me, Penny. Jess, Clare, the kids, Timmy." He paused at her intake of breath.

"I thought we discussed I'd stay at the ranch with Penny so you could concentrate on your riding." Her accusing tone shifted to disbelief.

"That was the plan before Trish called and threatened the whole lot of us." He hadn't told her about the latest call, not wanting to upset her.

"She what? When?"

He'd expected fear, not the rage shaking her

voice. He should have known she'd react like a she-bear.

"Right after I got home from visiting you, she called. I decided to talk to her and see if I could get her to fess up. Instead, she claimed no one ever sees her, but we'd all see her soon. That means she's planning something. I called Jess 'cuz I couldn't come up with anything logical. He suggested if we all traveled together and stayed in the same motel, you and Penny would always have people around, and Trish wouldn't have a chance to do anything."

"But what about you?"

He strained to catch the words buried in the soft tone of her question.

"What about me?"

"She said 'we'd' all see her. What if she plans to do something to you?" Fear vibrated in her voice.

His gut twisted that she had to go through this on account of him at the same time as happiness at her concern for his well-being expanded his chest.

"I'll have Jess and Timmy with me all the time except when I ride. She can't do anything then, too many spectators. Besides, it's you and Penny I'm worried about." He lowered his voice. "Especially you."

Chapter Twenty-Two

Gina walked into the small terminal. It overflowed with people, most of them waving and smiling at her. Holt strode forward, folded her into his arms, and kissed her.

His handsome mischievous face, earthy, spicy scent, and hard, strong body engulfed her in security. His kiss deepened, and her heart thrummed. If not for the bags in her hands, she would have participated wholeheartedly in the kiss.

She came up for air, eased out of Holt's arms, and stared over his shoulder at the patiently waiting group. "Wow, what a reception,"

Holt tucked her against his side and led her to the familiar and some not so familiar faces. Penny broke free, throwing her arms around her and hugging. Jess had his arm around the shoulders of a dark-haired woman. Her eyes sparkled as she nodded an acknowledgement. Two young children stood on either side of the adults. And Timmy stood a step back from the smallest child.

"Gina, this is Clare, Jess's better half." Holt waved a hand to the woman by Jess's side.

"I'm pleased to meet you. Jess and Holt have told me a lot about you." Gina extended her hand.

The woman stepped forward and pulled her into a hug. "I've heard only good things about you. It's good to finally meet." Clare stepped back. "These two ornery critters are J.J. and Rita." She pointed to the boy of about five and a girl of about three.

"I'm pleased to meet you." Gina bent down, shaking Rita's hand and then J.J.'s.

"You're prettier than Holt deserves," J.J. said, backing away from his mother's stern glare. Jess's face bloomed to a deep crimson. Obviously, the boy was repeating what his father had said on more than one occasion.

"She sure is." Holt pulled her back against him and kissed her cheek. Heat blazed a path from her cheeks to her ears.

"Hi, Timmy. Did you make finals?" Gina drew the attention from herself. Only a blind person would have missed the young cowboy's gaze drinking in Penny.

He shook his head and smiled at her. "Nope, but it's good experience for me to help out these two." He nodded to Jess and Holt.

"Well, I'm glad you're joining our little entourage." *My all these people.* How would she and Holt have any private time? Gina glanced at the baggage belt. "There's my bags."

"Grab those bags, Timmy, and let's get on the road." Holt twined his fingers with hers and headed to the exit. His rough palm and wide, strong fingers meshed with her hand and connected her to him physically and emotionally.

"So, who rides with whom?" Gina asked, scanning the small parking lot for Holt's truck.

"You, Penny, and Zip with me, Timmy with Jess and his family." Holt led her to the last row of vehicles where she spotted the maroon truck.

"Where's the truck and camper?" Noticing a high-end minivan next to the truck, she scanned the area.

The smirk on Holt's face quirked her own smile. "What?"

"Jess is driving the minivan. Clare insisted the camper wasn't fit for her and the kids. Not to mention better gas mileage."

"I agree with her about it not being fit for

children. It's not even fit for adults." Zip hung half his body over the side of the truck, wiggling and tongue lolling. Waiting for Holt to unlock the truck, Gina patted his head and scratched under his chin.

Timmy trotted up, tossing her bags into the large chrome storage box behind the cab of the truck. He stood a minute watching Penny, then hurried around and helped her climb into the passenger side.

Gina tipped her head toward the two and whispered to Holt. "May want to keep an eye on those two."

He stared slack-jawed at the young couple. Typical man. He hadn't a clue what was going on.

"They are kind of cute," he whispered and helped her into the truck.

Gina giggled. She wouldn't be a bit surprised if Holt didn't find a way to make the interest grow. He had a fondness for Timmy that ranked right up there with his fondness of Penny.

Settled in her position straddling the gear shift, she waved at the full minivan, and the truck fired up. The two vehicles pulled out of the lot and headed down the road.

"I haven't even glanced at a map. How many days will we be on the road?" She noticed Penny had a pillow behind her back and one to use to lean against the door.

"Two long days or three short. Depends on the kids and Penny." Holt sent a reassuring smile to the teenager and squeezed Gina's leg. "You tired of sitting by me already?"

"No, I thought it would take longer. When Penny and I planned to stay at the ranch, you weren't heading to the finals so soon." Gina looped her arm through his and squeezed. She didn't mind the change of plans. Being able to stay with Holt rather than at the ranch had softened the reason behind their going to Las Vegas and watching the performances.

"We decided to get there early so they don't give away the connecting rooms we reserved. That town is nuts anytime of the year but during Nationals it takes on a whole new level of craziness."

"This Trish thing has added expenses for all of you." She watched Holt. "What about you focusing to ride? Will all this ruin your chance at the championship? And why drag Jess into this?"

Holt ran his hand back and forth across her knee. "We've been over the pros and cons. If I can ride with bruised ribs and still come in the money, and Jess rode knowing Clare was rushed to the hospital having Rita, then we can both ride knowing you and Penny are safe." He kissed her forehead. "I promise."

He could promise all he wanted, but she'd never live with herself if he missed his chance at Champion Bareback Bronc Rider thinking about her safety.

****

Tired and fidgety, Holt was damn glad they arrived in Vegas a few days before the wild ride of promotion and riding started. It gave him time to rest up and make certain Gina and Penny knew the route to take every time they went to the center. It also gave the group a chance to get a feel for one another. So far, Clare and Gina hit it off. He didn't think there'd be a problem, but with women you never knew.

Timmy appeared at Penny's passenger-side door the minute both vehicles stopped in the motel parking lot. It tickled Holt, the way the young cowboy showed up by her side every time there was a chance. He liked the interest Penny also paid in Timmy. They'd be good for one another. He could stop worrying how Penny would take care of a baby if Timmy stepped in and took them on. At this point, it looked promising.

"You're exhausted. Why didn't you let me drive?" Gina rubbed his back as he raised the lid on the cargo box to retrieve the suitcases.

"My legs don't fit too well around that gear shift and in Penny's condition, I didn't think she'd fit either." He grabbed the bags, placing them on the ground and locking the cargo box. His riding gear would remain stowed in the box until he needed it.

"True. I just feel bad I didn't contribute to the driving." She wheeled her bag to the outside door where the Karlan family, Timmy, Penny, and Zip entered the building.

She didn't know it, but just her sitting next to him kept him energized. Slipping his hand up and down her leg when Penny napped and stealing an occasional kiss, it was the best dang trip he'd ever taken. Holt followed with his own bag and Penny's. Jess motioned to the rooms across the hall from his open door.

"Timmy's room connects to ours." He pointed farther down the hall. "Penny is across from him and you two are across from us and connected to Penny's room."

Gina slid the keycard in the slot, clicking entrance. Penny and Zip stood in the room, her connecting door gaping.

"Here's your bag." Holt set Penny's bag inside her doorway and ruffled the hair on Zip's head. The dog would stay in Penny's room when they were at the motel and in the back of the truck when they went to the coliseum for performances.

"Thanks. I'm going to take a nap. Wake me when we go to dinner." Penny hid a yawn behind one hand and closed the door. A click announced she'd set the lock. Holt wanted to object. At the same time, he didn't want to scare her or ruin her nap.

"Why's there indecision on your face?" Gina's

arms wrapped around his waist, and her head rested on his chest. A floral scent wafted from her soft hair to his nostrils. He loved her scent and the embrace of her arms.

He shook his head. Now wasn't the time to bring his fears to light. There had to be someone else helping Trish. In her usual drugged condition, she couldn't have stayed focused long enough to do the detective work to find Gina's unlisted phone number.

"I knew you weren't okay with me being here when you ride." The disappointment in her voice hit him at the same time she slipped her arms away and took a step back.

"Don't even think that. The list of pros for having you here far outweigh the cons." He grasped her hand, sweeping her into his arms. "What do you say we take a little nap, too?" He kissed her neck and smiled at the way her body sagged against him.

"Sounds like an excellent idea, cowboy."

****

Everyone gathered at the chain restaurant across the street at seven. Gina cast a glance around the table. Jess and Clare sat on one side of the booth with their children between them. Penny and Timmy sat together on the end and Holt blocked her into the window side of the booth. Ironically, they had the most room, but with her snuggled close to Holt they only used half the space.

More a strategy session than mealtime, she listened close. Having been to the event before, Jess, Clare, and Holt hashed out best times and modes of travel to the event and who would pair with whom and when. She didn't like the children and Clare drawn into this or the fact they conspired as though she wasn't an adult who could make judgments.

Gina clanked a spoon against her ice tea glass. The chatter around the table stopped and all eyes stared at her.

218

"You're all doing a lot of planning for something we don't even know will happen." She peered at each one of them, ending with Penny. "Do you really think your sister will try something here?"

Fear flickered in the girl's eyes before she pasted on a smile. "I don't know my sister any more. But I do believe she won't stop until she gets her fantasy." She shrugged and shot Holt an apologetic smile.

Gina swung her head to Holt. "Do you feel the same? She isn't going to stop until she gets you back?"

"She's not stable. I don't know what goes on in her head, but she's threatened people I care about, and I'm not going to sit back and pretend she's harmless." Holt held her hand, playing with her fingers. "You keep saying you want me to stay focused on my rides. The best way is to let me do what I can to protect you. Then I can ride, knowing you're in the stands watching and safe."

"Okay, I'll do as I'm told and cheer the loudest when you ride." She offered him her most supportive smile. If making plans helped him ride, then she'd play along. Secretly, she believed Trish incapable of anything other than threats. As if on silent command, everyone at the table fell quiet as the waitress set their food in front of them.

Holt stared at his food, not saying a word.

Gina nudged him with her shoulder. "You need to eat. You can't worry yourself over this and not be at your best."

He gave her a weak smile then stared at Jess. "I didn't want to bring this up, but I think it needs to be heard." Jess nodded. "I don't think Trish is doing this all on her own. For some reason, someone's helping her."

Penny's intake of air caught Gina's attention. The teenager's eyes widened with fear. That idea hadn't come to her.

Penny's gaze darted between Holt and Gina. "Who?"

A shiver ran up Gina's back. A delusional drug addict was one thing. Someone else of sound mind helping Trish put a whole new frightening twist on her vengeance.

"I don't know who. I don't think it's your father. No offense, but his horns are screwed on too tight." Holt stirred a fork in his potatoes and gravy. "Do you know of any friends she has that might help her?"

Penny shook her head and pushed her plate away.

Timmy slowly pulled it back. "You need to eat," his soft voice carried to Gina.

She witnessed the shy smile he gave Penny. The innocence of their budding relationship warmed her heart. Oh, to have had someone show her that concern at such a young age, her life may have been different. Holt's arm grazed hers. She peered into his eyes. No, she wouldn't have wanted it any different. If not for her past and donating her time to a cause she was adamant about, she wouldn't have found the only man for her.

"Okay, so we look out for Trish and anyone who seems suspiciously interested in Penny or me." She placed her left hand on Holt's leg. His muscle tightened.

"That's about all we can do." He gave her hand a squeeze.

She listened to the conversation turn to the people they might encounter and what everyone wanted to see while at the finals. But her mind went back to the vicious shove she'd received from Trish at the Payson rodeo. Her unhinged anger could be fed by someone else. That made her even more dangerous.

****

Back at the motel, Holt smiled when Timmy and

Penny asked if anyone wanted to play cards. Then snickered when J.J. jumped at the offer, and the three disappeared in Timmy's room for some fierce hands of war. He'd bet the two had hoped no one would take them up on their offer.

He and Gina bid the rest of the group good night. In the room, Holt still couldn't get the foreboding out of his head. This was his year to win, yet guilt throbbed in his head like a bad hangover. If not for him, Gina and Penny wouldn't have threats from a crazy woman.

"Come here." He pulled Gina into his arms and held her close to his heart, cherishing their time together. "What do you want to do for the next three days until all hell breaks loose in this town?"

"Whatever you need to do. I'll just follow you around like a besotted fan." Gina batted her eyelashes.

A hearty, deep-from-his-gut laugh erupted. Several seconds passed before he caught his breath. "You're full of surprises, lady."

"What?" She feigned innocence, but the smile curving her luscious lips gave her away.

"Here's what I have planned every night."

He led her to the bed and proceeded to remove her clothing.

Chapter Twenty-Three

People. More than Gina had ever seen in one place. She'd never been to any kind of professional sporting event or a concert other than classical piano or an orchestra. Nothing, not even the rodeo in Payson prepared her for the mass of bodies, noise, and adrenaline permeating the air. This wasn't even the event crowd. The performance wouldn't start for several more hours. The family members, media, and sponsors packed in the concourse milled about visiting and scheduling meetings.

She linked her arm in Holt's, fearful she'd get sucked away in the current of people. He squeezed her arm against his side and smiled down at her, pulling her along the outer wall of the building and acknowledging the people who called out to him.

Black and white photos with placards underneath lined the wall. Holt stopped in front of one of them.

"This wall has photos of the National Rodeo Association Hall of Fame Cowboys." He linked one hand with hers. "This is Ty Murray, he's won nine titles. He rides it all and does one hell of a job." The awe in Holt's voice drew her gaze from the photo to the man by her side. She openly admired her cowboy.

"You want to best him don't you?" Gina cringed, thinking of how many animals he'd have to ride to try and attain the prestige of the man staring back at them.

"At one time I did. But not anymore. I get as much satisfaction out of a finished piece of art as I do riding a horse, and a lot less pain." Holt smiled and pulled her to another picture. "This is Bruce Ford. He won five titles in the late seventies and early eighties in bareback riding."

They strolled along the wall, Holt naming and rattling off the titles and dates of the cowboys who rode their way to fame in a sport she still couldn't fathom.

"This is Jack Buschbom. He holds three titles, forty-nine, fifty-nine, and sixty. His riding style is used by most riders today." He led her along. "And this one—Jim Houston held two titles in the sixties and invented the hard hand-hold we use."

His knowledge of the profession amazed her.

"And these two—Oregon cowboys. Larry Mahan pretty much a poster boy for rodeo in the sixties and seventies. Sonny Truemon was a horse breaker in the forties who rodeoed and won a bareback title."

"It's amazing how you know so much about your sport." She stopped him and gazed into his eyes. His confidence had drawn her to him. He knew his sport. Its dangers and his ability. Gina didn't fear his riding any more. "I wish you the best rides of your life at this event." Sealing the wish, she kissed him on the lips.

Holt's arms wrapped around her, dissipating the noise, the press of bodies, her inhibitions. He deepened the kiss. She opened to him, heart and soul, savoring his strength, commitment, and love. Proving to him she accepted his goal.

"Reynolds, who's the lady? Any plans your fans would like to hear about?"

Gina jerked out of the kiss, facing the voice. Holt spun her abruptly as a camera clicked and flashed.

"Get the hell out of here, Scott," Holt said in a growl worthy of a German Sheppard.

Fear and uncertainty tapped inside her chest. Why was Holt so upset? Who was this man?

"This the pregnant little lady we heard has been living with you?" The potbellied, balding man continued to move toward them.

Holt shifted Gina, directing her away from the man and through the crowd.

"Who's that guy, some kind of paparazzi?" Apprehension clenched her chest, making her light-headed. "I didn't know your life was so interesting." Gina didn't glance over her shoulder. She didn't want to take the chance the man had his camera ready. Ducking from cameras was new to her, and she didn't like it. If she wasn't behind a piano, she didn't like being the center of attention.

Holt nodded to someone over her shoulder. She followed his gaze. A sophisticated looking couple well beyond retirement age smiled and walked toward them, arms outstretched.

Holt's arm tightened around her. She didn't miss the woman's eyes scanning the length of her. *Not another confrontation.* Gina didn't know if she could go in public with Holt if this was the kind of turmoil that surrounded them every time. She liked her privacy, and so far this afternoon, she felt more vulnerable than she had in years.

"Gina Montgomery, I'd like you to meet Mr. and Mrs. Canfer. They've been two of my biggest supporters since I joined the pro ranks." Holt shook hands with Mr. Canfer and hugged his wife.

Gina shook off her anger to force a smile for the couple.

Mrs. Canfer continued to eye her up and down. "You look like a good solid citizen, unlike some of the floozies I've seen this man with over the years."

Holt coughed.

Gina's tension eased, and she smiled at Mrs. Canfer. "Thank you, I'll take that as a complement to my choice in wardrobe and Holt's maturity."

Holt gawked at her. Mrs. Canfer burst out

laughing.

"Young man, I think you've finally found a gem in this one." Mr. Canfer took Gina's hand. "It's a pleasure to meet you, my dear."

A camera clicked, and the Canfer's pivoted toward the flash. "Scott, wonderful, I'd like a photo of Claude and I with Holt and his lady," Mrs. Canfer said, positioning herself against Gina's side.

Gina started to shake her head, but lost her objection when she caught a glimpse of Holt's traveling buddy, Sam. Was he here to ride? Why wasn't he hanging out with the rest of his buddies?

"Gina's not my lady, she's my fiancée."

Holt's firm statement warmed Gina and drew her attention back to her cowboy and his exuberant smile. It was his first announcement to anyone other than their close friends. Witnessing the pride on his face as he captured her hand and drew her closer, she gazed into his eyes relaying her happiness.

Mrs. Canfer clapped her hands. "Oh, that's even better! Did you hear that Claude? Fiancée." She put her arm through Gina's. "Oh, you're going to break a lot of hearts taking this man off the market."

Gina glanced at Holt. She wasn't worried about many hearts—only one. They both knew who wasn't going to take kindly to seeing the picture and the caption underneath.

"It was good talking with you both, but I need to catch up with a few more people." Holt tugged her hand, weaving them through the crowd to a door. The muggy warmth and flashes of people and colors made her woozy.

Once outside, away from the horde and dull hum that permeated the interior, she gulped the cool crisp air. Two gulps and dizziness swept over her. Her knees buckled and everything went black.

Holt noticed Gina sway and moved beside her in time to catch her limp body. His heart drummed in his chest as fear pulsed at his temples. What caused her to faint? The threat of Trish? The crowd? He held her in his arms and fervently scanned the vacant area for a place to sit. He opted for a concrete retaining wall.

"Gina? Honey, wake up." Relief washed over him the moment Jess and Clare, followed by Penny and Timmy herding the kids, stepped through the door.

"What happened?" Clare hurried to his side. "We saw you duck out the side door, was it because Gina wasn't feeling well?"

"No, I just wanted to get away from the mob. We came out and... she fainted." Holt's heart thundered in his chest. Worry shredded his gut. "Why would she faint? She did great in there. Holding up under Scott's accusations and winning over the Canfers." Was bringing her to this madhouse event too much for her? She had kept an almost hermit like existence up until she met him.

Her head moved, and she came to on an inhale of air. Holt held her close. She blinked and focused on the people gathered around. Her pale cheeks brightened, growing redder with each face her gaze absorbed.

"What happened?" Gina glanced over her shoulder at him. Her body shook in his arms.

"I don't know. We came out the door and you collapsed." He ran the back of his hand down her cheek. "You scared the daylights outta me."

"I'm sorry." She pushed at the hair sliding into her face. "We came outside. The fresh air and sunshine were refreshing, then dizziness hit."

Holt helped her stand. She leaned against him, her legs still not strong enough to hold her. Guilt rumbled in his gut. He was putting her through hell with Trish and all this exposure to his world. His love for her could hurt her physically. If that happened he'd be no better than her father.

"The boys need to speak with their sponsors, how about we girls head back to the motel?" Clare put an arm around her shoulders.

He didn't like the ladies leaving or Gina out of his sight. After her fainting, though, he wanted her back at the motel resting and away from the crowds.

"That's a good idea," Jess said, leading J.J. over to Clare.

The relief on Timmy's face reminded Holt he'd promised to introduce the young cowboy to a sponsor. Holt took Gina's hand and gazed into her eyes. "Call me as soon as you get back to the room."

She nodded and walked away with Clare, Penny, and the kids.

Holt watched them, torn between helping his friend and following Gina.

"She'll be fine." Jess slapped him on the back. "Come on, that boot company was asking about you."

How the hell did he talk coherently with a possible sponsor when Gina wasn't well?

****

Day seven of Finals and he sat right where he wanted to in the standings—in the top five with Jess. Holt glanced at the clock on the bedside table. Time to head to the event center.

"You know," he said, dressing and watching Gina stretch her arms above her head, "you've been just what I needed." He leaned over her, capturing her mouth in a soft kiss. She wound her arms around his neck, tugging him down on top of her. He deepened the kiss and roamed his hands under her shirt, enjoying the feel of her silky skin.

"I've enjoyed watching you ride more than I thought I would." Her admission rocketed his admiration and adrenalin, filling his heart with joy.

"I'm glad. If I knew you were cringing up in the stands, I don't know if I could focus."

Pounding rattled the door. "Come on, Romeo, we

need to head to the center."

"Yeah, yeah!" Jess could be a real pain at times. Holt kissed Gina, pushing off the bed and grabbing his hat. "See you at the end of the performance after the bull riding."

She smiled and waggled her fingers. "I'll be there."

Holt opened the door, slipping out, and closing it snug behind him.

"I don't know why you can't get all the hanky panky done before it's time to leave." Jess started down the hall. Timmy trotted alongside grinning from ear to ear. Zip circled his feet.

"You're just grumpy you don't get any hanky panky time with the kids around." Holt high-fived with Timmy and caught a sinister glare from Jess.

"I've already told Clare, you and Gina asked to watch the kids tomorrow afternoon." The triumphant grin didn't dampened Holt's mood. He sat well in the standings going into tonight's round, and he had a good draw for the horse. He'd walk away tonight one step closer to his dream, and with the woman he loved by his side.

****

Gina dressed in the jeans, shirt, and boots Holt bought her the day before. The outfit wasn't over the top western, and she had to admit, he picked a warm, feel-good color that accented her coloring. They planned to meet with his biggest sponsor for dinner after the rodeo. It didn't make sense if he quit riding when he won, why he was interested in schmoozing this sponsor. Maybe he had doubts about winning?

She brushed her hair and stared at her reflection in the mirror. His confidence over his position last night had been addicting. Holt promised if he drew good horses, he'd win the title. His air of confidence should have appeared cocky, but it made him more desirable. His self-assurance was sexy.

Even though she had come to enjoy watching him master staying on a horse for eight seconds, she liked the idea of him hanging up his spurs. They'd discussed how he'd still travel to the larger rodeos to put in an appearance and to accompany his stock.

Penny waddled through the adjoining door, her face pale.

"Are you feeling okay?" Gina rushed to her side, helping her to the bed, and easing her down.

"It feels funny." The fear in Penny's eyes switched Gina's attitude from friend to nurse. She grasped Penny's wrist, monitoring her pulse. Fast. She placed a palm against Penny's forehead. Clammy. Gina placed a hand on the teenager's swollen belly. A faint quiver moved against her palm.

"It's probably false labor. Just lie back. I'll tell Clare to go on without us. If this passes and you feel up to going later, we'll meet them for dinner after the performance." Gina left the door open and crossed the hall to knock on Clare's door.

Chaos rained around Clare as J.J. and Rita whooped, excited to head to the rodeo. They liked hanging out in the nursery, an area with professional babysitters where children played games and worked on crafts during the event.

"You and the kids go ahead. Penny's having false labor and doesn't feel up to the crowd." Gina smiled at the children's exuberance.

"I'm not supposed to leave you two alone." Clare stared at her.

"We'll be fine. Besides, I need you at the arena, so I can call and keep everyone updated. If this passes, we'll be there for dinner. If it doesn't, you need to give Holt the message so he doesn't worry." Gina didn't like the idea of Holt finishing the night and not find her waiting.

"I don't like it, but I'm the only one you'll be able to contact. You know the boys will have stuck their cells in the lockers so they can stay focused." Clare glanced across the hall. "Keep your door shut and locked."

"Nothing's going to happen. My guess is the false labor will pass, and we'll be there in a couple hours." Gina smiled and backed away from the door.

"You're probably right." Clare shot another glance at the door then whispered, "How early is she?"

"She's still got a month. Nothing to worry about. I'm sure it's just false labor. She's young and this is all new to her." Gina stepped into her room. "We'll catch up to you later." She shut the door and faced the bed and Penny.

The teenager clutched her stomach, her face drawn and rigid. Her brown eyes widened with fear. "What's happening?"

Gina smiled confidently and flipped on the television. If they couldn't be there, they could still watch the event. "It's false labor. Lots of women have this experience. It's just your body's way of preparing for the birth." She adjusted pillows behind Penny and settled her with a glass of water.

Fifteen minutes later, Penny's eyes widened and her face paled. "This is too..." She breathed in pants. Pain dulled her eyes.

Gina placed a hand on Penny's swollen stomach. The muscles rippled under palm. This was more than false labor.

She hurried across the hall and pounded on Clare's door. Nothing. They'd left. Gina took a calming breath, pasted on her emergency room façade, and entered the motel room. She had to treat Penny like any other patient. It was the best way to keep her own fears from showing and upsetting

Penny.

"Let's gather our purses and go to the lobby. Someone there can get us a cab to the hospital." At the panic flaring in Penny's unfocused gaze, Gina placed an arm around the teenager's small shoulders. "It's okay. I just want to have you checked to see why you're having such strong false labor."

Gina willed her racing heart to slow. She had to think clearly and keep Penny focused on good thoughts.

Her words calmed Penny, and Gina helped her to her feet. She found her shoes in the other room, and they shuffled down the hall to the lobby. The Asian woman behind the counter picked up a phone.

"You want me to call the hospital?" she asked, finger poised to dial.

There wasn't a need for an ambulance—this was just false labor. And Penny didn't have insurance or funds for the expense.

"No, a cab will do." Gina kept moving to the outside doors. The fresh air would be good for Penny. "We'll wait out front." The registration clerk nodded, talking into the phone.

The door swished open. They stepped into the early evening dusk. When Holt said they'd stay in a motel far from the glitz and clamor of the strip, she'd liked the idea. Now, with night creeping in and bright lights of activity off in the distance, Gina wondered at the logic. How long would it take a taxi to get here? She'd seen few hovering about the entrance since their arrival. How far away was the hospital? She should have found out these things right away, but she'd stayed cocooned in Holt's world. Trusting all would be well.

"Uhhh…" Penny griped her belly and bent. The pains shouldn't be this strong for false labor or this early in a labor. The signs weren't good. Penny said everything was fine at her appointment right before the trip. Her doctor gave her the go ahead to travel.

"Hang in there. I'm sure a taxi will get here soon."

Where was that taxi?

A car pulled up to the curb. Penny froze, and then took a step back.

Gina's stomach curdled. The small leathery woman who'd bumped her months ago at the Payson rodeo stepped out. *Trish.* Where had she come from? Gina placed a protective arm around Penny's shoulders.

"What's wrong with Penny?" Trish's gaze bounced from Penny, to her, to Penny again.

"She's going into labor."

Something flickered in Trish's eyes. "What are you waiting for? Get her in the car. I'll take her to the hospital."

Trish stepped to Penny's side, taking her arm. The teenager stiffened and leaned into Gina.

"Come on, Penny." Trish stared into her sister's eyes, her own glistening with unshed tears. "We've had our differences, but I can help you. Let me do one good, big sister act. Let me take you to the hospital."

Gina scanned the street both ways for a taxi. Nothing.

Penny doubled over in pain, nearly toppling her emaciated sister.

Gina supported Penny and stared at Trish. The skinny woman's wheezy breathing and jittery eyes worried Gina. Did they dare trust her? Trish seemed sincere. A glint of tears sparkled in the older sister's eyes. Maybe she really did want to help. Did she dare hope Trish was feeling guilt over her sister?

"I haven't been a good sister. I know that, but let me help you. I'm here, I have a car. I can get you where you need to go," Trish begged.

Gina watched her. Was that sincerity in her

eyes? Maybe in this time of crisis she was coming through for her sister.

Her gut and head ping-ponged facts and what ifs until a headache started.

Penny groaned again. The pains were coming too close together and with too much force. She couldn't let her biased feelings cause Penny to lose her baby.

"Okay. Come on, Penny. If your sister is willing to help you get to the hospital, let's go." Gina opened the back car door. Penny lowered her body to the seat and slid over. Gina scooted in beside her and closed the door.

Trish plopped behind the steering wheel, and the car roared down the street. Gina looked back at the motel. Penny moaned drawing her attention to the interior of the car. For Penny to be in this much pain something was wrong. Their only choice was to hold on to the faith Trish was sincere.

Chapter Twenty-Four

Holt and the other fourteen bareback riders sat in the locker room watching video of their rides from the night before. The adrenaline, anticipation, and taking care of business hummed in the air like a live electric current. He welcomed input from the others about form and how to ride the horse he'd drawn for tonight's go-round. Everyone focused on their next ride, except Sam.

His traveling buddy had remained aloof the past seven days. He carried on a conversation, but something else had his attention. Even Jess had tried to find out what was eating him.

Right now, Sam moved about the room like a caged animal. He couldn't sit still, didn't focus on last night's ride. Not a good sign when he was the third up on a bronc. Watching the other man's nerves, Holt was glad he'd drawn a horse in the second string.

He disregarded Sam and thought about Gina. She finally accepted what he did. Her love had changed his outlook on riding broncs, his art, and living alone. When he won that belt buckle and title, he'd present it to her. And tonight, he'd put out feelers to the company they were dining with to see how they felt about sponsoring rough-stock. Once that was set up, they could work on funding for Gina's dream of a rehab ranch.

****

"Are you sure you know where the hospital is?" Fewer and fewer buildings flashed by the window. Fear curled in Gina's throat. She shouldn't have trusted this woman.

Penny stared at her with wide, frightened eyes. The girl had trusted her to make the right choice and look what she'd done. They were headed to who knew where with a deranged woman behind the wheel.

"I know exactly where I'm taking you." Trish's wild eyes peered at her in the rearview mirror. "I'm getting what I deserve."

Penny clutched her belly and moaned. Gina rubbed the teenager's back, giving reassurance. She got them in this mess. She'd figure a way out.

"What do you deserve?" She had to keep the woman talking and maybe she'd figure out where they were going and what to do.

"I deserve a cowboy to take care of me and the baby."

Gina glanced at Trish's reflection in the mirror. A tear glistened on her cheek.

"What cowboy. What baby?" she coaxed.

Trish's eyes gleamed with possessiveness, and her prominent jawline jutted out. "Holt and our baby."

Gina's heart slammed into her throat. What was she talking about? The woman didn't look pregnant. Holt said he hadn't been with her since the one episode. When was her abortion? Was it his baby her parents made her abort? The thought made her queasy. All the questions stuck in her throat. Would asking make Trish more agitated?

A tug on her sleeve drew her attention to Penny. She crooked a finger. Gina leaned down, and Penny whispered. "What do we do?"

Penny depended on her to stay calm. Gina had to find out as much as she could about Trish and Holt, and what the woman had planned. She couldn't think of Holt with Trish, it hurt too much. Even knowing they were together before she met

Holt, offended.

Gina shook her head, pushing her hands in her pockets to keep from chewing on her cuticles. Her fingers wrapped around the cell phone. She flipped the top up and slid the phone out of her pocket near her leg, shielding it from Trish's sight. Gina punched number one and held her thumb over the earpiece to keep Holt's voice, if he answered, from being heard. She raised her thumb. Voicemail. She poked the off button. Did he turn his phone off once he entered the center? Would she be able to contact him? Should she try Clare? The phone was their only hope of getting help.

Penny cried out and hugged her belly.

"Breathe, just like we practiced on the drive here." Gina massaged Penny's back. The teenager didn't need the stress of her psychotic sister.

"Where are you taking us?" She settled Penny more comfortable in the seat.

"Where Holt and I can get our baby and dispose of you."

Gina glanced at Penny. She shook her head and grimaced, clutching her belly. Someone had to know Trish had them. Gina leaned next to Penny and whispered, "Talk to her, keep her attention. I have to look for Clare's number."

"It was a miracle you happened by to help." Penny forced a smile and rubbed her belly. Gina smiled encouragingly and flicked down the numbers Holt installed in her phone after they arrived in Las Vegas.

There it was. Clare's number. She hit the dial button and once again held her thumb over the ear piece.

"It wasn't a miracle. We planned it." Trish's triumphant voice, tensed Gina's jaw.

"Planned what?" she asked, raising her thumb enough to hear Clare's hellos. *Please Clare, listen long enough to figure out what's happening.*

"Planned you two would be headed to a hospital tonight."

Penny searched her face. Gina leaned forward "How did you plan that?"

"We gave Penny something to start her contractions."

"We who?" Gina squeezed Penny's hand. Maybe the contractions would go away, if they, whoever they were, just wanted to make them look for a taxi to go to the hospital.

"A friend."

Great. Gina's stomach twisted with dread. Probably another person on drugs. "Why did you want Penny to go into labor?"

"So Holt and I can have the baby." The matter of fact way Trish said it scared her more than the statement.

"Uhhhh!" Penny clutched her stomach. Her frightened eyes beseeched Gina.

"Breathe," Gina grasped her hand, but kept the phone uncovered. "What baby are you talking about?"

"Why mine and Holt's. The one my baby sister is giving us." Trish cackled and swerved the car onto a side road.

"This baby isn't Holt's or yours." Gina put conviction behind her words. Holt and Penny had both said it wasn't his.

The woman stared at her in the rearview mirror. "How can you be so certain that baby isn't Holt's? Those two been cozy since before she got pregnant. Kind of convenient the way he's taken her in, paid all her medical bills."

The thought the man she loved could—Gina swallowed the disgust rising in her throat. Her father said he loved her and look what he'd done. Was Holt just like her father? Like all men? Fear for

Penny and stress she'd put them in this position spun her thoughts from the present to the past. Her father degrading her for childish mistakes then crawling into her bed putting his hands on her and whispering he loved her. She shuddered and battled the memories.

"This isn't Holt's baby. How many times do I have to tell you that?" Penny shouted and kicked the back of the seat. "He's a better friend than you are a sister!"

The action and frustration in Penny's voice sliced through Gina's thoughts, exonerating her love for the man.

The baby wasn't Holt's. He was nothing like her father or any man she'd ever met. And she loved him. She had to get out of this mess so she and Holt could spend their lives loving one another.

Trish slammed on the brakes and shoved the shifter in park. "It is! Once I get the baby and get rid of you." She leaned over the front seat, her eyes wide and angry, her mouth twisted in an ugly sneer. "Holt and the baby will be mine!"

"Even if you get rid of me, Holt won't raise the baby with you. He doesn't even think you're fit to take care of yourself." This kind of talk was dangerous, but she had to do something to stall and hope Clare had gone for help.

Penny reared up, screaming and clutched her abdomen.

"If you want this baby you need to get us to a hospital. Making her go into labor early you've increased the potential for problems. We need professionals. Especially, with this baby coming premature."

"You're a professional, or did you lie about that to everyone? What do you have that attracted Holt?" Trish's bloodshot eyes stared at her. "You aren't so special?"

A piercing scream ripped through the confining space.

Trish flipped on the interior light and stared over the back seat.

Gina used the light to examine Penny better. Amniotic fluid drizzled down Penny's leg in a pink line.

"What's happening? Why is it pink?" Trish pulled a cell phone out of her purse and dialed. "Sam! Something's wrong. She's bleeding! My God, Penny's bleeding!" Trish's hysterics and white knuckle grip on the phone raised Gina's hopes they could play on the woman's sympathy.

Gina mouthed the word *Sam* to Penny. Could it be Holt's traveling buddy? If so, why would Trish call him? The girl shook her head and tried to move out of the wet spot on the seat.

"Stay there. This is natural. It's just the membranes bursting, preparing for the delivery." To save the baby and possibly all their lives, she had to stay in her professional nurse mode. Her heart ached for the frightened young woman and prayed Holt didn't find out about this mess until after his ride.

"Yes, I want Holt. Yes, I want our baby," Trish said into the phone and started crying.

Gina leaned over the seat and yelled. "Who the hell are you, and why are you pushing Trish to a nervous breakdown?"

Trish remained intent on the phone. She held it away and pushed a button.

"Ah, you're tougher than you appeared." A voice Gina knew erupted from the small phone.

"I thought you were Holt's friend?" Why would Holt's traveling buddy be filling lunatic Trish full of false hopes? Causing possible harm to Penny and herself?

A sarcastic laugh echoed out of the cell phone.

"I've never been a friend of Holt's, not after what he did to me. Sleeping with my fiancée and turning her thoughts to him." He laughed again. "Haven't you ever heard the saying, *keep your friends close and your enemies closer*? Well, I've kept my enemy close ever since he made me look like a fool over the woman who holds your fate."

Gina gasped. Trish was Sam's fiancée? Why was he helping her get Holt then? She stared at the mask of makeup on Trish, her red-rimmed, sunken eyes, prominent cheek bones, and anemic body.

"Trish is smarter than you think. She knows when someone is using her. Don't you Trish?" Gina had to either get Trish on her side or confuse her. Anything to stall whatever the two had planned and hope help found a way to get to them.

"Trish." Sam uttered in a controlling tone. "Stick with the set up. You get the baby and the man."

"Holt isn't going to go with you, Trish." Gina kept eye contact with the confused woman.

Penny screamed and clenched Gina's arm. "Hee, hee, hee, hoo. Hee, hee, hee, hoo," she breathed, her face paling.

"Good. Keep breathing." Gina focused on Trish.

Somehow she'd bring this child safely into the world, and get back to Holt.

****

"Holt! Holt!" Timmy ran towards Holt, knocking people right and left.

"I'm just about to get on my horse." Holt backed away from his friend. He didn't want anything interrupting his routine or his focus.

"You gotta..." Timmy gasped for air. "You gotta listen to this." He shoved a phone at him.

"Timmy, I'm climbing into the chute in five minutes."

"Listen!" He slapped the phone against Holt's ear.

"Breath Penny, You're doing great." Gina said in a controlled voice.

"She better have that kid soon."

The screeching sound of Trish's voice froze his heart. The lunatic had Gina and Penny. How the hell did that happen?

"Where'd you get this phone?" he demanded, staring at the wild-eyed kid watching him.

"Clare. She said she knew you needed to hear this. So she found me and had me bring it to you, 'cuz they wouldn't let her down here."

Holt pressed the phone to his ear and scanned the staging area for Jess. His head pounded. There was no telling what the lunatic Trish would do. Fear for Gina and Penny circled his heart, squeezing tighter and tighter.

"What plans do you and Sam have for us?" Gina sounded more in control than he did riding a bronc.

"God damn, him!" Holt heard Gina suck in a breath and realized she heard his voice. He covered the mouth hole and looked at Timmy. "How much of this have you heard?"

"Enough to know Trish has Penny and Gina, and Sam put her up to it."

Holt stared at Timmy. Sam had a grudge, but he never guessed it went this low or mean. The man had pulled in the deranged Trish to do his dirty work.

"We're going to have a talk with our traveling buddy."

Timmy nodded. "What about your ride?"

He held the phone to his ear and listened to the professionalism in Gina's voice laced with an undercurrent of fear. His heart thundered in his chest for her plight. He put her in this situation.

"I'm not going to lose another person I love."

Chapter Twenty-Five

"Screw the ride. Round up Jess, fill him in, and take Sam to the locker room."

Timmy tipped his hat and headed through the crowd. Holt stared at the phone. He raised it to his ear as he walked down the ramp to chute four and Greased Lightning, his best draw of the year.

"Me and Holt, we're gonna be real happy with this baby." Trish's voice scraped his nerves like the sound of a horse slamming into the arena rails. How did she get such a delusional idea? He would never have anything to do with her.

All the helpers smiled and moved out of his way so he could check his rigging. He shook his head and moved on down the ramp to the chute official.

The man looked up from where the next rider sat on his horse.

"Scratch my ride." Holt's gut didn't even twitch. A scratch would drop him in the standings. There would be no way he could win the title now.

"Why? You look fit to me." The official scowled, eyeing him up and down.

"Personal." Holt spun on his heel to head to the locker room and find out what Sam had to do with Gina and Penny.

"You know what this means don't you?" the official called.

He waved his arm and kept on walking, right by chute four and the horse that would have clenched his victory. The cowboys behind the chutes parted, making a clear alley to the locker rooms. Their faces mirrored disbelief and confusion. No one walked away from the finals. They might be carried out on a stretcher, but they never walked away.

Holt slammed his palm against the locker room door, ramming it open. Jess and Timmy had Sam backed into a corner. His anger spun through his head like a whirling, bucking bronc, kicking his brain and making his head hurt. He stalked between Jess and Timmy, stopped in front of Sam, and wrapped his hand around the man's throat.

"Where did Trish take Penny and Gina?" The son-of-a-bitch didn't even flinch.

Sam smirked. Hatred snapped in his eyes. "That lunatic? It's hard to say."

"There's no way Trish could pull this off without help. Where did you tell her to take them?" The rage rushing to Holt's extremities and blurring his vision tightened his hold on Sam's throat. He may have lost the title tonight, but no way in hell would he lose Gina.

"Holt, he can't talk if you kill him." Jess's calm voice broke the shard of control he'd had.

"Maybe I want to kill him." Holt tightened his grip. The gurgling sound Sam emitted did little to appease the wrath burning in his gut. Jess and Timmy pried his hand from the traitor's neck and held Holt back.

"We won't find the women if you kill him," Jess said.

"Yeah," Sam croaked. "You kill me you won't find the women." The snide lilt to his voice rammed Holt's fist into the man's gut.

"Let's beat it out of him." Holt didn't wait for the other men to agree. He launched forward, punching. Sam's head snapped back, and he buckled forward, too stunned to retaliate.

"Enough!" Jess put Holt in a full nelson and dragged him away from Sam. "This might help your anger issues, but it sure as hell isn't getting us any answers. Timmy, go get someone from security."

Holt fought his friend, but the man had always been better at wrestling. The hold they'd practiced on one another many times in college had him restrained.

"We have to think of Gina and Penny. Not this scumbag."

Holt shook, releasing some of his tension, and Jess released him.

"Where's the phone?"

Fear and frustration washed over him. What did he do with the phone? He scanned the area and dropped to his knees, looking under benches.

Shit! Their only connection to the women, and he lost it. He sat on a bench and dropped his head into his hands. He lost the title and possibly Gina.

His world wasn't worth spit without her.

****

"Trish, Penny needs to get to a hospital." Gina glanced up from checking the teenager's dilation. "She isn't dilating. The baby is being forced into the birth canal, and Penny's body isn't ready, it's resisting. The baby, and possibly Penny, will die if you don't get us to a hospital." She squeezed Penny's hand. She'd made sure the young girl knew the truth—things were going along fine, but their only hope of getting help was to convince the confused woman to take them to a hospital.

"Please, Trish. I'll forgive you everything and even give you the baby if you'll take me to the hospital." Tears streamed down Penny's cheek. "I don't want to die."

Gina sent Penny a reassuring smile and tipped the phone a little more toward the front seat. She'd heard Holt speak shortly before Trish had started the car moving again. Since then it had been quiet, but she could tell the line was still open.

"Trish, any hospital will do. You don't have to

take us back to Las Vegas." There hadn't been a road sign in a while making it hard to determine which direction they were headed. The black beyond the car lights gave little insight into the land.

Trish's eerie reflection in the rearview mirror revealed an unsure mind. "There's a small town ahead. Do you think it will have a hospital?" Trish had lost her bravado since losing contact with Sam. Her voice warbled and whined like a frightened child.

This could be their chance to persuade her to take them to a hospital.

"I don't know. What's the name of the town?" Gina held her breath.

"Searchlight." Trish laughed. "It sounds like a soap opera. Soap operas have hospitals." She smiled. "Yeah, they'll have a hospital." Trish's hand shook as she pushed hair out of her face.

A car came up behind them fast. The lights glared in the mirror. Trish yelled a curse. The car slammed to a stop. Gina sailed forward as the ripping crunch of metal tearing metal assaulted her ears along with Penny's screams.

****

Timmy brought the phone back to the locker room along with the head of security at the Events Center. Holt listened to the phone as Jess filled the officer in.

The officer radioed for men to come take Sam.

Holt strained to hear the conversations on the phone. The pounding of his heart and whoosh of blood in his ears hindered his hearing. "Searchlight, like a soap opera." Trish said.

Hope flared. "They're headed to Searchlight," he said, turning to the security officer. Timmy slapped him on the back.

Screams and ripping metal shattered his hope and stilled the people in the room.

"Gina!" Holt yelled into the phone clutched in his hand then listened.

Silence.

Chapter Twenty-Six

Holt sat in the hospital lobby barely holding himself together. Gina was out there somewhere hurt. The security officer had radioed the state police and 911 right away. Holt knew they'd found the car and were headed back to Las Vegas. He sent an inquiring gaze Jess's direction. His friend shook his head. When would the ambulance get here? The shredding of metal and a woman's screams played over and over in his mind.

Holt shot out of the chair and paced. He couldn't lose Gina now. Not when he'd finally realized what was important. Her love was all he'd ever need. He'd never set foot in another rodeo arena if it brought her back to him safe.

"Mr. Karlan?" A woman called from behind the counter. Holt started toward the woman.

Jess held up a hand. "Stay there, we'll get answers faster if you contain your emotions and let me gather information."

Holt didn't like keeping his distance, but the rage and fear engulfing him surpassed the grief and shame that shrouded him after Sherrie's death. Jess had been there then, listening and guiding him. He wanted answers, but knew Jess would have his back no matter what and tell it to him straight.

He flexed his hand. The knuckles still ached from their encounter with Sam's face. What he wouldn't give to have that S.O.B. in front of him right now. His hand fisted, and he faced the wall. He couldn't lose Gina. Couldn't lose another person he loved. Tears burned at the back of his eyes.

A hand rooted on his shoulder. He couldn't move.

"Five minutes and they should be here." Jess squeezed his shoulder. "Penny had the baby. They're both stable."

Holt swallowed the knot in his throat. "Did you tell Timmy?"

"I will in a minute."

"They..." he couldn't get the words out.

"One of the women was airlifted to a larger hospital."

Holt spun around. "Which one?"

"No one knows for sure." Jess put a hand on Holt's chest when he started toward the desk. "The nurse doesn't know anymore than we do. Hold tight." He stared over Holt's shoulder. "Looks like red lights coming this way."

Holt shoved his friend aside and strode to the emergency room doors. The wail of sirens dissolved into the night, and the irritating beep of the vehicle backing ticked at his nerves.

"You need to move," a male voice said, drawing him away from the door.

"I have to see..." He stood still as the attendants pulled a gurney out of the ambulance. The dark brown hair told him they had Penny and not Gina. A small bundle rested in her arms.

The gurney rolled by. Penny focused on him. "Gina..." They rolled her down the corridor carrying her words away.

A high-pitched siren riveted his attention from the activity in the hall to the doors again. Another ambulance backed next to the first.

The doors popped open. An attendant jumped out and pulled on a gurney. Gauze wrapped the head of the occupant. Fear chewed at his gut. His hands shook and shivers wracked his body. *God, let it be Gina and let her live.*

Holt shuffled forward, pressing through the crowd around the gurney. He grabbed the bloody hand resting limp against the blanket. Relief swelled into his throat. He stared at the ring he'd placed there.

"Gina?" He brushed a hand down her cheek and jogged alongside the gurney.

"Sir, you have to let go." A nurse with a surgical mask hanging around her neck tugged on his arm.

"No. She needs me." He drew his arm out of the woman's grasp, trotting with the rushing gurney.

"Holt." Jess's tone broke through. He clutched Holt's arm, leading him back to the desk.

Holt stared at the swinging doors shutting Gina away from him. She was alive. Could they keep her that way? She needed to know he was here.

"Pull it together. Let's talk to the paramedics and see what's up." Jess put an arm around his shoulder, moving him toward the men filling out charts.

"What can you tell us about the woman you just brought in?" Jess's patient tone soothed Holt.

He would forever be in debt to his friend. Jess knew how to handle a crisis.

"We can't say." One of the attendants said, brushing them off.

Holt put a hand on the man's shoulder, spinning him back around. "That's my fiancée, and I want to know what's wrong with her." He needed answers about the woman he loved, why couldn't the man see that?

The attendant raised his hands in supplication. "I'm sorry, but we can't discuss the people we bring in with anyone but the doctor."

Holt stalked to the desk. "Where's the doctor in charge of the woman who just came in?"

The nurse lifted an eyebrow and stared him in the eyes. "He's evaluating the patient. Please. Sit down. We'll fill you in as soon as we know her condition."

Timmy and Clare rushed into the area dragging J.J. and carrying Rita. Would he and Gina ever get the chance to have children? He watched Clare and Jess hug. They gained strength from one another. Just as he and Gina had learned to do.

Timmy walked over to him. "How's Penny? The baby?"

The concern on his friend's face echoed the turmoil boiling Holt's insides. He put an arm around Timmy's shoulders. "They looked good, considering."

"Can I see them?" Timmy's question verged on pleading. What Holt wouldn't give to be able to beg information out of the staff in this hospital.

"I don't—"

Jess tugged on his arm and pointed to a man and woman dressed in surgical scrubs headed their direction.

Holt swallowed the fear bubbling in his throat and strode forward to meet them halfway.

"I'm Doctor Phelps," the man said. "And this is Doctor Manning." He indicated the woman next to him.

"Who here is related to Penny Landers?" Dr. Manning asked.

Jess stepped forward. "All of us in a way. We may not be blood, but she's like a sister to Holt and me and a little more than that to this guy." He slapped Timmy on the back.

Dr. Manning narrowed her eyes on Timmy. "Are you the father?"

"N-no." Timmy squared his shoulders. "But I'd like to be."

She nodded. "Then I guess it wouldn't hurt for you to see the mother and the child. They were lucky. They only suffered minor injuries."

A grin spread ear to ear on Timmy's long, thin

face. "That's great news. When can I see them?"

Holt stepped forward. "What about Gina? How is she?"

Dr. Phelps put his hands behind his back. "Are you the next of kin?"

Holt swallowed the lump creeping up his throat. "Yes."

"She's in a coma, we had to set her leg, and there are no internal injuries." He slapped Holt on the back. "It's a good thing. They could have caused a miscarriage."

"When will I be—" Miscarriage? Didn't a woman have to be pregnant to have a—He peered at the doctor, then Clare. Tears spilled down her smiling face and glistened in her eyes. *Gina was pregnant.*

Holt didn't want to smile, not with Gina still in critical condition, but a baby. His baby! "When can I see her?"

"Give us another half an hour to get her settled in a room. Then only one person at a time. Remember, though she's in a coma, it does a patient good to hear the voices of their loved ones."

Timmy followed Dr. Manning. Holt turned to Jess and Clare. He wanted to shout, *I'm going to be a father.* He never knew how much it meant to him until the doctor said Gina was pregnant.

"Did either of you know?" he asked his friends. They had moved to chairs, each cradled a child on their lap. Jess shook his head.

"I wasn't positive, but after Gina fainted, I started watching her closer." Clare smiled. "Congratulations."

Holt sobered. "I can't get too excited. Gina still has to come out of the coma." He stared at the woman. "Do you think she knew?" He wasn't sure how he felt about Gina keeping the news to herself.

"I'd say given her profession, she probably had an inkling. Why?"

"I guess I'm wondering why she didn't tell me." Did she have second thoughts about getting married?

"She probably wanted to wait until the time was right. Like when you won the title." Her expression darkened. "You lost that chance this year didn't you?"

"Yeah, but I wouldn't have had it any other way. I'd rather spend the rest of my life loving Gina than a title. She's a heck of a lot warmer to cuddle."

Jess and Clare laughed.

"Mr. Reynolds?"

Holt faced the young nurse. "Yes?"

"You can come see your wife now." He didn't correct the woman. In his mind, the minute Gina accepted his ring they became one.

Chapter Twenty-Seven

Warmth filled her hand and slowly radiated out to the rest of her shivering body. Gina struggled to open her eyes. A deep, soft voice, one she'd heard during her fight to consciousness, spread the warmth deeper. The heat grew, strengthening and reassuring, wrapping her in comfort and security.

Effort and pain opened her eyes. No less than a foot from her face, she peered into the loving eyes of a man she thought she'd never see again. Her heart swelled and ached with love.

A tear trickled down the side of her face. His gentle thumb whisked it away.

"Hello." Holt's raspy voice throbbed with emotion.

"H—"

He placed a finger to her lips.

"Don't talk, just look at me." He leaned down and kissed her lips. "I thought—" Tears welled in his eyes. "I've been sitting here for days hoping you'd open those eyes and look at me."

"D-days?" How many days had she been asleep? Where were they? Why did her head and leg hurt so bad?

"The only thing that matters is you." His deep confident words steadied the budding panic.

"How many… days?" She swallowed. Her tongue felt thick and dry.

Holt held a glass of water with a straw up to her lips. "Six. The finals have been over for four days."

The hospital room, rather than giving her comfort, made her vulnerable. Gina twisted her head to peer into his eyes and regretted the movement. Pain ricocheted inside her skull. She shoved the discomfort aside. Holt's future was at stake. *The finals.* "Did... you stay... the whole time?" Her low raspy voice sounded strange.

He nodded and kissed her forehead. "I only left you long enough to clean up. They were good enough to bring trays in here for me at meal times."

"But—your dream." She ached knowing he passed up his dream for her.

"The only dream I have is watching you walk down the aisle to become my wife." He glanced at her mid-section. "And holding our child."

Heat scorched her cheeks and feathered down her neck. She hadn't had a chance to tell him about the baby. Now he knew. "I was going to tell you... after the finals. I didn't want—"

"Me to not be focused." He kissed her hand. "How?"

"How could I... keep it from you?"

"No, how did it happen? We used protection."

Did he really not want a child? Had she been right to keep it from him? Gina studied his weary, handsome face. The laugh lines around his eyes deepened, and his eyes glowed with happiness.

"Are you okay with me... being pregnant?" The words came easier as she sipped on the water. She tried to shift her right leg to ease the ache, but it felt like a boulder.

"I'm delighted. I just don't understand how it happened."

Memories of the shower and hot tub flashed through her mind and her cheeks heated. "There were a couple times... we got carried away... and didn't use protection."

He sobered. "That's why there are so many girls like Penny."

"Penny! The baby! How are they?" She'd almost

forgotten. The baby had been close to breeching when the car struck them.

"They're both fine. In fact, they headed home with Jess and Clare. Timmy talked her into staying with him for the winter." Holt twined his fingers with hers. "I told them to all make plans to come to our ranch for a Christmas wedding."

"Christmas?" Her heart hammered in her chest. She didn't want to waste another day not being Mrs. Holt Reynolds. "How long till Christmas?"

"Seven days."

Gina tried to sit despite the throbbing in her head and leg. She couldn't lie around when there was a wedding to plan. *Her wedding.* There was a time when she didn't think she'd ever have that occasion.

Holt held her down. "You're not going anywhere until the doc says so."

"But, seven days. I have to call Jerry—"

"I already did. He'll be at the ranch the day before."

She narrowed her eyes and glared at him. "You didn't call my father did you?"

"Nope."

"Good. I'm starting a new life. He isn't going to have a place in it." Gina grabbed his shirt, drawing him down to her. "I plan to start making new memories."

"Can I help?" he asked against her lips.

"Definitely. You'll always hold the title to my heart."

Epilogue

Cast propped on a pillow on the coffee table, Gina sat on the couch in front of the fire, watching her husband try to find a station hosting the New Year's Eve celebration. She ruffled Zip's hair with her bare foot. After having a crowd for their wedding Christmas day, they both opted out of all the New Year's invitations.

"Finally." Holt dropped onto the couch beside her, wrapping an arm around her shoulders. "You know, I've never had someone to kiss on New Year's before." He placed a gentle kiss on her lips.

"Me either." She peered into his eyes. Her love for him grew stronger and stronger with each moment they shared. "And you're the only one I ever want."

Holt squeezed her hands. "I can't believe I almost lost you all because of being drunk and stupid."

"You couldn't have known Sam held that much hatred for you." Gina raised his hands to rub them gently across her cheek. They both came so very close to never experiencing this moment. She shuddered at the thought of what could have happened in the crash.

"I should have known. He asked questions about you and overheard my side of our conversations when we were on the road. I should have known something was up when he'd hide in a corner to talk on his phone. He was calling Trish and getting her all riled up." Holt pulled her into his arms. "He got your number off my phone and gave it to Trish. Then he also found your brother, knowing he was a ski instructor from my conversations with you, and got the number so it would throw us off."

"Sam is one smart, and sick, man." She rubbed the arms circling her, protecting. "But who planted the note in your house and when?"

"Penny's father. Come to find out, he'd been working there almost from the start, but staying hidden. Sam pulled him into the plot for a portion of his National winnings. Landers watched and knew when Penny left the house for town. He snuck in the first time, when Zip ate my best boots, just to see if he could, then planted the note the second time."

"I'm glad everything worked out in the end. Trish will get treatment. Sam will get some time in jail. I can't believe all he went through to get back at you and Trish. And that she was so drugged up she didn't even see he was being malicious." Her heart went out to the woman considering her past, but she still couldn't forgive her for putting her sister at risk and nearly killing them all.

"Let's talk of pleasant things." Holt placed his hands over her stomach. "Like our family."

Gina smiled at the ardor growing in his dark eyes. He pulled her onto his lap, slipping a pillow under her casted leg, and covering her mouth with a long, hot kiss. Her body roared to life, simulating the flames in the fireplace. She ran her hands up and down his back. This she could get used to.

He pulled back. Dropped brief kisses on her face and settled his gaze on the stack of papers on the coffee table.

"Next week we send in the paperwork for the camp." He twined their fingers together. "I'd like to see kids here this summer."

"I'll have the baby in July. Are you sure that's going to work with your rodeo schedule and opening the camp?" She'd argued this point with him several times since he told her *Camp Sherrie* would open this summer.

"Penny and baby Josh will come help. Timmy will be on the road with me. But I promise. No rodeos for a month around your due date. I'll be here for you and our baby."

She kissed his cheek. "I'm glad you're going to give the title one more try. I'd feel bad if you thought you couldn't rodeo anymore."

"Only this year. If I get the title great, we can do more for the camp. If I don't win the title, I'll have used every chance I'm interviewed to promote the camp. I'll make sure the announcers at every rodeo mention Camp Sherrie and what we do."

Pride filled her chest. Holt had pushed the camp from a dream to a reality, and they'd both agreed the name was a fitting memorial to his sister. Working together to help others would only make their bond stronger.

Counting from the crowd in Times Square drew her attention to the TV. "...Three, Two, One."

Holt caught her head in his hands. "I love you."

He leaned forward, capturing her lips, igniting her desire, wrapping her in security, and giving her unconditional love. If not for his persistence to unbridle her heart, she would have never known true happiness or that life can have new beginnings.

A word about the author...

Award-winning author Paty Jager lives in Oregon running a ranch with her husband of thirty-one years. Her first contemporary western earned an EPPIE award for Best Contemporary Romance. She also has seven historical western romance books available through The Wild Rose Press.

More Wild Rose Press titles by Paty Jager:

Contemporary:
Perfectly Good Nanny

Historical:
Marshal in Petticoats
Outlaw in Petticoats
Miner in Petticoats
Doctor in Petticoats
Gambling on an Angel

Historical Paranormal:
Spirit of the Mountain